Prologue

"Full speed ahead," ordered Captain Harrison, pointing confidently towards the horizon. "Hold nothing back. The target is dead centre." The crew jumped into action like startled cats in an alleyway: climbing the rigging, hoisting the sails, no action too much to please their faithful captain. The motif of the ship became a little clearer now; a skull and wings - pirates.

*

Lazily, the two farmers sat back and gazed over their bountiful fields in front of them. After a full morning of ploughing their land, they were glad to be enjoying their simple dinner. The dry, crust of bread and lump of hard, waxy cheese, though not filling, was satisfying for the ravenous workers.

*

"Prepare the incendiary devices. Steady now. We are almost upon them." The crew lifted the clumsy devices and lit the fuses, looking cautiously over the side of the ship, waiting for the target to come into sight. Some held Piscis bombs, with a smooth wooden finish, a silver tip and the fin-like tail to propel it through the air. Others the winged Tempus grenade, with an adjustable clock face to set the device between the regal looking pair of wings below the pin; or even the Bombo - a strange device with a fuse protruding from the top and a couple of wind up feet below. When wound up its eyes lit green, and it squealed - the friendliest of bombs if that were possible.

*

Frantically, the wife of one of the farmers came running down the lane and up through the field. As she approached, she pulled back her red and white checked headscarf that had blown into her face and gasped for air.

"Can you not hear the thunder? It's coming from the west," she nervously called, pointing above their heads. The two men laughed at each other and then the first man's wife. Thunder, on a dry day like today. There had been no rain for months, so why now?

*

"Steady, we will enter the clearing soon, and the target is about come into range. Be ready," Harrison ordered.

*

As the farmers eventually contained their raucous laughter, the wife - who had almost given up hope - stood like a terrified statue, gazing over the farmer's heads into the distance. She gasped and pointed. Her mouth opened to scream but nothing came out. She slowly edged backwards, retreating from whatever was striking fear into her heart. The two men turned to see what had panic-stricken the woman.

There, moving through the field in their direction, were three men. But these were no ordinary men. These men were at least ten feet tall as they had what could only be described as extended mechanical legs, like stilts. The sheer height of them was daunting enough, but the way the men moved menacingly towards the country folk, with slow, methodical bounces, created a panic as one

6

had never known before. In their arms, they carried what looked like a gun, covered in an array of dials and levers. From the back of the firearm was a thick brown pipe that led into a backpack each man carried behind him. The elaborate golden handle and trigger gleamed in the sunlight until it was squeezed then a river of flames poured from the mouth of the weapon and sprayed the land in front. Unlike life-giving water, it brought bright flashes that lit up the handle even further, as if it were on fire itself. As the men progressed through the charred, blackened remains of the field, the new life of the crop disappeared with the flames as quickly as they had appeared.

As they moved towards the farmers and the wife, the men looked further still. For in the distance, behind the giant walkers, came the thunder the wife had spoken of. Gigantic mechanical beasts lumbered across the fields towards their position. Massive artillery loomed from the front of these giant walkers. Pistons and cogs drove the thunderous tyrants forward, steam blowing from every slit in the horrifying grey shell. A small window at the front peered into the souls of these mechanical, soulless beasts. There, the goggle-wearing, breathing mask of the secret army stared back with no remorse as they destroyed all around them.

*

The ship continued its course.

"Are we ready gentlemen?" Emerging from the mist, the bow of the ship poked its head through to see what was happening. Above it, the vast balloon, which kept the boat in the air, followed. This vessel was no ordinary ship. This was the resistance's premier ship - Ducis; the one that had survived so many treacherous missions; this belonged to the Caeli Pirata. The crew hung over the sides ready with their munitions, some clinging to the rigging, some in the multi-paned ammunition booths, others just over the edge of the ship. Harrison prepared his command.

"FIRE!"

Chapter 1
Archie

The boy ran. Desperately and frantically. The vision of the hideous monster had returned to haunt him. He had caught a glimpse of one of the characters; a metallic skull that looked inhuman. The courageous woman protected him as best she could to give him enough time to run away and hide. He recalled how she stood in front of the three characters and said no to them.

"You will not take him!" she had shouted defiantly.

"He's not yours anymore," came the reply. What they discussed, he did not know, but when he heard her final words, he sprang into action.

"Archie, run!" He set off down the tired, dirty streets and looking over his shoulder he saw her following. The three sinister figures captured her and, as he swivelled around, he tripped and fell to the floor. Banging his head on the hard, stone ground, he recalled the final thing he saw before darkness came. The skull; reflecting in the morning sunshine, the image that was engraved in his memory from that moment onwards.

The vision of the mask loomed deep in the heart and soul of the boy. He awoke from another nightmare, out of breath and damp from sweat. Panic had overtaken him, and he needed to calm down. He reached to the side of the large, comfortable four-poster bed for a glass of water and gulped down several mouthfuls. Feeling slightly more at ease and refreshed, he placed a hand on his chest to feel his heartbeat. Pounding like a madman at the door, he realised he still wasn't as calm as he should be. Archie thought of getting out of bed, maybe to speak to someone, but the dawn was nowhere to be seen, and everyone in the house would still be asleep. Instead, he decided to make himself feel at ease by checking outside. Pulling back the covers he chose to look into the night. He stood at the open sash window and pulled aside the intricate net curtain floating in the cold night air. Outside not a soul moved for there were no souls to be seen. Archie's eye was drawn to the movement of a bird; its silhouette flapping around in the moonlight, hopping from sill to sill. Carefully, the bird appeared to be edging closer to the window were Archie was stood. Perhaps it was as curious of Archie as the boy was of it.

He left the bird and the window and moved cautiously through the dark to the bathroom. He poured the icy water from the fine porcelain jug into the large bowl and splashed his face. Considering the mirror in front of him, the young man rubbed his defined cheekbones and almond-shaped eyes. The dream had passed, and now the tired eyes that daily had the clarity of a mountain stream struggled to stay open. He scratched his head through the thick, wavy hair, sweeping his fringe from his eyes. A handsome young man, even at this hour of the early morning, he gleamed with the vigour and delight of youth. Archie returned to his bed, closing his eyes, trying to sleep. It was no use. The dream had brought back memories of that day when he was much younger.

Archie Roker lived a very well to do life. As far back as he could recall he always had all he wanted. Splendid clothes from the tailors, Clovis Tudor, in the town;

regular bathing in a beautiful roll top, double ended bath; the plumbing standing proud next to the tub while four feet proudly held the magnificent tub aloft. A plethora of dishes at every meal, ham, eggs, bacon, bread and fish for breakfast, a light lunch, then afternoon tea, followed by the numerous courses of the evening meal. A vast selection of cheeses, milk, butter, potatoes, onions, garlic to eat. Not to mention the beef, goose, ham and turkey, along with the exotic spices with which they were seasoned. And the food that was left? Thrown away. Life indeed was to excess.

To keep him entertained, Archie had a room full of expensive and handmade toys: a kaleidoscope, with repeating psychedelic patterns; a zoetrope, that which he would sit and wonder at the marvels of moving objects; a hobby horse and rocking horse, both made from some exotic wood from the other side of the world - apparently. These along with his diablo, skittles, marbles, yo-yo, spinning top, toy theatre and of course, his favourite, his pride of place, shiny red clockwork train, made from soldered tin. He had recalled days visiting the zoo and getting very close to rare, beautiful animals - and there had been talk of a pony - but that did not interest him. That, he thought, is more of a girl's thing. Archie had heard of children working in mines or factories - living, working, eating and often dying in damp, filthy conditions - but no such thing for him.

He had a governess, Ms Buddington, who looked after him every day and was almost a parent as his father spent all his time at work as a surgeon. Archie had been brought up by Ms Buddington for as long as he could remember. Ms Buddington was the primary person in

Archie's life. She was always there. She was the closest thing to a mother that he'd ever had. But not a mother in the conventional terms. Archie had never known his mother, and furthermore, there was never any mention of her. So, there was Ms Buddington. She acted as mother but also a teacher, disciplinarian and often, the fiercest enemy. Archie's relationship with her was very unusual. He knew she would protect him, take care of him, do anything for him, but he also felt like he would be in trouble at any moment if he didn't follow her instructions. And she gave a lot of instructions.

Her personality matched her appearance. She was strict and harsh, and she looked strict and harsh. Always in black, with a lace embroidered dress she certainly looked the part. Her face was as white as snow with cherry red lips and dark eyes. Very dark eyes, like they held a cold secret from the past. Her hair was always tied up and never out of place and on her chest, was a brooch of a silver heart with a robin for decoration. Archie very rarely saw her appear any different. She would be like that when he went to sleep, and when he opened his eyes to a new dawn, she would be there pulling back the curtains in the same pose. Archie often thought Ms Buddington must sleep in her clothes to always be ready, but inevitably that would crease them he thought. However she did it; she always looked immaculate.

"Preparation is everything, Archie," she informed Archie. "Know what you like and stick with it. That way you will never be disappointed."

The only change in appearance would be on an outing which was very rare. Then she would adorn a lady's top hat and her ebony walking cane topped with a silver orb.

The top hat and the cane were accessories the day he had met those people on the street. She had been there again; his guardian and his protector. Because of that, his father insisted he spent all his time at home with Ms Buddington or at work with him. Archie's home was spacious - substantial. It was a vast city house with several floors. Most of the rooms on the fourth floor were Archie's or somehow linked to him. He had, of course, a bedroom, but conjoined to this was a dressing room. A dressing room for a child and a male child at that - who had heard of such a ridiculous thing. There was a bathroom where the elegant roll top bath stood like a throne; the schoolroom where he was taught daily by Ms Buddington upon a small wooden desk with a lifting lid and inkwell, in front of a large blackboard, on which Ms Buddington would scratch her nails to demand his attention; the playroom, where his extravagant belongs lived, but in a controlled, obsessive tidy manner and finally Ms Buddington's room. He had caught glimpses inside - plain and simple - but he dared never enter. Staying here all the time saved Archie from trouble on the street, but not from his nightmares.

There were other people in the house of course. Smetherly, the Butler, ensured everything ran smoothly and Santini was an eccentric Italian cook. Smetherly was not a very pleasant person and very rarely spoke, except to utter "Sir" or "M'lady". He looked very dapper in his long black serving jacket, grey waistcoat (buttons trying to explode open) and black cravat (stained with dribble and beads of sweat). Over the years, he had gained a few extra pounds, so now sweated a great deal - most of the time in fact - so he invariably looked red and breathed heavily. Archie could always hear him coming as his shoes clipped the wooden or tiled floors in the house, like a shire horse over cobbles. Under his arm, as always, was a silver platter - upon which he brought and collected items that Archie's father or guests required.

Santini, on the other hand, was a different entity entirely. A small man from Italy, but with a personality that could fill the world. His hair was always neatly greased back, and a smile continually adorned his face, but above his top lip, there was a masterpiece. Moustaches were commonplace among sophisticated men of the time, but this was perfection. Smartly trimmed under his nose, the whiskers extended out at both ends and entwined like a cobra being teased in a circle - waiting to pounce on its prey. The time that it must take to get that ready each day must be tremendous Archie thought. Santini was always cooking. Archie would often visit the kitchen to try the latest recipe he was creating. Whether it be boiled calf's head, crimped fish, soused pig's face or pressed duck, Santini had a knack of turning exotic food into culinary delights.

Through living his life at home though, Archie's interaction with other people – let alone children was very minimal. The only other child he was friends with was Katrina Biggs (Kat)– the niece of Ms Buddington – who also lived in the house as a scullery maid. Although in most homes of this sort, the young gentleman talking to a scullery maid would be frowned upon, Archie did not care one bit. The time he spent with Kat was the only time he felt like a proper child because they had fun, lots of it.

"You try first…" dared Archie.

"Ok," came the reply from Kat. "Watch this!" The pair of them sat in their favourite position, at the edge of the bannister on the fourth floor. Sometimes they let their legs dangle through the rails, but today they were leaning over the railing looking down to the basement. There, they knew Smetherly would appear shortly, and the aim was to drop things onto him as he passed so far below. Bits of food, rolled up paper, toy soldiers; whatever the dare would allow. Kat's favourite was paper that she had chewed a good while so was nice and soggy. This was today's weapon of choice. Because of the distance between the fourth floor and the basement, it was all about timing. One had to aim at the place the person would be rather than where they were at that moment. Kat dropped her missile. They both watched with breath inhaled. Missed. But only just. Smetherly had passed, and the stray rocket crashed to the floor. They both leant back and laughed.

"You were so close," complemented Archie, "you nearly got him right on his shiner."

"He would have gone crazy", came the reply. "Do you remember last week?" Archie creased up and the thought of it.

"I felt sure I were for it then."

The antics of the previous week had involved a lot of paper, patience and saliva. Archie had hung over the edge of the bannister with Kat grabbing his legs. Then, the selection of paper spitballs they had made were carefully attached to the ceiling below; just enough to stick on but enough to fall off at any sudden movement. The target was the kitchen door. When Smetherly, for they felt sure it would be him, came out of the kitchen, the heavy door would slam after him, and they planned that all their spit bombs would fall from the ceiling onto the unsuspecting butler.

"Hurry up, I can't hold you much longer!" complained Kat.

"I'm almost there, just a few more."

"You weigh a tonne; too many crumpets for breakfast today?"

"Be quiet you," whispered Archie angrily. Kat loved winding him up, and he fell for it every time.

"Yes, Master Archie, whatever you say Master Archie, three bags full Master Archie." The teasing continued.

"Right, I'm done. Pull me up." Kat heaved on Archie's legs, and he swung back to safety over the bannister. Smetherly would know who had done the prank. He knew both would be involved, but he dared not say anything to Archie's father as he would fear for his job. Regarding Kat, he would not dare think of speaking to Ms Buddington as he feared it would be more than his life was worth. They retired to the floor above and took up a safe viewing spot between the rails. Time was against them as the spit would soon dry up and the balls drop. It needed to happen promptly. They heard a door open.

"This is it!" whispered Kat in anticipation. But the kitchen door did not open. They distinctly heard footsteps on the black and white tiled floor, but it was coming from the other end of the corridor - his father's study.

"Oh no." Archie could not bear to watch.

"Let's hope he's not hungry!" Kat responded. They could now see him walking down the corridor toward the door.

"Smetherly, Smetherly, where are you?" boomed the man's loud voice. He walked past the kitchen door.

"Phew," sighed both children in relief, but then the kitchen door opened. There stood Smetherly.

"Is there something I can help you with Master?" came the droll tone in an awkward manner.

"Have you seen Archie?"

"I believe he is with that young maid Miss Katrina."

"Right!" He almost pushed Smetherly back into the kitchen and the butler tumbled into a pile on the floor with a crash of culinary items. His father returned up the corridor, but as he moved, the kitchen door slammed with no Smetherly to hold it and, all at once, what seemed like hundreds of tiny paper spit bombs dropped onto the target below.

Truman Roker was a great man - a truly great man. To Archie, a giant of a man. But perhaps all children felt like that about their fathers. Six feet and two inches, slicked back, black hair, trimmed short at the sides and an elegant slug-like moustache, crawling across his top lip, trying to reach the small triangle of hair left on his chin. Square-jawed and often wearing a monocle in the left eye, Archie felt he could see into people's souls through that monocle. He was always smartly dressed. Dark grey trousers and jacket, a silver waistcoat, with a shining pocket watch and either a crisp white or darkest black shirt. This look was topped off with a smart cravat around his neck. The final piece to this attire was a black walking cane. A metal base at the foot which tapped on the floor as he walked and a solid silver headpiece of a fox at the top, a symbol that his father enjoyed, naming it after his son, telling Archie that one day, he would become the fox. When out and about, he would wear, like most men about the town, a long black figure-hugging coat and an excellent top hat. Archie thought his father's hat was always a little taller than everyone else's. The dark, dreary colour of his wardrobe made Archie believe it looked like he was a regular attendant at a funeral.

"Perhaps it's in case one of his patients dies?" he often wondered to Kat. She just looked at Archie. To her, he was Mr Roker or "Sir". The man who put a roof over her head and paid her aunt's bills.

A world-renowned surgeon who held high power in the country. He was private surgeon to the sovereign, Queen Mathilda. Roker had explained on numerous occasions that because of this prestigious role, he would have to be away from home - on call at the palace. Not only did he operate on significant patients, but he lectured to other surgeons about the techniques he used. He spent most of his time at his surgery or travelling to other such establishments in the country or throughout the world. Because of this, Archie only saw him once a week, on a Sunday. Archie had a strange relationship with his father – he felt like a burden, a chore upon him.

It was not that his father did not give him any attention; he could not as he was so busy. The times they were together; Archie travelled with Roker. His father would tell him about the places he had been or the people that he had met. How lucky he was to meet such famous and influential people and that one day, Archie would do the same. Archie recalled his visits to the medical surgery to Kat on numerous occasions; that his Father would explain that, one day, he would be like this, but he had to learn the family business. This confused Archie. He could see the attraction in saving people's lives as a doctor or surgeon, but, at times, his father seemed to almost experiment on bodies and then discuss his findings with other people. This wasn't for Archie. He often dreamt of travelling the world. One day, when he was older, Archie would take all the people he knew on a trip around the world – whether on the big steamboat or the zeppelin – he would leave the house and surgery behind and visit all the exotic places Ms Buddington had mentioned in his Geography lessons.

At the surgery, Archie would either follow his Father around or sit in the big leather chair in his office. He was sure his Father must be of importance for him to work that hard. He must be busy to not spend time with him. The surgery looked an exciting place, but after years of paying a visit every Sunday, it became very dull very quickly. There were many others there too, all dressed up in their top hats smart suits and pressed shirts. Archie recognised many of these men: Lord Burley Wilberforce, a man who had revolutionised the mental health system in England and many of his ideas were used around the world. In a time when inmates had equal rights and were treated humanely for once, Wilberforce had been the man to put all of this into place. Before his astonishing input people were admitted for many lunatic reasons including jealousy, laziness, religious enthusiasm, fighting fires or even grief. Not only did he improve the facilities in many institutes but also reassessed many of the people who were inmates at the time to allow them another chance at a normal life.

Edward Plundell was another reformer in the medical field whom Archie recalled. Although he had never met him in person, he felt he knew him from the number of times his name appeared in conversation or the numerous medical journals Roker read. Archie's father was a top surgeon in the country, Archie knew that, but the measures Plundell brought in ensured the success of Archie's father. Not only revolutionising basic hygiene through steam in the operating theatre, Plundell also inspired and helped develop many of the tools and equipment used in most working surgeries throughout the world. Through a terrible accident as a child where he lost part of his left arm, Plundell was inspired to help others so they may never suffer like he did at the hands of ignorant and ill-educated doctors.

"Is that why he doesn't come to the surgery much?" Archie asked his father, "because of his arm."

"Yes, it's a bit of a sore subject, and Plundell keeps himself to himself. He doesn't want people seeing him, or his arm." These men, along with Dr Borthwell (a pioneer in charity work, especially for children), Alphonso Meredeth (a statesman in the evolution of humans and genetics) and Eligah Bilton (at the forefront of disease prevention), were the most regular members who viewed surgery and then met afterwards in a very secretive manner.

The other regular character was Oliver Crowle, the head of the police. Crowlies had been set up in the capital, and their success was unparalleled. However, the tactics they sometimes used with specific groups of the community left little to the imagination. His success in the capital had led to other forces throughout the country and people from all over the world coming to see how the streets of London were kept safe. Although not a medical man, his presence was always prominent and a certain amount of security was always felt when he was in the building. A selection of Crowlies were ever present

Archie's father would give lectures and perform operations for many people including the pioneering gentlemen mentioned, but also many, many others; all wearing the identical, smart black suits. Archie often stood and gazed around the vast operating theatre. When empty, it had been a marvellous place to play when Archie had been younger; to run and climb and play with marbles. However, when full, the arena was a different place. Men, (always men), peering and stretching their necks to get the best view possible of what Archie's Father was doing. Of course, other surgeons performed, from around the world, but this was his Father's surgery, and he was the top dog. Sometimes, Archie could watch, others he was strictly forbidden. Occasionally it sounded like screams and cries, but Archie was sure he must have misheard. All the things his Father did would be to make people better, not hurt them.

On one occasion, when Archie was watching another slightly tedious talk on the brain, he heard a man screaming a lot of disruption coming from the high locked steel door at the back of the theatre. This entry was enormous, and Archie was sure it must be a safe. He had asked his father, but he always got the same reply.

"Behind the door are our world's greatest secrets. When you are old enough, you will see them for yourself. Till then, you must remain safe from them."

The technician in the theatre spoke to his father, and Archie knew something was about to happen as his father sent an assistant to move him away. Before he was taken, he saw the large bolted steel door with intricate locks and seals on it being opened. Cogs and gears turned most elaborately on the steel door - twisting, turning, interlocking - like a mechanical maze showing the path through. As the door opened a bright flash of light and a hive of activity seemed to be taking place on the other side. Archie always assumed it was another room in the medical centre, the vault, the safe. He had asked his father numerous times if he could go in, but he was not allowed. When you're old enough, he would tell him in a stern voice. Archie had tried to sneak a look numerous times and even tried to slip in but the head of security, Loren Kruncher, had other ideas. A huge man, whom Archie thought was as wide as he was tall. It always looked like he had his head-on upside down. On the top, not a single hair anywhere, but on his chin, the largest, bushiest, ginger beard you could ever see. He looked like a round version of a circus strongman or a street wrestler. He wore an ill-fitting suit due to his width and a small bow tie that disappeared into insignificance under his beard. Threats of a clip round the ear hole or telling his father was enough to send Archie on his way, but he still had questions.

"Maybe it's a place for dangerous secrets?" Kat had suggested. Archie was not sure, but he could not wait till he was old enough to go through the door and find its secrets out for himself. There had of course been other incidents. Fighting seemed to break out near the door every couple of months. Sometimes with one or two people or sometimes with larger groups but it always ended with Kruncher and his men stopping the proceedings and someone being taken away from the vast metal door. Sometimes, quite eerily, they were even taken inside.

One day, Archie was at the theatre, following his father around. He seemed more preoccupied than usual, worried about something, and he kept mentioning the great steel door. Even though it was a Sunday, the theatre was in full swing, lectures taking place and meetings with various men in suits. Archie's father was talking to a group of men in suits. That's when it happened. The door swung open.

Chapter 2
The Visitors

A vast billow of smoke blew through the doorway, filling the ground floor of the surgery. No one seemed to know what had happened or what was going to happen next. People were shouting and screaming at each other; panic was the order of the day. But why? What was through the doorway? What had made the door open so violently? Was everyone safe? Archie had many questions and thoughts running through his head but no time to stop and think about the answers. As the smoke cleared, a hot glowing light emitted from the opening; like the sun had fallen from the sky and was trying to pass through the gateway. Men scrambled to try and close the door, but in the process, knocked over shelves which contained row after row of bottles full of medical samples and trays that had surgical equipment, that looked more suitable in a torture chamber than a theatre of medicine.

"Get those people out of here," Kruncher ordered. People were ushered from the room. "We need more security! Get some Crowlies in here." Archie realised it must be severe if the police were involved. Not a shout for a maintenance team to fix something, but the police. But why? For who or what were they being called? Then Archie realised.

Amidst all the initial chaos and confusion, three people entered the surgery, unknown to Kruncher and his men.

"Where are they? Where have they gone?" Kruncher moaned. Various shouts came from his colleagues, but nothing to help find the strangers. They surrounded the doorway but, from Archie's high vantage point, at the back of the first-floor balcony, he could see the trio had already entered as the smoke choked the room. Now they were making their way around the room, in different ways; snaking from tier to tier, avoiding any noticeable movement. What was evident to Archie was that the security detail was looking the wrong way. All their eyes focused on the doorway, but they were too late. Archie took it all in, he did not feel afraid, moreover excited at what was filling, what would have been another ordinary, dull day. Feeling safe in his high, secure lookout, he carefully observed the mysterious characters as they wove between the rails in the lower half of the theatre.

The first wore a top hat, but unlike any other Archie had seen the fine men about town wearing. This was made from brown stained leather with a curved rim, brimming with random accessories – a key on a chain, a small bottle with what looked like red liquid, three bullets and a feather, long and brown as if recently plucked from a pheasant. The mask he wore wholly covered his face and eyes. The goggles, like circular cavities, were black and lifeless like pools at midnight. The mouthpiece, however, was blue and red leather, covered in gold and silver studs, almost like a ventilator of some sort – as if the air in the surgery were poisonous. The rest of his clothing was as equally elaborate, again with blue and red leather, decorated with studs all over, but the most striking element was one armful of golden machinery –

cogs, gears and levers – and something that looked like a syringe about to fire from his bicep.

The second, a lady with bright red hair like the setting sun, followed behind. She too wore goggles, but these rested on top of her head acting almost like a headband taming the fiery locks. She also wore a mask, and like her accomplice, this too was decorated with golden cogs and machinery. However, the rest of the cover was as if two pieces of brown leather were stitched to hold her face together. Like a pair of boot laces, it was pulled tight across her face, and press studs aided the job of connecting the two sides. She wore a highly decorative top – white with red pinstripes and elaborate matching ribbon bows down the front. Almost the front part of a fancy swimming costume, or a designer nightdress, but over the top, just above her chest and covering one arm was a green khaki material, the kind a soldier may wear, with leather trim, finished off with leather fingerless gloves. Buckles and straps adorned the arms and matched a similar pattern on the brown leather trousers she wore – again with chains, pouches and bottle attachments. Two vials of liquid – one red one blue, nestled safely against her left thigh.

The final visitor could have been either male or female – Archie didn't know. Grey and black pinstripe trousers and a black leather jacket with several buckles across the front were relatively modest in comparison to the others, but underneath a brown hood, this character wore a terrifying mask. Like the bird mask worn by doctors at the time of the great plague, this appendage brought fear to Archie. Black goggles again provided no clue to the soul of the character, but the elaborate design covering

26

the beak of the mask was almost mesmerising. What secrets did this mask and in fact all the disguises hold? Who were these people and what did they want?

As the trio continued their climb, now up to the first floor, Kruncher and his ineffective workforce realised their error. Like a gang of bumbling fools, they now tried to climb the tiers like the strangers. These men were neither the fittest nor healthiest ever seen. Many were overweight and a little light of brain cells. Not like the three athletic strangers who had come through, nimbly moving from tier to tier, avoiding any confrontation. Archie's concern grew as the strangers grew closer to his position. He decided it was time to move; to retire to his father's office and feel safe. Kruncher was shouting at him.

"Archie, get away from there. What on earth are you doing?" Panic was now starting to set in. He shifted and planned to run to the nearest exit, but as he turned, something was blocking his path. The first person he had seen - adorning the leather top hat - was standing in front of him. No face to look upon, only the black circles leading into the man's soul were in front of him. The mask made the breathing of this giant sound like he had a machine, performing it for him. He stood there; arms on rails at either side of him, blocking the path for Archie. The golden syringe, now more menacing than ever was facing towards Archie. He backed up, away from this strange being; scrabbling backwards as quickly as he could, hoping a door would appear behind him. Suddenly he felt something behind him, and as he turned, he soon realised it was not a door. There stood the creature with the bird face. Out of the three characters, this was the one that caused Archie the most fear - the mask had a long beak, looking like it was encrusted with either jewels or cogs; perhaps both. What monstrous look did this mask cover? What was the purpose of such a creation? If it was to strike fear into its viewer (as it did with Archie) then who would come up with such an idea. Surrounded on both sides, Archie scrabbled across the floor, under the rail and fell backwards from one tier to the next. The tumble was stopped by the third character.

"Careful Archie, you don't want to hurt yourself now, do you? You're far too precious." Archie didn't know what to do; was he more shocked that the mystery rescuer knew his name; that it spoke to him; or that it spoke in a soft feminine voice that felt so warm and caring?

"Who are you?" Archie finally stammered out the words.

"That young man, is something you will find out very, very soon," came the reply. The woman winked at Archie, lifted him to his feet. Suddenly he was surrounded again by all three characters from the doorway. He looked to see where the guards were, but they were still climbing the steep steps of the surgery towards the first floor; panting wearily and out of breath. In the next moment, without hesitation, the three strangers acrobatically flew over the top of the clumsy guards and headed towards the steel doorway again. Kruncher stood there, and he looked like a man on a mission. The lady who had spoken to Archie was the first to him. He stood there bracing for impact, but as she approached, she dropped to the floor and the first man in the leather top hat, used her as a springboard to propel himself through the air at Kruncher. He met the old man with two feet straight in his chest, knocking him to the floor. The other two characters followed; the lady tapping Kruncher on the head as she passed; the strange character with a mask, slowly turning and looking at Archie one last time, before they all disappeared through the doorway.

The scene that followed was nearly as chaotic as that that had preceded it. Archie's father, who had not been present during the "invasion", suddenly appeared back in the surgery. Where had he gone during that time? Archie wondered but more so why had his father not come back for him. His only son. While thinking of this Archie's heart sank. Although he was not close to his father, the realisation of this thought made his heart heavy.

As his father took command of the situation, Archie remained on the higher tiers, out of view and (probably as his father thought) out of mind.

"What on earth have you been doing you fool?" Archie's father shouted at Kruncher.

"I'm sorry Mr Roker sir. They were just too quick for us. We managed to contain them in here and not let them escape out."

"Not let them out? Really?" Roker retorted. "That's funny…" As he said this, he clapped his hands. The doors to the surgery opened and in they walked. Crowlies. Like nothing you had seen before. Kruncher and his men looked fierce, but these men were not to be messed with one bit. With Roker being good friends with Oliver Crowle they were at his beck and call. Smart, simple uniforms, with a black waistcoat and a long black overcoat; slicked back hair, shaven short around the back and sides; whistles on chains, attached to large brass buttons, in their pockets; and the stumper - the weapon of choice of a Crowlie. A long, thin handled hammer with a flat-ended mallet on the top, often held over the shoulders of the men as they awaited instruction. When they entered the room suddenly, everyone felt on edge.

"The room was secure because of these gentlemen. Nothing to do with you!" Roker explained in a sarcastic tone. "We almost had them. They couldn't escape from this room and the one exit that you had to block, the way they entered - you couldn't even do that."

"I'm ...I'm ... sorry, sir."

"What the hell did they want anyway?"

"I don't know sir. They came in climbed to the top where young Master Roker was and then came back down. We didn't stand a chance!"

Roker soon changed his tone.

"They went for Archie? Right..." Archie was still watching from above, and his father's shouting now turned into quiet words. He whispered something to Kruncher and then to one of the Crowlies. The next thing Archie knew, four large bags were brought into the surgery. From these, the men brought out some equipment. What looked initially like a gas mask was attached to each of the men. But this cover had a long pipe that led into the back of each man. They then also added a type of gauntlet into their right hand. From a distance, Archie could not make out the detail of them, but it looked like dials and cogs. When they were all suited and booted, a Crowlie stood by the door. He placed his gauntlet up against the door, and as he did a series of mechanisms began to move and steam came from around the door. The other Crowlies stood ready; as if their gauntlets were weapons. The door swung open and they charged through. Once they had entered, the door swung shut.

"Keep that door locked. We need to know what they have brought in or what they have taken out." Roker ordered.

He now turned to Archie. He beckoned him down. Archie was unsure yet he did do as his father said.

"Come here, Archie. You are safe now. What did those people do to you?"

"They...they didn't do anything. They just said that I'd find out everything very soon. What does it mean?"

Roker looked concerned but then changed to a more relaxed look.

"Archie, a lot is going on here at the surgery. A lot you need to know but when you are older. Not now. I can't risk that now."

"But..."

"No Archie. I know you must have lots of questions but that is all I can say now. I must sort out this mess that Kruncher has left here. I will make sure you are taken home safely and then in the coming weeks I will explain what is happening."

Archie wanted to ask more but he felt sure the response would be no. When his father said no that meant no. Archie was escorted home, not only by a troop of Crowlies but also Oliver Crowle himself.

Crowle sat opposite him in the carriage. He only looked a young man - perhaps in his early thirties - but he was always impeccably dressed. A salmon coloured waistcoat with two long strips of buttons on either side, covered a white shirt. Over this, ran a long brown leather strap that attached to his belt on the front and back. At the foot of this strap, in an elaborate holster, was a gun and a selection of bullets, though Archie felt this appeared to be more for display and effect than actual use. Over the top, he wore a long dark, leather trench coat; two strips of silver buttons running up his waist and chest on either side of his torso.

As he walked, or strutted as Archie felt more appropriate, the long tails of the jacket blew behind him giving him a majestic presence, matched only by the exquisitely, detailed design on the front; a design William Morris would have been proud of. The double-breasted jacket could remain open as it was now, be button up to the chest, or to hide whatever may loom below, buttoned up to the neck allowing two parallel lines of silver buttons gleaming through. He indeed looked a formidable character and Archie felt glad he was under his protection. However, he dared not speak to any of these men and when he returned home, the look on Ms Buddington's face told him not to ask her anything either. "Go to your room, get ready for bed and go to sleep," she ordered as he walked in.

He did as he was told and went straight to his room. He changed into his nightwear as commanded, but went to the window to peer out. The square upon which the house was situated was very private on a typical day. It was not on a through road and there were no other front entrances to other homes on either side of the courtyard. Merely two walls parallel belong to establishments on either side and a small gatehouse through which a carriage could pass if attending this residence. As he looked out of his fourth-floor window, he could see a different scene. Oliver Crowle was giving orders to a troop of Crowlies; rules which were followed out to the letter following as two Crowlies manned the gatehouse, two the front door and two disappeared, to the rear of the house Archie assumed. Crowle turned and looked at Archie's window. Archie swiftly closed the curtain and returned to his bed. The last thing he needed was Crowle reporting back to his father.

Archie lay in bed in the darkness. He could hear movement on the landing outside in the corridor. This was nothing unusual, merely Ms Buddington going about her business but he felt this time she would be around outside for quite a while. As he stared into the darkness, he thought of what the soft female voice had said. He was too precious - he would find out everything soon. How did these people know him? Why was he precious? What were they doing at the surgery? And where did they go? Where did that giant steel door lead to?

For the next few days, Archie felt different. He felt as if he were being followed. Whether it was the visitors to the surgery or the Crowlies (who were still present outside the house), he didn't know what to feel. Something in the air made him feel uncomfortable. He just wasn't sure what it was. He hadn't noticed any suspicious characters following him, especially with goggles on, but still, the feeling remained. One thing he had seen was a raven. First, it landed on the opposite side of the square, resting on the highest point of the gatehouse. Next, he spotted it on a window ledge nearby. Cawing out a strange sound, almost like it was being wound up. But that was just his imagination was it not? A raven following him? Really?

Often connected to the occult and many myths and legends; an ill omen with a diet of carrion. In certain parts of Europe, ravens were linked to death and lost souls; the ghosts of murdered people. In his religious studies with Ms Buddington, ravens were continuously mentioned. In the Book of Genesis, Noah released a raven from the ark after the great flood to test whether the waters have receded - the raven was a symbol of vice, unlike the dove - a symbol of virtue. God commanded ravens to feed Elijah. Ravens were an example of God's provision for all creatures in the Psalms. According to the legend of the fourth-century Christian martyr Saint Vincent of Saragossa, after St. Vincent was executed, ravens protected his body from being devoured by wild animals until his followers could recover him. His body was taken to what is now known as Cape St. Vincent in southern Portugal. A shrine was erected over his grave, which continued to be guarded by flocks of ravens.

Throughout history, especially regarding Vikings, ravens were key. In Norse mythology, Odin was depicted as having two ravens Huginn and Muninn serving as his eyes and ears – Huginn being referred to as thought and Muninn as memory. Each day, the ravens flew out from Hliðskjálf and brought Odin news from Midgard. The raven was a typical device used by the Vikings. Ragnar Lodbrok had a raven banner called Reafan, embroidered with the crest of a raven. It was said that if this standard fluttered, Lodbrok would carry the day, but if it hung lifeless, the battle would be lost.

Closer to home, according to legend, the Kingdom of England would fall if the ravens of the Tower of London were removed. It had been thought that there had been at least six ravens in residence at the tower for centuries. Archie knew the symbolism of a raven from his Greek lessons he had suffered. Ravens were associated with Apollo, the god of prophecy – symbols of good luck – the God's messengers to the mortal world. No, it must just be his imagination.

"I mean, a raven following me! What would my father say to that?"

Days passed and the feeling of someone watching him continued. He hadn't bothered telling Ms Buddington: she would never listen to such nonsense. And if he revealed this to his Father, he would probably get into trouble. That's what his father was like. Archie often thought back to the time he had been attacked when he was younger by the mystery gang and how he'd told his father his feelings about it, but his father had told him to man up, to not worry about it and to grow up. He never forgot that.

Chapter 3
The Raven

Things had calmed down over the next few weeks and months. The Crowlies were no longer positioned outside of the house; visits to the surgery became less and less; Archie felt like a prisoner in his own home still, but there was light at the end of the tunnel. His father had told him he would be going away with him soon on a special trip which would start to answer the many questions he had. For his trip, Archie was given a list of many things he would need to get from town. This pleased Archie no end: the thought of going out of the house and breathing fresh air. The list was long with many items already in his possession but some, he did not possess: a black velvet suit with a vulpes corvum lining (Archie did not know what this meant but thought it sounded very grand); black leather boots - like he wore daily but travelling much higher up his calf; plus, a long, red velvet robe - very specifically with a hood. The trip would also include a visit to the barbers, milliners, jewellers and bookshop.

Excitement grew as the day of the trip to town approached.

"Time to go Archie. Ms Buddington can you take Archie to the second carriage," Roker ordered.

"As you wish Sir. Come along Archie; you heard your father." Archie followed her out and wondered why the second carriage.

"Are we not travelling with Father?" Archie questioned.

"We will be travelling together. The first and third carriage are for security."

"Security? Security for what?"

"Don't you worry about that Archie. Just get in the carriage." As he passed through the entrance, between the grand pillars guarding the giant front door, into the courtyard, he saw the second coach in front of the doorway. Looking from left to right, he saw carriages on either side, not as elaborate as the one he was readying to board, nor as big. However, in each one sat a driver, with two Crowlies aboard.

As he climbed into the main carriage, seating himself on the plush, red seating, he noticed the blinds were pulled down over the windows. This made it very dark inside so he moved to open the shutter. Ms Buddington tapped his hand as she entered.

"Get off. Leave that alone. Orders from your father."

"But it's too dark!"

"Do you want to argue with your father?"

Archie did not. He sat down quietly, fiddling with indents in the seat, twiddling the little button around between his thumb and forefinger.

"And stop messing with that..." barked Ms Buddington. Archie tutted but very quietly. The day he had been looking forward to for so long was not going as he planned so far.

His father now climbed into the carriage and sat down.

"Can we open the blinds?"

"No,' replied his father, 'but I can do this." He leant forward and rotated a metal rod hanging down. As he did, part of the roof slowly slid open and warm sunlight flooded into the carriage. A smile grew on Archie's face as he could now see the world as he travelled along. The sound of the hustle and bustle of the town fascinated Archie. Street sellers calling out for the attention of passers-by. The sound of other carriages passing by and the general hum of daily life in a town. Boring for many but something Archie longed to see daily.

The jewellers was the first place to be visited. Siddons' Jewels was a distinguished shop in town. Only the wealthiest people could shop here, and if you were not recognised by Emmitt Siddons, you were denied entry. Archie accepted the familiar sight of Crowlies stood either side of the door as he entered.

"Ah, Siddons... excellent to see you. Now you recall the ring I asked you for. For my son. He is nearly ready for his first visit and we are preparing him with everything he needs."

"Of course Sir, I have it ready for you. I shall just get it from the safe." The old man shuffled off behind the counter to a dark back room.

"Now Archie, this ring is significant. It is the start of the next phase of your life. We will be visiting some compelling people soon and you need to be the part for it. It is a little bit like an exclusive club and being a club there are certain things you need to do, wear and rules to follow. The first is this ring. Have you heard of Ebenezer Dorrington?" Archie nodded. "Well, it is designed by him. It is extraordinary, and when I give it to you, you will wear it all the time. Wearing this ring will open many doors to you; quite literally."

Archie was unsure what his father meant, but he did not want to look like he was not listening, so he uncomfortably agreed. He had heard of Ebenezer Dorrington at least; a famous artist and designer. Many people wore jewellery or clothes designed by him, or hung paintings and positioned art created by him.

The jeweller wandered back into the room carrying a small black leather box. His glasses looked like they were about to fall off the end of his nose and Archie thought this man would be blinded without them. For such an elegant jewellery shop, the man dressed in very plain simple clothes. A stained, striped collarless cotton shirt, covered with a shabby waistcoat, dotted in flecks of dandruff like a brief snowstorm at night. The man could not do enough for Mr Roker and his level of grovelling made Archie feel a little uncomfortable. Roker opened the box and looked inside.

"Perfect. Exquisite work as ever Siddons."

"Can I have a look?" Archie asked as, after all, it was his ring.

"Not yet: the time is not right." Archie did not ask any further questions. Roker thanked Siddons for his assistance and, in return, he was praised for his custom.

"Shall I put it on the usual account, Sir?" Siddons grovelled.

"Of course," Roker replied giving the poor man a stony glare.

A similar thing happened at the bookstore; collecting a specific, ordered book but not showing it to Archie. The barbers followed with a fresh, short haircut that made Archie feel like a Crowlie. At the Milliners, Archie's head was measured and a hat ordered to be made specifically for him. Then at the tailors, Archie was measured up by the owner, Clovis Tudor, for his new suit. It felt bizarre to have all these things being made specifically for him for one event that he knew nothing about. What was the function his father was taking him to? Suddenly, a man entered the tailors. A Crowlie stood to block the breathless intruder, but Roker stopped him and beckoned the man forward. He handed Roker a note and spoke quietly to him as Archie was still stood in the middle of the room on a stool with his arms stretched out; looking like the smartest scarecrow to grace a field of corn.

"Ms Buddington, I need to leave, something urgent has come up and I need to sort it now, but I cannot take Archie with me. I will take the carriages as it may not be safe for you to travel in those. I wish you to leave this shop through the back entrance taking these two officers with you. We are only ten minutes from home. Take back streets and avoid the main road that people assume we will take. Get Archie home and safe." He then turned to Archie. "I know you heard all that. Do not ask any questions, leave with Ms Buddington and go home. Do you understand?" Archie nodded. Archie's father then left with and he could see through the door as he climbed back into the carriage.

"Right young man, follow me," ordered Ms Buddington. They were led to the rear of the shop and an old wooden door with two rusty bolts was opened for them. Back out into the sunlight they went.

"Why do we have to avoid the main roads?" Archie questioned.

"Let's just follow your father's instructions shall we," came the reply. Street after street, they walked down, but these were purely pedestrian. No carriages could fit down these. Many people were bustling in the streets, a side of the town Archie rarely saw. The hardworking folk whose lives were a million miles away from Archie's.

As they passed through these narrow streets (with the pair of Crowlies still nearby), Archie stopped and to listen to some street musicians; one playing a melodeon and another violin. Archie enjoyed music and was keen to practice his violin at home at any opportunity. Again, having not much contact with the outside world meant more time for things like that – things he really enjoyed. Ms Buddington beckoned him on but Archie recognised the song and wanted to stay until the end. She grabbed him by the forearm and tried dragging him away but he was not having that. He shrugged his hand away from hers and folded his arms in displeasure. What followed were a few choice words from Ms Buddington. Archie had always done as he was told, especially when outside, but something changed inside him today. He took a few steps back away from the continuous sound of Ms Buddington and then he saw the two figures of the Crowlies in the background head towards him. He continued to shuffle backwards, past the musicians and into the crowd. Still only being a short young man, he was not easily spotted in the massing crowd. He knew his way back home and he had looked forward to his day out so much he did not want it ruined by Ms Buddington, or indeed a couple of Crowlies dragging him home. He enjoyed the feeling of freedom even more now. He weaved in and out of streets, stalls and people. He came to confectioners and decided to enter. Jars and jars of sweets lined the walls and he looked up in amazement at the rainbow of colours in front of him: Bull's Eyes, Pear Drops, Rosy Apples, Bonbons to name a few. As he stood there wide mouthed and dribbling he suddenly realised - he had no money. He never carried money. He had no need - Ms Buddington would get him what he required, but she wasn't there. He felt a slight pang of guilt and decided to go and look for her. She must be panic-stricken now thought Archie. Out into the streets again he went. Weaving and ducking between stalls and people. That's when he saw it!

The mask - the long bird mask he had seen in the surgery. He did a double take, but it was no longer there. The long beak, covered in an elaborate design, trimmed with what looked like little rivets. And again, round black eyes which seemed to lead straight to hell. He continued looking for Ms Buddington, all around now. He saw it a second time. The mask. It appeared to be covered with a hood like last time, so other people around could not see it, but now Archie had seen it he was fixated. But the mask was coming towards him. He turned and ran, in the direction his nose was pointing. As fast as he could. He thought back to what happened to him as a child as he turned and looked over his shoulder. The faceless creature stalked him. He pushed past person after person. Angry shouts from passers-by as Archie bundled people over. One lady selling fruit on a cart was his next victim. As he repeatedly looked over his shoulder, he did not see the cart and he, the truck, and the poor lady ended up in a heap on the floor. Apologising profusely, Archie stumbled on leaving her to pick up her apples from the floor. He could see the mask gaining ground, so he ran down a secluded side street. Dodging and diving, eventually he found a small gap in a wall – low enough for him but too small for his pursuer to pass through. He appeared to be safe.

He sat there in silence – listening to the footsteps pass away and the regular street sounds take over again. And then he heard the flap of wings and a caw. There on the wall directly opposite him sat the raven. The raven that had been following him? How could he know? Well, he recognised the strange sound from before and upon looking at it, he realised why the noise it made was so strange.

Upon closer inspection of the raven, Archie was astounded to see that it was like no other raven he had seen before. It had the same structure and was the same size, but its body was not covered in black feathers, but what initially looked like pieces of scrap metal. As it turned his head towards Archie, the familiar caw came, but Archie could now see cogs and gears moving. It looked like a clockwork bird that had just been wound up. Archie rubbed his eyes as surely something like this was part of a dream and he must be in it. Something about the bird made him at ease and forget the situation that had occurred before. He moved from his hiding place and approached the bird. Although the creature moved very slow and methodically, it still seemed to be a friend, a companion. He half expected it to speak to him, but that would be ridiculous. He imagined telling Ms Buddington or his father about this. They would never believe him. Upon closer inspection, this magnificent mechanical creature had many working parts inside. Like machines he had seen on trips to factories with his father, it was so intricate. He reached out his hand in friendship, not knowing the possible result. He stroked the cold steel and felt the rust, rough against his fingers. As he became more confident, he noticed a ring on the bird's leg with what looked like a note attached. He wondered should he have a look? Would it be for him? Surely it was, and that is why the bird is here he thought logically to himself. And if it isn't I'm sure the bird will let me know. He leant forward and took the note. The Raven stood majestically as if he had won a prize. Archie unrolled the note and couldn't believe what he had in front of him. It read:

Archie - do not be afraid. We are your friends and we're here to help you. Trust nothing; open your mind to everything. We will protect you from those who wish you misfortune.

Archie was confused. Not only was he questioning why a mechanical raven was giving him messages, but who was after him? He thought back to the events earlier in the day and to the attack when he was younger. Who could it be and who is trying to protect him? It must be his father. He must know someone who can create magical machines like this and it was his way of protecting him. Protecting him from the masked individuals. That must be it he assured himself. He would ask his father about it when he saw him next. He wrapped the note up and put it in his pocket. He looked up at the raven, but it had moved from the wall; now sitting on the roof of the old run-down building in front of him. The cawing of the bird was soon drowned out by the cawing of Ms Buddington. She argued and shouted, but she seemed relieved to have found him. He decided not to mention the raven as he could see out of the corner of his eye it was still there.

On the walk home, Archie decided to question Ms Buddington about that eventful day as a younger child, when masked individuals attacked him.

"It must be linked," he answered her back. She didn't like his tone and made him know, but Archie didn't back down. Something was obviously going on. "All I can remember from those years ago was someone attacking us, and you defended me. I can picture you screaming for help and holding me tight as those people hit you demanding you set me free. What was it all about?"

"I cannot and will not say," she retorted in her usual demeaning manner, but Archie continued.

"If you don't tell me I shall tell Father that you left me alone in town and he will not be happy at that." He didn't feel happy about this threat, but it unquestionably wasn't idle. He thought he was old enough to know the truth and know who was after him.

"Master Archie, it is nothing for you to worry about. People are after you as your father is very well to do. You know that."

He begged and pleaded all the way home, but she refused. Even the threat of his father seemed to have little effect.

"Your father wouldn't believe you; he would only listen to me. He knows what boys are like!" she added trying to calm him down.

"Ha, well he wouldn't believe me about a mechanical raven then!" muttered Archie under his breath.

"What did you say?" Ms Buddington's mood changed completely.

"Nothing," replied Archie. Tales of the secret bird would only cause more trouble if he mentioned this.

"No. Say that again. What did you said about the mechanical raven?" she insisted. "Repeat what you said exactly."

"Father wouldn't believe me about a mechanical raven."

"And where might I ask have you seen a mechanical raven?"

Archie didn't know what he was more shocked about. The fact that she wasn't shouting at him or the fact that she was not questioning a mechanical raven.

"There are many things afoot Master Archie and many things you will find out that will change your life forever."

"What?" Archie didn't know what to think now. The one thing in life he felt Ms Buddington would never believe was now the thing she focused on and now she was telling him there is more.

"I cannot tell you now, but all I ask is that you do not mention this to your Father. You know what he is like and mention of this will only cause trouble for him, me and especially you. I cannot tell you all the secrets now. There is not enough time, but I know someone who can, and I will take you to see them the next time your father is away on business."

Chapter 4
Alium

Archie was perplexed: he had so many questions, but he could tell by the tone of her voice and the look in her eyes that Ms Buddington was severe, solemn and sincere. He considered her differently now. Something about her made him feel at ease, more so than ever before. Their relationship had been strange and unorthodox over the years of his life, but always close. She was strict, very strict. Too harsh at times he felt, but she was unfailingly there. No matter what. As solid as a rock. She had been more of a parent to him than his father had ever been. She had taught him to read, to spell, and to play the violin. She had cleaned his knee when he'd fallen, rubbed his back when he was sick, told him it would all be ok when he'd awoken from a nightmare. She was always there, and without reason, that had all come flooding back to him at this moment. Perhaps the way she had shown trust and belief in him had changed his views.

After feeling alone for most of his life, Archie suddenly sensed he had someone close. He reached out and hugged her. Something he had refrained from most of his life. His father would not approve, and Archie always believed neither would Ms Buddington. He closed his eyes and wondered what the response from his governess would be. He felt a warm, calming hand on his back and felt safe.

The journey home from this point was quiet. And quick. The Crowlies had eventually found Archie and his guardian and were now escorting the pair home at a rapid pace. One led the chain of people; walking menacingly; like a bulldog unhappy with its supper or the person trying to take it. People were either knocked out of the way if they had not seen the Crowlie, or fled to the side of the alleyways as quick as they could, for fear of the repercussions if they said anything or did not move. Next came Ms Buddington, focused on the task at hand (making sure Archie got home safe). Following, Archie glanced around, questioning what had happened still in his head and gazing up, looking for the mechanical raven; and behind, for the masked character. Finally, the second Crowlie, who walked with one eye continually behind him, unlike the bulldog at the front, more like a buzzard hovering high above, ready to pounce. A couple of times he would stop and grab someone, pushing them, aggressively and arrogantly, to one side, but always within a couple of metres of Archie.

They entered the courtyard, in front of the house, after passing through the gatehouse - again with extra Crowlies present. As he walked towards the front door, across the vast, elaborately paved square in front of the house, Archie gazed at the windows - almost thirty on the front face, each giving a glimpse into life in his unusual life. The elegant stone pillars guarded the front door and above was the ornate first-floor window, an excellent viewpoint - both for inside and outside of the house. Above that window, the mighty pillars on either side of the door reached their peak, with what looked like a sentry tower but only for a tiny person. It was here that he saw it again; the mechanical raven.

"Ms Buddington!" he burst out.

"No Archie!" came a stern reply, but one he felt was more protective than argumentative. The look on Ms Buddington's face said that she had seen it but with Crowlies around, it would probably be wise not to mention anything.

As he walked into the house, Archie was led immediately upstairs. The grand, ebony staircase coiled through the centre of the house like a snake, slithering and sneaking into the rooms of the house, searching for its prey. Past the first-floor window that he had gazed on only moments earlier from outside, stepping on the plush carpet that covered most of each step. The same pattern was adorning every stair. Trying to escape from each end was the matte finish of black wood, supporting the magnificent bannister that twisted and turned. Unlike the day of the attack in the surgery, Archie was not required to go straight to bed. Instead, he was placed in the music room.

This grand room was one of Archie's most favourite places. No one could fail to be impressed as they entered this splendid tribute to music. No matter what instrument one may play, it could be found in this room: a grand piano, that once belonged to a member of the royal family; a harpsichord from Venice dating back to the sixteenth century; a selection of ivory recorders and a tortoiseshell covered oboe that belonged to a famous Italian composer. Or a sitar, brought from India by some chap his father had said was called Lowther; and of course, the usual selection of stringed instruments, violin

(Archie's favourite), cello, guitar and, the largest of all, the one Archie dreamt of being able to play, the double bass. The room had two floors of windows along the front of the house, but along the back wall was a balcony with a huge comfortable chair sat near a stylish gramophone. Archie had spent many a time sat on that chair with Kat, listening to the strange sounds coming from the enormous bell at the end of the crackling stylus. The walls of the balcony were a collection of the wax circles that were played, often late into the evening. Looking over the rail to the view below, an enormous grand piano was the real focal point of the room, but other instruments joined to create an excellent orchestra, bursting to be played at any opportunity.

It was here again that Kat entered in a rush to greet Archie.

"What's happened?" she gasped.

"I have no idea Kat," Archie replied.

"My aunt has just come into the kitchen and she ain't happy. I thought, Archie must have done something now."

"Thanks a lot. I have not done a thing. But things just seem to be happening to me at the moment." He proceeded to retell the tale of how he had gotten separated in town, the face he had seen in the crowd and the mechanical bird.

"Hold on a minute! Stop the press! You're telling me you've seen some wind-up bird?" questioned Kat.

"Yes!"

"It's no wonder my Aunt is going off her head. I think her precise words were 'that boy will be the death of me'. She is having a cup of tea now."

"But I have not done anything wrong Kat," Archie defended himself.

"I believe you, but I'm sure I saw steam coming out of her ears she was that cross. I was going to say something, but I thought against it. Mechanical bird? Really?"

"Yes!" Archie protested. "Look, come with me." He almost dragged Kat to the window. "It was just out here, on the ledge. It's followed me back here." Kat looked at Archie and made a spiralling signal with her finger at the side of her head.

"Cuckoo, cuckoo," she teased, "Wilberforce will be coming for you soon. He's gonna lock you up. You're crazy!"

"No, I'm not, I tell you I saw it." Archie was getting increasingly frustrated by the second. "Where is my father?"

"He's in a meeting. A group of people turned up earlier this afternoon and your father came back from town. He has been in the meeting ever since."

"Right, let's see what he has to say!" Archie marched towards the door, feeling defiant. He'd show Kat he thought. She did not believe him, but he would show his authority over her by going straight to his father. That would teach her. After all, she was just a maid. The feeling of anger started to subside, and a sense of confusion came over him next. Archie desperately wanted to say something to his father. He felt he was going to burst, but upon further thought what would he say? How could he bring this up with his father? Archie decided to go for it. He paced across the room, reached the door, grabbed the handle and pulled it open. There was Ms Buddington.

"Get back in there. NOW!"

Archie paused for a second, unsure what to do. He had decided to try and show Kat that he was the boss, but this was a whole other level. The look on Ms Buddington's face said to try it and it will be the last thing you do. She made no effort to stop him physically, but the glare was enough. Archie sighed and backed into the room. His mind was cluttered with confusion after all he had seen and heard that day, and he had so many questions. He wanted to shout out at her and ask her everything running through his mind, but she gave him a silent look that said: "Don't you dare open your mouth!"

The longer he stayed in the room, the more he calmed down. Looking out the window, he observed the comings and goings of visitors to the house. Most of them he did not recognise except for Crowle and his Crowlies. Eventually, he saw his father leave, and any plan of speaking to him disappeared like the carriage as it passed from the square. Archie did not see him again for the next few days and, the following week, he was informed by Smetherly, that his father was away on business. Archie took this as his opportunity to speak to Ms Buddington.

"All sorts of things have been going through my head the last couple of days; I have so many questions, so many things I need to know? You said you would tell me when Father went away."

"And I will," replied Ms Buddington. "Perhaps it would be better if we went to see a friend of mine, that way you will get the bigger picture."

"Tell me now; I need to know. Why is there a mechanical raven following me around?" Archie listened to the words coming out of his mouth and realised how crazy it sounded. The feeling of desperation grew inside him, and he could feel his emotions running high. The tears welled up, and he could hold them back no longer. Tears ran down his face, and he slumped to the floor, almost as if the life was oozing out of him. Ms Buddington could see the effect it was having upon him.

"Right, tomorrow, we will get a train to the seaside where my friend lives, and you will get all your answers. I promise."

The following day, they set off early to the train station. The carriage took them from the house as usual, but this time they were not followed by Crowlies. Ms Buddington, through an elaborate plan of deception, had made sure they were alone. As they approached the towering station, Archie felt it looked more like the House of Parliament than a train station. He imagined all the Members of Parliament rushing around inside, trying their best to sort out the problems of the country. Or at least that is what his father had said. Something about powerful men gathering together to solve the issues in this country and, indeed the world. The station was a splendid building to look upon. Archie had seen it many a time and often wondered what went on in all those windows at the front. Surely all those intricate and elaborate windows were not offices or a place for the steam engine drivers to sit. The colourful brickwork above each window made this building stand out in, what would be, quite a drab city. The only thing that impressed Archie even more, was how the station looked at night. Glistening under the street lamps and plumes of steam, which populated this area more so than many other areas of the centre. They entered through the gaping archway - like a giant mouth, ready to eat the choicest fillet steak.

"What about tickets?" Archie quizzed Ms Buddington.

"All in hand," came the reply. They now passed the giant forecourt and entered the main terminus of the station. Down one flight of steps they went, to a parting in the path. Archie felt like he was walking onto a stage and all the passengers bustling below him were the audience. At the break in steps, Ms Buddington went stage left - he decided to go stage right. As they separated, he could hear her call.

"What on earth are you doing? This isn't a dance routine you know. Get back to me."

They both rushed around their part of the stage and met gracefully again in the centre as they descended the final set of steps to the concourse. The smell, smoke and steam filled the cavernous ceiling at the station. Steel girders rose from the floor and intertwined like a metal forest above their heads with a canopy of glass protecting them from the elements. Archie gazed in wonder at the many people passing through the station. The majority were men, in the traditional dress, long dark coats and either top or bowler hats. Women followed behind: some pulling irate looking children, screaming and crying; others dressed so smartly it look as though they were visiting the Queen; a nun passed followed by a group of young girls, walking piously with hands joined.

Archie then spotted a figure that stood out. Workmen were not unusual to be seen in and around the station: hard hats, goggles, a spade or pick over the shoulder, dirty, soot-filled faces. But this person stood out to Archie. Only after closer inspection did he realise it was a woman. She had a helmet on - though this one had a matte, golden finish - goggles resting on the front - though these seemed more elaborate, like something Archie had seen before - and a blackened face, like an inverted panda that Archie had learnt about in Geography lessons. But the thing that made her stand out to Archie were her two, long, blonde pigtails hanging down from either side of the helmet. That and the strange contraption she held in her hand that looked like a cross between a weapon and a bug spray - with a large plunger at the end of the barrel. Archie was unsure as to what it was.

"Ms Buddington? Do you see…?" he started

"Yes, I see, now let's keep moving," she replied as they moved onto the platform for their train. Archie did not know what to think. Panic began to set in, but Ms Buddington maintained her path. He continued to look behind and saw the golden-crowned woman stop at the fence where the guard was. They had just swiftly passed through there, but the woman stayed there, staring at Archie and then turning around, checking behind her. As Archie continued to glance, she repeated this.

"Just a little further and we will be in our carriage."

The pace seemed to quicken over the final part of the journey until eventually, a slight jog was required for Archie to keep up with his ward. Entering their first-class carriage, they settled privately for the long ride ahead of them.

"Now we can talk," Ms Buddington remarked as Archie sat up intently. As he did, he felt the judder of the carriages as the steam train set off. The loud train whistle blew to signal departure and slowly, the train began to move. Archie did not know where to start.

"Who was that woman at the station? Did you know her? It seemed like you knew her. Is she involved in this somehow?"

"Slow down Archie. We have a long journey ahead and plenty of time to answer questions. Yes, I do know that lady - her name is Maria Fizkin. She was not at the station to harm you. She was in fact there to protect you. I did not know it would be her, but I knew someone would be there." Archie sat astounded.

"Protect me? Protect me from who?"

"Well as you know, your father is a very well to do man. He has lots of contact with many important people in this country and throughout the world. But because of this, he also has a lot of enemies. A lot of enemies who want to hurt your father, and the best was to do this is by hurting you."

"There are lots of things," she continued, "that have been put in place to protect you. There have been attacks and attempts to get you. So, your father feels it is important to keep you safe in the house away from the rest of the world. But you are getting older now - a fine young man, and because of this, it is time you knew further things. Archie, you have been contacted. The raven is a sign. It has been watching you for a long, long time; since you were born. It has always been with you, and always will be. As this train travels towards the seaside, the raven will be flying above also. It is your Angelus Custos. It will be with you all the time now, and now you have reached the age of shifting, it has contacted you. Have they said anything else to you?"

Archie thought long and hard about this. He recalled the note he had received from the raven and wondered should he tell Ms Buddington about its contents.

Archie - do not be afraid. We are your friends, and we're here to help you. Trust nothing; open your mind to everything. We will protect you from those who wish you misfortune.

He pulled the crumpled note from his pocket and showed his guardian. He always kept it on him as he did not know where else to keep it or if he could ever mention it to anyone else. A knowing smile grew across Ms Buddington's face. "Yes, this is them. They are contacting you."

"Let me try and explain. There are a group of people in this country who want to rule everyone and everything. I cannot go into too many details as I do not know many details but this I do know. These people form a secret society. People can only guess at who the members of this group are - but they could be anyone. The combined power and wealth of these people make it very hard to uncover what they are up to. There are a group other people who disagree with these evil men. These brave people live in hiding and only come out at certain times, or they will be hunted and killed. They hide behind masks, in dark alleyways, only appearing when they have a purpose."

Archie sat with his mouth wide open. He couldn't believe what he was hearing.

"Who are they?" he questioned.

"They... are Alium."

Chapter 5
Ida Redgrave

The final part of the journey followed the coast, and they could see not only the sea but the seaside town they were visiting. The train pulled into the station, and it felt very different from that in the city. Archie had never been here before, and usually, he would be filled with excitement at visiting a new place like this. Today, however, other things were in his mind. They departed the train onto a platform. Gone were the dark, sober-looking faces; now people looked happy. Like it was a different country. They walked from the single platform through the modest station and out onto the road.

A horse and carriage awaited them and took them along the coast road. The road narrowed and became a little more secluded. After travelling for what seemed a while, the carriage pulled up at some giant gates with a strange emblem on them. The highly wrought, iron gates looked as if a giant spider had confused the iron for web silk and had made its home there. An old gentleman came from the gatehouse and stumbled up to the carriage door.

"Can I help you sweetheart?" he said in a kind but croaky voice.

"We are expected. I am Ms Buddington."

"Ahhh, I was told we might have visitors today. Not a lot goes on here. It's nice to see some new faces, especially one as pretty as yours!"

Ms Buddington smiled weakly at the old man. Archie could not contain the laughter inside of him.

"And who's this young whippersnapper? Is he yours? Your son?" He continued.

"He is with me, but he is not my son. He also has an appointment with Miss Redgrave."

"Very well," muttered the old man. He seemed to be losing interest in the conversation now and was heading towards his gatehouse. The pair sat in the carriage unsure what was happening.

"Is this blithering idiot going to open the gates or do I have to do it myself?" cried Ms Buddington in an angered voice. She sighed and grumbled repeatedly and looked like she was about to get out of the carriage and start a fight with the man (one Archie felt sure the man would lose) when the iron gates gracefully swung open. The carriage trotted through, the old man waving as they passed the gatehouse.

"Well at least we are here," sighed Ms Buddington.

Now they had passed the gates they proceeded down a long, windy driveway. As the looped backwards and forwards, it enabled to see what lay ahead. On this side of the gatehouse, the compound was made up of many small buildings. It was obvious which was the main house with its whitewashed walls and flowering baskets, but the other buildings looked just like derelict farmhouses. But there seemed an awful lot of them for land which apparently was not used for crops or livestock.

As they pulled up outside the shiny painted red door, Archie was struck with how beautiful yet innocent everything looked. The house was nowhere near as grand as his, but it almost seemed better through simple charms. Above the scarlet door was a modest covering that would shelter a visitor from the rain while awaiting entry (though this was not needed today). Archie looked to the minute spire at the top of this shelter and again noticed a familiar trait of this home - a spider was crawling up the edge of the pole or was it. Upon closer inspection, Archie noticed it wasn't real.

The front door opened as they climbed down the steps. Out stepped a pretty young lady. She had long, flowing hair with curls rippled throughout. She wore a plain white blouse, a long black skirt and an apron over the top, covered in white marks, which Archie assumed was flour or some other after effect from cooking. Her eyes lit up as she saw Ms Buddington.

"Layla. How wonderful to see you," she exclaimed. Layla! This revelation was a complete shock to Archie. He had no idea what Ms Buddington's first name was. Everyone referred to her as Ms Buddington. He did, other staff, her employer, everyone.

"Ida, it's been too long!" The pair embraced, and Archie realised they were apparently close friends.

"This must be Master Roker," Ida returned.

"Indeed, it is. And it is Archie. There'll be no ideas of grandeur here."

As he passed through the front door, his eyes were drawn to the elaborate stained-glass window in the centre of the door panel. A checked pattern covered the glass in an array of colours but in the middle, was a framed circle with a familiar sight in the centre... another spider. This Miss Redgrave must have a severe spider fascination thought Archie to himself. Stepping over the Dorchester patterned floor, being careful not to leave dirty footprints on the tiles, Archie noticed how white and bright the room and indeed the whole house seemed. It was as if sunlight was flooding in through a huge window, but there were only simple, small windows. In his room at home, he had substantial sash windows, but his bedroom still felt dark and dingy in comparison to this.

"Sit down, sit down, you must be tired after your journey. I have some tea and scones ready for you. I shall return in a second. Please make yourselves at home." The pair sat down. Ms Buddington removed her hat and coat, and Archie did the same.

"Layla?" he quizzed.

"Never you mind that," came the response. The comfortable chairs were covered in a variety of shawls and throws and covered in what seemed a mountain of cushions. In the centre of the room sat a glorious chest. Four-foot-long, three-foot-wide and one-foot high. On the side, in front of Archie, was an immense black clasp, and upon it was a locked padlock. The cabinet seemed a strange thing to have in the front room of a house, but after everything Archie had seen in the last few weeks, he then thought it seemed quite tame really.

Ida returned with a tray: a considerable teapot emblazoned with a selection of pink roses and green branches as its handle and spout; a plate with scones stacked up, butter, jam and a collection of knives; and three teacups. They were delicate white china but upon the side of each one was a golden spiders web. What was it about this creature that fascinated the woman so much?

"Archie obviously has a lot of questions, and I have brought him here, as you know, to get some answers.

61

However, I realise what he is about to hear is quite possibly hard to believe so Ida, that is why I have brought him to you, as you have some things that can back up what I say."

Ida nodded and sat up straight.

"Indeed. Now, Archie, before we begin you must promise to sit and listen to everything. Please do not interrupt. Listen to everything you are told and then ask questions at the end. Agreed?" prompted Ida.

"Agreed," replied Archie.

"Right," began Ida, "where to begin? Well, as you are probably aware there have been a lot of strange things going on around you over the last few weeks, months even years. This is no coincidence. It revolves around you being your father's son. Layla says she has explained about the secret society - well I can tell you this. The organisation is called Imperium. They are a group of people. I am not sure who the members are - no one is - but they are wealthy and influential people in all areas of society. If they need something or want something, they take it. No one can stand in their way. Their goal is to make themselves more powerful and not think of others in the process. They control everything. If people don't do as they say, they will either threaten them or kill them. This is what is happening with you. Your father is being threatened. If he doesn't do as told by Imperium, they will hurt you. So far, he has done as they have said, but they are starting to threaten you as they probably want your father to do something dangerous. Do not ask me what as I do not know. Only know that your father is a very gifted man with lots of influential friends."

"On the other side of this are, as Layla explained, Alium. These are a group of rebels who stand against Imperium. They believe in freedom and equality for all. They want a society where everyone has the same rights and access to everything."

"Imperium know and control lots of technology. Technology that we should all be able to access. If we were all able to access the tech, it would make life easier for everyone in society - especially the poor. But, in typical imperium fashion, if they keep the tech they have the power. Let me give you an example. Your angelus custos, who I believe you have met now, could be used for many basic tasks for humans. But if a machine did this for us, what would the human do? Think? Rebel? Fight? So, Imperium control it all. Would you like to see my angelus custos?"

Archie nodded. That was all he could do. The amount of information he had been given was struggling to register in his head. Ida moved her right hand towards the wristwatch on the left. She appeared to fiddle with a dial and then what followed amazed Archie more than anything he had seen before.

From the corner of the room on a table, what had earlier looked like a simple lamp, came a fantastic looking creature. Archie could only describe it as a cross between a light bulb and a spider. A mechanical body similar in size to Archie's fist, with what looked like screws for eyes, had eight appendages, each one triple jointed. However, the most unexpected part was the abdomen. For in this mechanical wonder the belly was a light bulb, and as the creature moved from the table to the floor the lamp illuminated. The faster it went as it crossed the ground, the brighter the bulb grew. He sat open jawed as the spider climbed onto the broad chest in the centre of the room.

"This is Milo. My angelus custos. He does as I say. He requires no food or to be cleaned up after. He is technology and can be used as required." The creature moved towards Archie. Milo climbed up onto his knee, and Archie felt at ease, as when he met the raven.

Archie sat and thought for a moment. Here, in front of him, was a woman who by first appearances would appear like any other lady of the time. She looked a rich lady with very stylish clothes: long flowing emerald skirt, white blouse encased in an ebony lace throw with an oversized silver buckle on a black belt. But crawling around his lap was a mechanical spider. What other secrets did this lady hold and what would he find out next?

"Let's go into my study and see what you think of that." Ida stood up and beckoned Archie to follow her. He carefully stood with the spider still in his hand and followed her as Ms Buddington followed him. From leaving the bright and airy front room, they walked down a narrow corridor which was remarkably dark and dingy. There was a door at the end of the passage, which looked like it may lead 'to a bathroom or bedroom. They stopped halfway down the corridor in front of a huge bookcase that was set into the wall.

"In a second Archie, you will continue to see things that few people have seen. You must understand that you cannot tell anyone about the things you have seen. Not only is it dangerous for you but people will think you crazy for suggesting such things."

"What's beyond that door?" questioned Archie, ever more curious as the minutes passed.

"That..." replied Ida, "is the bathroom." Archie stared at her blankly. "Nothing exciting in there, unless of course, you need to go?"

"Err...no," blushed Archie slightly confused, but not wishing to ask any further questions.

"Look here," Ida said as she gestured towards the bookcase. Archie could make out a couple of books on the shelf. Oliver Twist and Bleak House by Dickens; In Memoriam by Tennyson; The Strange Case of Dr Jekyll and Mr Hyde by Stevenson. Archie felt a little bit like Jekyll and Hyde now. One way one moment, another next. There was also a large carriage clock, which looked like it was made from black marble, smooth over the front and sides but rough around the edges. Ida opened the glass doors over the front of the bookcase and carefully pulled back the glass face of the clock. After this, Archie noticed her turning the hands of the clock anti-clockwise. As she performed a revolution of the clock face, a tiny chime sounded out. This continued until Archie had counted ten chimes. There has a loud click, and the cupboard in the wall appeared to drop a centimetre. "This is where you want to be." She pushed on the bookcase and it swung back like a door. Archie peered into the darkness. He saw Ida disappear into the dark and then she was gone, but only for a couple of seconds. A bright light flooded the room and Archie could not believe the things he saw.

In front of him was a vast study. Although he was on the ground floor of Ida's house, he stood on a balcony overlooking an Aladdin's cave of an office. As he gazed around him on the "first floor" of the study, he noticed bookshelves interwoven with stain glass windows. Many colours and patterns adorned these windows encased in black and green steel frames decorated with a hundred rivets. He gazed at the titles of the books on the shelves but there were no longer any works of Tennyson or Dickens; instead names of books and authors he had never seen before. A History of Imperium by Lowe; The Truth of Romani Grove by Blundell; The Idiot's Guide to Airships by Jacob.

He approached the rail of the balcony and peered over the edge. He could see Ida walking across the room and he glanced around as to how she had moved down so quickly. To his right was a spiral staircase. A plush, patterned carpet led from the balcony and twisted down the stairs. As he started to walk down the stairs, he noticed a considerable painting in an elaborate golden frame. A giant skull covered the canvas but this was like no other skull he had seen before. Around the eyes and across the jaw, rivets were painted in; over one eye was a golden pocket watch, held in place by a brown leather strap. From where the ears should have been, came two copper pipes; one dropping down and disappearing behind the jaw; the other firmly rooting itself into the temple of the skull. Around the skull there appeared to be a splattering of liquid which Archie was unsure if it was blood or ink.

"One of Ebenezer Dorrington's pieces. When he was good!" Ida laughed to herself. Archie had no idea what she was laughing about but he now noticed Dorrington's signature at the base of the painting. Dorrington was a well-known celebrity of the time. A giant of a man with a mammoth dark mane of hair, only matched by an impressive amount of facial hair.

The rest of the room was as equally fantastic. Some lights looked industrial with large dials coming from various parts. Thick velvet chairs were scattered around the room as if people had left a meeting in a hurry, with one sat in front of an upright piano, appearing to be too small for the person trying to compose or perform. A globe table was positioned towards the centre of the room similar to the one his father owned. Archie had seen many bottles and glasses being taken and served to guests from the one at home. Ida noticed him looking and flipped open the casing of the globe. Inside there were no glasses or bottles but a device that looked like a mechanical brain. Upon closer inspection, Archie noticed it was made up of many tiny keys with letters of the alphabet upon them.

Ida next moved to the piano. After playing a selection of untuneful notes on the piano, the front lifted slow and graceful and the keys slid forward. Inside were three black screens with another type of keyboard in front of them.

"Wow, what is that?" quizzed Archie like a child on Christmas morning.

"This is a Vigilate station. From here, I can see what Alium are doing, where they are and I can keep an eye on you," Ida replied. "Let me show you." She casually flicked a switch and the three screens lit up. Archie had never seen anything like this before and he felt it was some magic trick. He could see what looked like a map on the black screen outlined in a pale blue hue. Observing carefully, he realised that the plan was, in fact, the area he was currently in.

"Look closely," explained Ida, "you see those flashing dots? These are us three and the Vigilate is showing me our position."

"But that's amazing, "responded Archie, gobsmacked at this technology in front of him.

"Looks like we have a visitor approaching - Randall. Here look." Archie glanced at the screen and saw a new dot blinking its way across the screen towards their position. "Don't worry, he is a friend, I am expecting him." Archie remained mouth open in awe of all he had seen and his hostess obviously realised this.

"Right, I think Archie has heard enough for now. I think we should give him a couple of minutes to let all this soak in Layla, don't you?" Ida suggested.

"Time for a fresh pot of tea. I need a chat anyway. Let's leave him with Milo for now," Ms Buddington replied.

They all left the secret study and returned to the parlour. Archie sat back down on the chair and Milo returned to his lap. Both ladies left the room for the kitchen. Milo remained sat on Archie's lap. He found it a little strange sitting stroking a spider, let alone a mechanical one, but something was strangely satisfying. The warm glow from the abdomen of the spider almost warmed Archie inside. As it moved side to side, it gradually went brighter then dimmer.

"What other secrets do you hold I wonder?" Archie whispered to the arachnid. Suddenly the spider illuminated more than before. It moved from Archie's lap to the floor. Archie got to his feet and followed the spider. It circled the tremendous chest in the middle of the room.

As it did, Archie followed, like a child with a new puppy. What on earth was Milo doing? After circling the chest several times, Milo stopped and slowly started to climb the side of the chest towards the lock. All eight legs now grabbed the padlock and the spider swung underneath like an oversized pendulum. One of the legs slowly protruded out forward and Archie heard a clicking noise. Milo placed his leg into the keyhole of the padlock and Archie heard the lock turn inside. The chest was open. What secrets lay inside here? Why had the mechanical arachnid only opened this when Ida and Layla had left the room? And the central question that ran through Archie's head - should he take a look?

Milo removed his leg from the keyhole, and the padlock swung open. With a flick of one of its legs, the spider knocked the lock from its hook and it clattered to the floor. The dilemma of whether to open the box was playing hard in Archie's mind but he soon realised he need not worry as Milo was now placing his array of legs between the gap of top and base of the trunk. Archie looked at the chest top. It had been cleared of cups, saucers and teapots but a vase of flowers and other decorative ornaments remained. The spider began to stretch its legs and the chest started to open. Archie did not know what to do. He just stood dumbfounded.

This creature that he would not have thought existed an hour ago was now opening locked padlocks and potentially causing a mess. Archie saw the vase and ornaments starting to move. He rushed to catch them as they slid towards the floor. He juggled them to safety and returned to watch the spider. The chest was now starting to open wide, and Archie could see inside. There looked like many things in the chest, but they were all covered in a thin piece of material. What secrets lay under the cloth? Milo walked cleverly from the centre point of the most extended edge where the padlock was to the right-hand corner, always holding the lid open. He then moved down the shorter edge towards the hinged side of the cover. As he did the opening grew wider and wider until the spider could push it open completely.

Archie worried the noise would make the two adults in the kitchen come rushing in, but nothing. He looked at the finely woven cloth that covered the contents. He wondered should he uncover it, but this was again solved for him. Milo now sat at one edge of the fired a web across the width of the chest to the far end of the material. Then, like a winch retracted the fibre ever so slowly. The cover started to move back.

Underneath was a selection of boxes and cloth bags which looked like they had been there some time as a thin layer of dust covered them but it was the other objects that sent a shiver through Archie's spine. The first thing he noticed were two vials of liquid in a leather holder. These triggered memories for Archie; they were just like those he saw at the surgery the day the steel door opened. But it continued as the cover moved. Next, he saw a pair of goggles and then the face mask. These were the things the second mystery person had been wearing that day. He picked up the face mask in his hands and looked carefully at it. Yes, leather mask with press stud fasteners and leather bands crossing zig-zagged to keep it in place, and black goggles. Did this mean Ida was one of the people in his father surgery? After all he had found out today, he would not be surprised.

One thing after another; everything he thought he knew, now different. He thought back to the message the mechanical raven had provided for him. Trust nothing; open your mind to everything. Ida had said she knew of a secret group; one that wanted something better for the society. Was she a member? If Ida was, then why was she in his father's surgery that day? Did this woman know the mysterious bird masked character? Who were they protecting him from? Imperium? He had learnt his father was in trouble but all this? And Ms Buddington? How was she involved in all this? So many questions Archie did not know what to do. He stood up and took a step back away from the chest. As Archie did, Milo moved away from the jaws of the lid and it snapped shut. Startled, Archie jumped backwards, but he felt something behind him. He turned around and the next piece of the puzzle appeared. The first masked man who had entered the surgery was now stood right in front of him.

Chapter 6
Randall Krewler

"Keep tha' britches on lad!" boomed a large, thunderous voice. "Tha's nowt to fear here."

There in front of him stood a giant of a man. Archie stared at the boots. Black leather with brown trim and numerous buckles and rivets positioned all over in a decorative manner. Up the outside of the right boot were three small pouches, each emblazoned with a different golden motif. The dark, smart trousers were masked by what looked like the most complicated belt and holster ever seen. Again, an overload of numerous buckles covered the design and supported the weapon that nestled close to the man's thigh. Though it appeared like any ordinary gun, it had a wooden and gold finish to it that Archie had never seen before. The oversize chamber of the weapon was a dull silver but surrounded by wooden fixtures, attached with metallic cogs and dials. A series of copper wires travelled across the top of the gun, and a green diode hung from a silver spring above the solid silver trigger. At the end of the barrel, there appeared to be three small chimneys of various size that Archie could only assume gun smoke flowed through when it had been set off. Even more remarkable was the other side of the belt, for attached in a neat, tidy holster was a white teacup, clipped in for added security.

The gentleman wore a pinstripe waistcoat with an extensive overlap of lapels. At the shoulders, Archie could see a fancy pair of colourfully striped braces that appeared to match nothing else he was wearing. On the right shoulder, he wore leather padding, covered in a selection of brass plates, riveted to the leather underneath. On the inner pad, below the shoulder, there appeared to be a bullet holder with six brass bullets shining through. However, it was what was below that stuck in Archie's mind from the visit at the surgery. On the elbow and forearm was the unnatural golden syringe, attached to a copper and leather holster, which was press studded onto the man's arm. A top hat still perched upon his head, but the dark goggles he wore to cover his eyes previously now sat upon the rim. Over his right eye though, the man now had a mechanical monocle, which was connected to a piece of machinery on the side of his head. In this mayhem of gears and cogs, a tube left and circled the back of his head, back to the front of the waistcoat and entered the top left-hand pocket. The machine makeover was complemented with the human element of the face. A finely trimmed beard with bushy hair only below the bottom lip. Above the top, a see-sawing moustache exquisitely finished off with the choicest wax to enable it to protrude three or four inches either side. Archie scrambled across the floor towards to kitchen door where the other ladies were.

"Where's tha' goin' now? I am flummoxed as to what's goin' on here. Ida, Layla, come and sort this tyke out."

The kitchen door swung open and the two ladies appeared. Archie scrambled across the floor behind the long dresses of the women.

"Randall! I knew you were coming but I thought you might knock," Ida exclaimed. "Archie, it's fine, this is Randall Krewler. He's a friend."

"But he was in the surgery that day and the mask in the chest - was that yours? Were you in the surgery that day? What's going on? Who are you people?"

Archie sat on the floor and shook his head. He did not know what to think anymore. Everything he had known had now changed. Something he never expected and the shocks just kept coming.

"Archie, we are Alium. We are your friends and we are here to protect you." Archie recalled the note he had received from the raven. His heavy breathing gradually slowed and he began to sit calmly on the floor. Ida continued, "We have been watching you for a while. Myself, Randall here, Madeline, who I believe you have seen a couple of times with her favourite mask on, and of course, your angelus custos, with which you will shortly be reacquainted."

"Let's all sit down and have a nice cup of tea," Ms Buddington suggested. She disappeared towards the kitchen again.

"That'll be a grand idea, Layla, I is parched," boomed Randall. "So, what does the lad know? Have you told him everything?"

"Everything he needs to know at the moment," Ida responded. He knows that he is not safe because of his father's position. And he now knows that we are here to protect him."

"Grand, grand job ladies. Maddie will be reight proud. Now Archie, tha's lots still to tell, but what tha must know is that tha shan't tell tha' father about any of this.

I'm reight serious lad. He can know nowt about this. He don't need thee mithering him turning him into a whittler." Randall explained. Archie sat dumbfounded. He sat and looked at the friendly giant in front of him but daren't say he had no idea about what he was saying. Whittler? What on earth was a whittler?

"Randall, it may be best if I explain. Archie, Randall is from Yorkshire as you may be able to guess from his accent. A fine man, and a loyal member of Alium, but not the best person to pass a message onto someone who has been brought up with the Queen's English from day one. So, under no circumstances must you tell your father about our meeting. As Randall said, we don't want him worrying about you and what may happen to you. We can protect you Archie - but your father must not know about us. If he does it will put him in danger and that, in turn, will put you in danger, and that is something about which he will worry. Archie, promise me now you will not say anything to your father."

Archie was confused. After everything he had found out today, he now was told he had to keep it secret.

"But I have found out so much today..." Archie responded.

"Archie, you cannot tell your father it is as simple as that. Layla will be there for you to talk to, in secret of course. But no mention of this to your father or anyone else. We will protect you if need be."

"Will I still see you?" Archie questioned.

"You will see us when required," Ida responded.

"I will not tell my father anything, but I want regular contact with you. I need to know more about Alium. I want to be part of it."

"Ok, ok," Ida answered, "we can come to some arrangement. Archie, you must swear to not tell your father about this. It could put his life in danger."

Archie finally agreed. The final comment by Ida had set the deal for him as he did not want anything to happen to his father.

"So… the doorway in the surgery; the one you came out of - what is that?" Why were you there?" Archie's mind had been working overtime with the amount of information he had been given and he was starting to put it together.

"That is a passage that leads to a secret place; a place that is different to here. Someday you will be able to visit, but that is not possible now. Things are different there, isn't that right Randall?"

"Aye, that's for sure!" he replied. Ida continued.

"You will find out about this but we have to make sure you are safe. That is the most important thing here. "

"Why were you wearing the masks, and why are your clothes so different?" continued Archie inquisitively.

"Well, we wear these clothes as it is a way of living for people in Alium. We are not confined to the restraints of normal society. People dress the way they do here because the majority of people have little choice. They earn a certain amount of money, decided by people in power - Imperium - and they are told to wear certain things. They are not given the opportunity to buy other things. Free choice has been taken away. Only the rich can choose the way they live but many of them are either Imperium or under the influence of Imperium. There is nothing or no one they cannot control. Forward thinking for the masses is not encouraged. People may think they have their own opinions, but in fact, there is little independent thinking by most people. For example, what do you think many people would think about what you have found out today? Imagine a street seller, selling fruit in town. What would he make of this? Or people working in factories - if they knew some mechanical creatures or beings could do the work? What would the response be? Chaos. So, what do those in command do? I'm not talking about the factory managers - they are as blind as the workforce. I'm talking about the factory owners. Imperium."

"I don't know," Archie replied.

"Let me give you some examples," Ida continued. "You have heard of Eligah Bilton."

"Yes, Father has spoken of him. I have seen him at the surgery a few times. Father says he is a great man as he has cured many diseases and helped thousands of people who would normally have died."

"Yes," sighed Ida, "that's the view many people have. But what if I told you the very diseases Bilton has prevented were created by him."

"What?" gasped Archie.

"Yes, everyone in this country has had an inoculation against basic childhood diseases. But in this serum, is a formula which has been created to dull the sense of people - to stop them overthinking. Not a huge dose; nothing too obvious, but enough to stop people questioning things. And if they do - they are called lunatics, or insane, and end up in Burley Wilberforce's asylums. There has been a marked increase in the number of people committed over the last few years and Imperium are planning something to combat this."

"But that's…" Archie stuttered.

"Crazy. Bloomin' crazy," joined Randall. "Who'd ever believe such claptrap. Well, there you go."

"Have you heard of Emerson Ackerley? The prominent author?" Archie nodded. This name had been championed by the working classes as someone who wanted better rights and conditions for them. "Well here is someone whose writing is almost followed to the letter. What he writes people believe. And guess which group he belongs to?"

"Imperium?" guessed Archie.

"Exactly," continued Ida. "If Imperium can't get a message to the masses using a famous author what else can they do. Leave it to Calvin Coleman inventor of the postal service. He can make sure a message is delivered to every house in the country if necessary. People believe what they read - fake news. What they are told to believe. It goes on. Want to control the younger population? Speak to Enoch Howlett. He may well be a prominent businessman who owns Howlett Chocolate Company, but he is also responsible for putting in an addictive drug which makes children want to eat it increasingly. And what if the population gets too high? Howlett can add something to his chocolate to take out part of the population. Nothing stops a rebellion like close family dying."

"But why doesn't anyone stop this?" Archie responded, almost pleading.

"Who's going to stop it?" The police? Crowlies? They are Imperium's own personal army."

"I can't believe this." Archie slumped back in his chair. "I have met Oliver Crowle many times. He seems strict, but he always looks after my father."

"Does he look after him, or does he make sure he does what he is told to do? Remember Archie; you must question everything now. As I said before, there are much bigger things going on here than just you and your father. That is why we must keep quiet about this. Do you understand?"

Archie lied and nodded his head. He knew what Ida was saying but did he understand - no, not at all. The conversation died down for a while. People sat and contemplated what had been said. Many truths had become known and it was vital to give them adequate thought and not just dismiss them as fantasy.

"So…" boomed Randall, interrupting the silence, "is it time to meet Abe?" This seemed to lighten the mood slightly.

"Ah, the angelus custos," replied Layla, who had returned to the room with a fresh pot of tea.

"Crackin' - tea and a cheeky raven. What could be better?" returned Randall. "Have you any biscuits?"

"You sort the angelus custos, and I'll sort the biscuits. Deal?" bargained Layla.

"Deal." Archie grinned to himself. This giant of a man who looked like he was invincible was almost brought to his knees by Ms Boddington at the promise of a Custard Cream.

"Right Archie, me lad. The first thing you'll be needin' is this." Randall opened a pouch attached to his belt. In it was what looked like a timepiece on a leather strap, very similar to the one Ida wore and pressed when she attracted the attention of her spider. He handed it to Archie. "Slide it on your wrist like a glove. There you go. Grand. Now let's open a window." Layla moved to the large bay window at the front of the house and slid open the sash pane. "Now you see the button between your thumb and forefinger? Press it. Good an' hard like."

Archie did as instructed and at first, nothing happened. Then a few moments later he heard the cawing sound he had begun to detect over the last few months. The next thing he knew Abe, the mechanical raven, had appeared on the window ledge. He had swooped down and landed on the sill.

"He's been on the lookout for us. Circling above and perched in the trees around, in case anyone wanted to interrupt us. Call him to you - if that's ok Ida?" Ida nodded and Archie responded.

"Err... Abe?" The bird looked up. "Abe," he repeated with a little more conviction this time. The bird flapped its mechanical wings and swooped into the room, landing on the broad chest in the middle of the room next to Milo. Milo scrambled to safety in Ida's arms, his abdomen flashing wildly as if on fire.

Archie took a good look at the creature in front of him. As he noted on their last encounter, the bird looked alive in every way shape and form, but the way its body was made up of metal; bits that looked like they were from a scrap yard; some rust, some finely polished, fascinated him. Most noticeably, the array of cogs and gears that spun; almost like a heartbeat of the creature.

"This is Abe," Randall introduced. "He is your angelus custos. From now on he will be with you always. If not in your presence then very close by and he can be called anytime with a press of that button. Of course, as you have probably realised, you will not be able to wear that all the time or questions will be asked. Layla will ensure you can keep it somewhere safe, but not to worry this daft bird will be around to see thee reet."

Archie was a little lost for words. He had never had a pet, let alone a mechanical one that would do his beck and call. He wondered what kind of tasks he could ask it to do. Initially, Archie spent too much time wondering what pranks he could concoct at home getting Smetherly into mischief with Kat. But would he be able to tell Kat? Suddenly, this new exciting thing seemed pointless if he could not share it with anyone. Like opening a birthday present but then having it taken away straight away.

"You must remember Archie; Abe is here to protect you and watch over you. To get help if required, to guide you when needed. Do you understand?" Ida instructed. Archie nodded reluctantly. "He is not a ..."

Suddenly, a beeping noise started from a machine in the corner of the room, nearby to where Milo had appeared for the first time earlier. The ornament which looked unusual in this place, but would have fit perfectly in the study below, was flashing. It initially looked like a clock, but upon closer inspection, there was a considerable valve on the left that was glowing blue. Underneath a dial was spinning around. On the right-hand side, two smaller devices glowed white. Ida went over to it and started turning the three dials below the shining white valves. What was an opaque, black circle in the centre of the ornament, suddenly lit into life. From a distance, Archie could see it was a much smaller version of the screens he had seen in the study before.

"We have visitors," announced Ida.

"Abe was keepin' guard, but that's stopped since he came in here," Randall added. "Abe, go and see what's goin' on."

The silvery bird flew out the window without hesitation. Everyone else in the room seemed very calm despite what had just been announced.

"Randall, you better disappear, I'll sort out here. Layla, Archie - in the study. Layla, you know what to do." Ida ordered.

"Indeed, Archie follow me," demanded Ms Buddington. Back down the dark corridor they went; to the bookcase and through the secret passage. Down the spiral staircase to where the piano, housing the three screens sat. On top of the piano sat a metronome, something to keep time in a moment of chaos Archie thought. Ms Buddington opened the front and pressed a button. The entire piano lifted slightly and swung away from the wall as the bookcase had done earlier. "In you go, I'm right behind you."

Archie did as he was told and went into the darkness, for the second time in as many hours. He heard Ms Buddington enter behind him and the grand piano door swung shut behind them. As it did, the passageway they had opened lit up. Again, a series of valves grew brighter as they walked past but then dimmed when they had passed. Down the dark passage, they continued for what seemed an age, until finally, they reached a door. By the side of it was, what looked like a box on the wall. Ms Buddington approached it and put her eyes toward it, looking through it like a pair of binoculars. There was a pause as she gazed into the corroded viewing station.

"It's safe," she said, and with that pulled a considerable lever by the door. A series of locks moved across the door in a hypnotic, rhythmic pattern and the heavy door swung open. Rushing through, Archie found himself running on a soft floor towards a light in the distance. As he thought about it, he realised he was in a cave and the surface below him was sand. Continuing through the ever-decreasing darkness, Archie soon found himself on a beach. He looked around. Ms Buddington was behind him, pressing down her dress and rearranging her hat. He looked up and saw Abe circling above, giving seagulls a run for their money.

"Archie, stop," came the command. "We are on the beach; we are on holiday. If we run, we look conspicuous. If we walk casually, we look like holidaymakers."

"But what about the others?" Archie questioned.

"They will be fine. I feel there has been a visit by the Crowlies. They must have suspected something, and when they saw Abe disappear, they have moved in."

"But Ida…"

"She will be fine, believe me. Her house will be on lockdown, and they will not be able to get anything from her. You are the critical thing here. We must get you to safety and back home. Would you like an ice cream?"

Chapter 7
Through the Door

Archie sat in the red velvet chair, in the music room back at home, plucking the strings on his violin. There were so many things going through his mind he did not know where to start. He felt like he needed to talk to someone but who? Archie was shocked at Ms Buddington for keeping all this a secret from him and even if he did speak to her she always hushed him as others may hear. He had been warned not to mention it to anyone else, and he begrudgingly agreed with his new friends that he would not. But would speaking to Kat be acceptable? She would not say anything. Would she? He put the violin down, and a hollow thud was followed by a discord as the strings rang out tunelessly. He set off in search of his friend.

Down the flights of stairs Archie wandered, and into the kitchen. Although hopeful to find Kat, his quest was interrupted by Santini.

"Heeeeyyy, Master Archie…" came the unmistakable tones of the chef. "You wanna me to make a you una merenda?"

"No thank you, Santini," Archie replied. He was not in the mood for a snack, only a conversation. Perhaps this was his chance. He may not be able to talk about what he had seen, but he could find out the eccentric chef's thoughts. "Santini, do you like working here for us?"

"Well a, of course," came the reply in a broad Italian accent. "I get to-a make-a a lot-a food for a lot-a of people. That is my passion. Being from Italy, I is a passionate person; you know what I mean-a?"

"But are you happy?"

"Of course-a, I got-a roof over my head and a kitchen that's stupefacente!" came the response as he kissed his fingers. "If it weren't-a for your papa, I'd be with the chaps selling ice cream on street corners. This is the life for Santini."

"But is this what you really want to do?" questioned Archie.

"Well-a, if I could do what I wanna, then I'd sing musica lirica." What followed was a usual routine of Santini singing tunefully, but very loudly, a selection of old Italian operatic pieces. This was no use, even if he did disagree, he was not going to tell the master's son that he was unhappy.

Archie continued his search for Kat. Smetherly, however, was the next resident he came across. Unlike Santini, Archie did not care much for Smetherly. As little conversation as possible was the order here.

"Excuse me Smetherly, but have you seen Kat?"

"Miss Biggs is in the scullery attending her chores, and she needs to finish them. Is there anything I can help you with Master Archie?"

"No, no, I'm fine. Thank you." Archie retraced his steps out of the kitchen, away from the scullery, with Smetherly keeping a close eye. When his back was turned, Archie took a detour and hid behind the counter in the middle of the kitchen. When Smetherly had collected the hot water for the teapot, set on the silver platter, he set off exiting the kitchen. Archie waited for his moment and dashed through into the scullery. As he barged in, he was met with a face full of steam. The temperature of the room was almost unbearable as if Archie had taken a wrong turn and entered a sauna. As he peered through the steam, he saw Kat in the corner by the sink; next to her a vast mountain of crockery (like that which he ate his breakfast off earlier that morning). As the mist dissipated, he gazed around the room and saw what other tasks were waiting for Kat. The household silver was next - a never-ending chore Kat always said. Smetherly was not happy unless he could see his face in each item. There were many other tasks Kat had to partake in; some so menial, Archie pitied her at times. As scullery maid, she was the servant of the servants. Many a time they had laughed as Kat boiled Smetherly's sizeable off-white underwear in a large saucepan. Now, however, these tasks, along with the many others: awakening early before everyone else to prepare the house, lighting fires throughout the house and emptying chamber pots, made Archie contemplate for the first time. He had always taken it for granted - the way life was in the house. He was friends with these people, but they were his servants. They did as he asked. They never refused his orders. What would he do if they did?

"Kat? Do you like it here?"

"Yeah, it's great," came a sarcastic reply.

"No, tell me please," he responded.

"What do you mean Archie?"

"Working here? Living here? Would you not rather be anywhere else?"

"Really? Where else would I go Archie? I am a scullery maid. It's not like I'm the same as you. You have everything you need or want. I have to do this or I'd have nothing." Archie had never thought of it like this before and felt taken aback.

"It's not my fault!" Archie defended himself.

"I'm not saying it is Archie, but it is a rather daft question don't you think. I work hard here and my life is not easy, but I have a roof over my head and food on the table. I am lucky for that. You have everything to hand and always will. One day, this house will be yours, and you will be able to look down on people like me as an adult and have as many servants as you want."

"I don't want that!" Archie retorted.

"Well that's what is going to happen isn't it, like it or not!" replied Kat.

Archie did not like this response, and he stormed away from Kat, leaving her to her chores. He knew she would not, or indeed could not, follow him as she had too much work to do. This annoyed him even more - his closest friend, and he could not speak to her properly. He ran from the kitchen back out into the main hallway of the house. As he did, with a tear in his eye, he charged straight into his father.

"Woah there Archie. What's going on here then?" Roker gasped in a shocked voice. He had just entered the house and hardly expected to be charged as he walked through the door.

"Sorry sir, I... I... I didn't mean to."

"I know Archie, I know. Calm down and tell me what's wrong." The soothing tone of his father's voice shocked Archie. He was never like this. This was Ms

Buddington's job. She was always the one who looked after him when he was upset. The one who calmed his nerves or told him everything would be ok.

"Right Archie, come with me and tell me what's the matter." He led Archie into his study. Archie had been in here a few times before, but most of the time was not allowed in under any circumstances. As with Ida's study, it was set over two floors, but there were no elaborate technical machines here. Here, there were books; lots of books. So much so any reasonable person would think they were in a library. To the right, as he entered, was a large desk and to the left was a grand fireplace with an exquisitely carved mantelpiece; on either side stood the carvings of two men, holding a long, coiled serpent above their heads. A small table sat in the centre of the room with an array of leather Chesterfields surrounding it. High above their heads was what looked like a gold chandelier. Light flooded in from the numerous windows facing them, and the smell of leather-bound books was potent in the air. These books, Archie assumed, were innumerable editions linked to the medical profession; some of which he felt his father may even have written himself.

"Now then, tell me what has upset you." Archie held back and thought carefully about what he may say next.

"It's Kat. We've had a falling out."

"But why? I thought you two were good friends?"

"We are, but I just asked her if she liked living here and she ended up making me feel like I am some horrible master. I can't help that can I?"

"No Archie. We are very fortunate. We have a nice house, nice clothes, a nice life. We cannot take it for granted though. We look after Kat and the others, and in return, they work hard."

"But is that right?"

"Where have all these questions come from?" Roker asked, puzzled and confused.

"I've just been thinking about it, that's all. The world seems so unfair for some people. I'm not complaining about our life; I'm just saying," Archie responded.

"You're growing up Archie. You're thinking like a man. Maybe it's time you met a few people, and we spent a little more time together. Would you like that?"

This shocked Archie almost as much as the things he had seen at Ida's house. His father wanted to spend time with him! Archie nodded.

"Then tomorrow you shall go with me to the match!"

Archie had never been to a football match. Archie had never been to any sporting event. Here he was though, at a game, with his father. Not only were they together but sat in the owner's enclosure - the private boxes. The owner was a friend of Archie's father - one Arnold Harrington. Archie asked his father about the owner.

"How does someone own a football team?"

"Arnold Harrington is a newspaper editor. Well, he is the editor, but he also owns the paper, plus a couple of others. Imagine owning a newspaper. And that is where he has acquired his money. And being a friend means we can enjoy the comfortable seats and meet the players."

After the game, they were waiting to meet the captain of the team. None other than Gabriel Shapter. He was a big centre-half, playing in the heart of the defence. He approached Archie and his father and Archie could not believe the size of the man. He seemed like a giant. As the game was complete, he was covered in mud and sweat but still held a presence in the room. The tight-fitting woollen shirt clung to his toned frame; his pristine white shorts were no longer clean, and his boots and socks looked well-worn and used. Under his arm, he carried the match ball, sodden and dirtied, but still welcomed as Archie received it from the captain. Even after ninety minutes of football, his hair was always immaculate only matched by his taintless moustache.

Archie had had a splendid day with his father at the football, something he thought he would never do. All the fears of security and keeping safe were gone and he just was glad to spend time together with his dad. However, the visits did not stop there. Roker decided to take Archie with him on most of his engagements for the following weeks.

First on the itinerary was the surgery. Archie had been here numerous times before, but now, now it felt different. He felt like he was a V.I.P being given a grand tour. All previous occasions, he had remained in his father's office or sat high up in the surgery listening to the many talks that took place. Today, it was very different. The infirmary was like a ghost town: no one was there. As he entered the grand entrance with hints of Greek architecture above him, the echoing of his and his father's footsteps reverberated around the corridors. They headed straight for the surgery in the lecture theatre, and Archie felt his heart race as he saw the door; still closed with its elaborate locking mechanism apparent for all to see. He felt a burning desire to question his father about the door, but something inside him told him he should not. He felt a tight, tugging sensation inside him and he was about to ask the question when his father walked straight over to the door and started to open it. Archie was amazed. He pulled himself together and tried to look calm, but inside the excitement was welling up.

"What's in there?" he asked, believing he knew the answer, but truthfully, he did not have a clue.

"There are many things that at first look one way but they are, in truth, completely different. I would imagine that this, to you, looks like a safe. But, in fact, although like a safe, it holds many secrets, it is where it leads, rather than what it contains that is the secret." As fascinating as this sounded, Archie had to think carefully about what his father had just said to get a full understanding.

"Let's have a look, shall we?" His father looked as if he had punched a panel on the doorway. The intricate locking system swung into action and the mechanism started its opening process. Archie could feel the knot in his stomach tightening. What if the others appeared again? What would he say to them? How would he pretend that he did not know them? What was he to do? The door swung open...

And nothing happened. The door just opened and his father walked in. Archie did not know whether to follow or not. Carefully deciding what to do, he was interrupted by his father.

"Are you coming?" Archie walked through the doorway, the only response he could think of to his father's call. What would he see?

A staircase. A rusty, metal staircase. On the wall, tired but technical lighting showed their path. Archie followed his father down the stairs, taking them below, what

Archie thought, ground level. Another great door stood in their way at the bottom of the stairwell. Roker pushed it open, and they entered onto a metal balcony; a skilful pattern garnished the floor below them and wrought metal bars protected them from falling over the edge. He looked over the rail, again unsure of what or who, he might see. Below him was an array of rusty machinery. Large pipes and cylinders wound intricately around large chambers; pistons drove up and down in a rhythmic manner, creating steam and loud thuds and clunks. Archie felt he was in a factory. Above him, substantial rust covered beams protected the machinery below, like an ageing rib cage of a robot. Numerous lights hung on long wires; swaying in the burst of steam that sporadically emitted from the belly of the machines below. Like a sleeping dragon, parts of the device moved up and down, preparing to breathe a fiery end to anyone who got too close. Archie held back his imagination and realised it was only a furnace at the end; probably powering the dragon into life.

"Come with me," Roker ordered, and Archie dutifully followed his father along the balcony to a gantry that led straight over the belly of the beast. Though perfectly safe walking over the gantry, Archie felt something may spring up from below and grab him, so he walked in his father's shadow. At the other end of the bridge was another door. Archie's father placed his fist onto a black panel next to the door and it swung open. Was that some sort of key? But how did it open with just his fist? Archie wanted to ask but dared not to, in case he was ridiculed or taken back. What Archie saw next took his breath away even more than before. For now, he could see row after row of drawers. That alone may not sound impressive, but the scale of coverage of these drawers was immense. The football pitch Archie watched the game on previously was dwarfed by this. This went on as far as he could see; an endless sea of drawers - a filing heaven.

"Meredeth?" shouted Roker, "where are you?"

"I'm here," came the reply in a strange accent. From the endless corridors came a man, a man of short stature. His short legs carried him towards Archie and his father. Archie had seen this man before at his father's lectures, but had never spoken to him, nor knew who he was. He had a smart, velvet jacket on; black with a white trim around the edges of the lapels and pockets. On his head, he had, what looked like, an oversized pair of glasses with thick steel rims. Wild hair stuck out from every angle; a curly mop that had had no attention for a long time. However, a fascinating feature of this minute gentleman was his bushy moustache. Excessively thick in the nasal area, but waxed to perfection as it looped to an end at either side of his face. As he approached, he was stroking his bushy but neat beard underneath.

"Meredeth, this is my son Archie. Archie, this is Alphonso Meredeth."

"The pleasure is all mine, of course," came the reply.

"Meredeth is a leading scientist in our age Archie. You will be so impressed with what you see here today. Please, Meredeth, explain to Archie your greatest contribution to our society."

"Well Archie, when people are born, they usually visit the doctor. If they are one of the unfortunate poor folk, they may only visit a doctor when they are sick. Something happens in these visits. Normally a patient would pay for such a visit, but we have introduced a system whereby this first visit is free. Your father and I hope one day to introduce a system in this country where health care will be free for all people, no matter how rich or how poor they are. In this first visit, we do two things. We take a sample of blood and we take a set of fingerprints. "

"But why?" questioned Archie rashly, then suddenly sunk back into himself almost embarrassed for interrupting.

"A good question Archie. Well at first some parents complain asking that same question, but after it is explained to them about our plan for the future, nearly all people are happy to have their children's prints and blood on record."

"What if they refuse? And where do you keep this information?" came the next question.

"If they refuse, they refuse, it is their choice. And as for where the records are kept - you're looking at it. Here are the records of some of the population of this country." He turned and beckoned his arm into the distance - the unfathomable distance that seemed to disappear into nothing.

"What do you do with them all?" Archie inquired.

"Well, that is where your father and I come in. We have a team of scientists who use the samples to help us prevent disease. If a certain proportion of the population dies for a specific reason, we can investigate why. A man named Eligah Bilton has a large role in this. He is at the forefront of his field - a medical mastermind." Archie knew this name and held back the comment that first came to mind. This was a sharp contrast to what Ida and the others told him. Both people sounded so convincing in their tales; he was unsure which story to believe.

Archie attempted to think about what he had just heard and that he had listened to previously. If he applied a little logic, surely he would be able to arrive at the right answer. Ida had told him a great many things; most of which Archie found incredible; and if he had not seen the angelus custos himself, he was ninety-nine-point-nine percent sure he would not believe any of it. For why would his father be involved in this. What he had seen today, could not have been further from the other tales he had heard. Whereas Ida made certain individuals seem evil and wicked, what Archie had heard today made him believe the complete opposite. How he wished he had someone to confide in, but again, the same feeling returned; Ms Buddington would not take him on, and Kat would not believe him.

As he returned home, he thought to himself how little he had seen of Ms Buddington recently. He had fallen out with Kat, and that looked in no way like it would be sorted soon. Even seeing Abe proved to be complicated. The only person he could talk to was his father. Archie decided on his next outing, he would ask his father what exactly was going on, and as it turned out this was much sooner than he thought.

Chapter 8
The Firmamentum

"The seaside?" questioned Archie, "why are we going to the seaside?"

"There are a group of people I would like you to meet. I think you're old enough now to know what is actually going on in the world. Let us embark on a grand tour to The Grand Hotel." Archie could not believe his luck. Not only was he getting to spend more time with his father, but it appeared as if he would be telling him many secrets that he wanted to know.

Archie's last trip to the seaside had been eventful and in a private first-class carriage. However, that looked like third class in comparison to his journey this time. For the coach, he and his father walked towards gleamed in the dull, smoky station. The panelling on the exterior of the carriage was so polished that Archie was sure he could check his hair and waistcoat in it. A golden number one was framed in each door to emphasise the importance of this carriage along with the letters F.W.D. - perhaps the initials of the man who built the wagon.

"Which door is ours?" Archie asked inquisitively. His father laughed.

"Archie, this whole carriage is ours."

"The whole carriage," gasped Archie in awe and wonder.

"Yes," replied his father, "now quickly on board."

As the door opened, Archie looked at the familiar pattern, (like that on his father's Chesterfields at home), which adorned the back of the door. The plush, rust-coloured leather; buttoned and studded into place at the bottom; the word FIRST, delicately painted above the window. Upon entering the carriage, he was greeted with what could only be described as luxury. The first part of the cart was like an exceptional restaurant - immaculately set tables with glimmering silverware and a beautiful oak bar to the left. A similar standard of oak trimmed the windows and ceiling, and a thick, red carpet spread out beneath them. Into the next section, Archie found a more relaxed, less formal area - more informal seating and desk with two familiar Chesterfields pulled up to it. Finally, at the rear of the carriage was the most extravagant element, for there, completing the effect was a bedroom. The same wooden finish adorned the outer rim of the room, but long drapes hung over every window, covered with an elaborate design of which Ebenezer Dorrington would be proud. Archie had managed to close his awe-struck jaw by this point, and a new feeling overcame him. This train carriage that he and his father would take a relatively short journey on was far better, far more luxurious, far more wasteful than any of the housing provided for much of the population - and this did not sit well with Archie.

"How do we get to travel in a carriage like this?" he questioned.

"It belongs to a wealthy man I know. I have done him a good turn and he has returned the favour. I know it is a little extravagant, but whether we like it or not, this carriage is going to the seaside. We can stay in it or move elsewhere, but if we do not use it, it will be empty."

Archie felt inside like he should say that he wanted to move but a large part wished to travel in style.

The journey moved on, and Archie did indeed travel in style. He ate a five-course meal with his father: oysters, soup a la Reine, lobster Newberg, beef collops au bordelaise followed by fresh strawberries and then relaxed in the lounge area of the carriage as his father drank strong, black coffee and a Cognac - the burned wine - to end the hearty meal. The industrial landscape soon disappeared behind them, leaving smoking chimneys and tired factories behind. The countryside greeted them next with rolling fields and fresh, flowing rivers. More apparent was the cleaner air and sweeter smell. Finally, the conclusion of the journey; sea air and the sight of the sea brought delight to them. They were at journey's end, and though they had travelled in luxury, they would be glad to stretch their legs in the sea air.

"What are we going to do at The Grand?" questioned Archie. They now travelled in a carriage through the town to the hotel. The seaside seemed to be a higher class place than the city. Of course, the town had many wealthy areas, but the seaside, more importantly, had no deprived areas, especially on the strip close to the coast. Gentlemen strolled in choicest suits and top hats, tapping canes on the pavement as they passed; ladies showed off their dresses and carried parasols over their shoulders, protecting their fair skin from the sun. The streets looked clean and tidy, the air smelt sweet and the presence of the prominent hill at the west end of the bay was ever present.

"We are meeting with some of the greatest minds of our time. You will have your eyes opened today, believe me," Archie's father responded. They pulled up outside the hotel and met by the concierge who opened the carriage door.

"Good afternoon Sir. Good afternoon young man. I hope you enjoy your stay at The Grand," he muttered in a dower, sombre voice. Archie's father just walked past the man, as if he were not there, so Archie followed smiling weakly, as he passed the old man.

They were shown to their rooms by a member of staff, and Archie was as equally impressed as he had been in the train carriage. The front of the hotel led straight out onto the main road, but the back of the hotel, and the view from Archie's room, looked out over the bay in into the distance to the sea. He noted how his quarters and his fathers were by the tower section at the far end of the building. Again, separate from the rest of the guests. This was becoming a familiar theme for Archie. He was used to it at home as he grew up, but he now was beginning to realise it was happening in every element of his life. What was the reason behind this?

Later that evening, just as the sun was setting over the bay, Archie was summoned to his father's room. When he entered, he noted how much more like an office this room was than his. His father was stood talking to another gentleman, but this was no gentleman like Archie had ever seen before. The gentleman was dressed as most men of the day did: cravat, shirt, waistcoat, trousers and jacket, but there was more to add to this. First over the top of his slightly average blazer was a green and black pinstripe throw with a scarlet red trim. On his feet, he wore, what looked like, oversized, black, leather boots; one of them sporting brown straps with some unusual attachment. He had a sprouting of hair at the side and back of his head - thick, curly brown locks - but on the top of his head, nothing - only the reflection of the light in the room flickering like a beacon on a dark winter's night. On his face, there was almost a beard; above and below his mouth was smoothly clean shaven, but on either side, sideburns that fanned out like an exotic lizard from a faraway land. He wore tan brown leather gloves and a satchel across his body. As Archie entered, he opened the bag, decorated with the letters H.C.L, and took out a handsome calabash pipe and began tapping it in his glove.

"This is Hudson Carbey-Lowther. He is a prominent explorer who has travelled to every corner of the globe. A bit of an adventurer, wouldn't you say Hudson?"

"Oh, yes indeed," replied the eccentric gentleman in a strange, slightly effeminate voice.

"Hudson has been on many trips for many people. His skills are second to none, and, for the right price, he will perform any task or retrieve any item desired," Roker continued.

"So, this is Master Archie Roker. I have heard a lot about you young man and I assume as we have now met you have reached the age to find out the truth."

"That is correct. I have arranged a visit to the Firmamentum here. I think it's time he met Keiler and The Engineer," Roker continued.

"A wise choice. That will certainly put the young man in the picture," the explorer confirmed.

The time in his father's suite passed as standard now, or as normal as his father's meeting usually went. A discussion or two about the state of the country, several drinks from a decanter of an unknown brown liquid and a lot of strange laughter coming from Carbey-Lowther. His laughter almost sounded like a fake laugh that the recipient may believe was a lie.

An hour or so later, Roker stood up and explained to the gentlemen present it was time to go. However, instead of heading for the door, he ventured to another doorway in the room - one Archie had assumed a cupboard of some sort. As they approached it, Roker placed his hand towards the handle and the door opened. Immediately in front of him, was a metal zig-zag grill. The squares squashed and disappeared as the mesh was pulled to one side by Roker, and Archie could see in the dim light, it appeared to be a small room. Roker entered first and beckoned Archie to follow him.

"Come on Archie, in you get." Archie felt a little unsure and hesitated. "It's fine Archie, trust me," Roker said holding out his hand in reassurance. Archie stumbled forward and felt the presence of Carbey-Lowther behind him. It was not a pleasant feeling as if he were being stalked or entrapped. He hurried his stumbling and entered the room with his father, followed by the hunter.

As he entered the room, he realised he was in a lift. Archie had been in one before, he recalled, when he stayed at The Grosvenor with his father on a business meeting when he was much younger. That one had been much more spacious than this with an attendant and even a plant on a pedestal. This one however barely fit the two men and young adult. Archie considered for a moment why this room had a lift in it. Why was it not out in the hallway for others to use? Why was it so small? Where did the one button on the wall take the occupiers if pressed? These questions were soon answered, but a few more would become more pressing.

"Going down," Carbey-Lowther explained in a strange tone. The lift plummeted downwards causing a peculiar feeling in Archie's stomach as if it were still left on the top floor of the hotel and was rushing to catch up with the rest of its body. The light flickered on and off sporadically, and suddenly darkness engulfed the box. The journey, which seemed to last an age, in fact, took less than a minute. Archie could feel his breath getting more rapid and more burdensome as he found himself stood in the darkness. He felt as if he should reach out to his father but was unsure where Carbey-Lowther was in relation to his position. Suddenly he heard the metal gate swing open and he could see the door reveal the light as it entered the carriage.

Archie stepped out of the claustrophobic container, expecting to be in the lobby of the hotel but instead he appeared to be on a small train platform.

"Where are we?" questioned Archie.

"We are taking a very special train, Archie," came the reply from his father.

"Take a seat here," gestured Carbey-Lowther. Archie looked at his father for reassurance. Following a nod of approval, Archie sat in the seat on a small machine. It was a curious contraption: two sets of chairs faced each other on top on a small platform; a cog sat close to one of the positions with a chain that linked to one of a set of six wheels on the track below. At the rear of the machine was a large funnel that looked a lot like the bell of a tuba, though this was not a shiny, gleaming metal as Archie had seen with an orchestra; this was tired and worn covered in a thin coating of grime and grease. Smoke began billowing from the funnel and steam shot from many nooks of the machine. Archie sat apprehensively at his father's side with Carbey-Lowther facing him. Carbey-Lowther grabbed a long lever next to him with a squeezable handle at the top and thrust forward. The carriage rocketed into life. Weaving through a narrow tunnel like a snake after its prey, Archie could feel his breath took away. It felt at times that the carriage may topple over as it rode up the sides of the chamber.

Another trip that felt longer than it was ended as the carriage came out into a vast underground cavern. Archie could not believe what he saw. Inside, what Archie could only assume was a mountain or under the ground, was an enormous cavernous expanse. Wherever he was, it was apparent solid rock surrounded him as when he gazed upwards the sheer rock face was still present; rough and coarse if he were to touch it. However, the rest of the cave looked utterly different. The walls of the cavern had been carved and excavated, what Archie could only associate as if it were a church. Ornate doorways dotted the lining, mingled with pictures that were cut into the wall: some showing hands shackled with chains, others showing a man, who Archie thought looked Egyptian, whipping slaves. Looking down at the ground, the floor was expertly polished and, for being in a cave, perfectly level. A simple but elegant pattern of interlocking squares and octagons paved the way forward.

"What is this place?" Archie stammered dumbfounded.

"I shall explain all in a moment Archie, but let's find somewhere more comfortable to discuss shall we." Archie nodded and remembered to close his mouth. Carbey-Lowther spoke quietly to Roker and set off further into the cavern. Archie and his father continued through the symmetric walkway and entered through a carved doorway on the left. There was a stone table with large chairs (or thrones as Archie thought of them) surrounding it.

"Now Archie, I want you to listen very carefully. Some people will be coming soon, and I won't be able to tell you much after that. Do you understand?"

"Yes," Archie lied. He had no idea what was happening.

"What I tell you, you must keep secret. Do not mention it to anyone you meet today, do not mention it to anyone at home. Do you understand?" His father seemed quite adamant about this. Archie nodded.

"I am being forced to do work for a secret group. It is made up of lots of rich and powerful people. The control and power they have Archie is unfathomable. They run everything. Including me. I must do as they ask or they will harm you. Do you understand?"

"Yes," replied Archie somewhat unconvincingly.

"The things they ask me to do are not important or relevant for today, but you need to be aware how powerful these people are. Don't get me wrong, we live an excellent life because of this arrangement, but it is not ideal. These people hold secret meetings. They conspire, collude and connive. They control everyone and everything."

Roker suddenly went silent as three gentlemen entered the room. The first was a gentleman of senior years, short and uncomfortable in his movement. He was dressed all in a military style, brown, hessian material that looked like it had seen cleaner days. He wore round-rimmed spectacles, but, by far, his most prominent feature was a long thin grey moustache that appeared to sprout from his nose before extending horizontally away from his face.

The second man was much younger and had his head shaved entirely on one side of his head. The crown and other side of his head was covered in thick black hair, slicked back from his forehead, down the rear of the skull. He looked as if he were wearing a padded jacket with thick tubes circulating his arms. Around his neck, he wore a large leather collar piece, inscribed with various symbols and detail Archie could not recognise.

The final man with a long jacket trailing behind him. Dark brown lapels stood out in comparison to the light, sandy coloured material that made up the rest of the coat. Underneath he wore a smart waistcoat matching the fancy cravat carefully tied around his neck. Upon his head, he wore a top hat, though not as high and elegant as those worn by gentlemen Archie had seen around the town.

These three men all appeared entirely different, but one thing linked them all. On their left arms, they all wore what looked like a leather fingerless glove, strapped in position with golden buckles, and upon this attachment were an array of dials and canisters like nothing Archie had seen before.

"Ah, Roker, I see you have brought the boy," exclaimed the third man

"Yes," replied Roker, sounding a lot less self-assured than he usually did. "As I was told." This made Archie feel uncomfortable. He had never heard his father speak like this. His father was always the man in charge and Archie had never seen him answer to anyone. He was the man who gave instructions.

"Do you know who I am boy?" barked the man in the top hat.

"Err… no Sir. I'm sorry I do not," quivered Archie in response.

"My name is Marsden. Roker, I thought you would have briefed the boy before now."

"I'm sorry, I thought…"

"Thought? Well maybe stop thinking and start doing. What do you say to that?"

"Of course," shuddered Roker. Archie was panicking now. His father was scared; he could see that. Apparently, the threat of these people that his father had told him about was clear and present.

"Archie, Mr Marsden is the leader of a group of fine individuals who are trying to make our country a better place. Mr Marsden has been influential in developing electricity to bring it to the masses. To make life better for the average man on the street. Some people want to stop us achieve our goal, so we work in secret and silence. We have developed places, like here, where we can meet and work collaboratively, and try to move humanity forward. Do you understand Archie?" Roker was hopefully looking at his son for some positive sign of affirmation.

"Yes father, I do."

"Excellent boy," bellowed Marsden. "Your father has done some tremendous work for us, and he has been splendidly rewarded. Do you like your house and lifestyle? That is because of us. Your father has informed us that you are of age to see more and that you are keen to develop your father's work. Is that correct?" Archie looked at his father again, and the same affirming look was reciprocated.

"Yes," answered Archie in a much more positive manner.

"Excellent boy, then we shall arrange a meeting. Sit yourself down." Archie and his father sat at the stone table. "Time for introductions. This is Floyd William Davis. However, we do not use that name - he is called 'The Engineer' due to his remarkable skills combining old and new technology. This young man is Mr Bertram Keiler; he is responsible for taking the human potential to the next level. Along with The Engineer, they have driven humankind to the next level. Let me explain further." Marsden lifted his left arm and pushed a button on his forearm. A few moments later, Carbey-Lowther entered the room with another man. "This is Edward Plundell; a man who has reformed surgical techniques to aid the medical profession. However, as a child, through a horrific surgical incident, he has injured himself, leading to the amputation of his left arm. These gentlemen here have developed the next step in human evolution. Plundell - show the boy."

The man in question was smartly dressed, like Marsden, but from behind his back, he produced his left 'arm'. It appeared at first as if the man was holding a machine in his hand, but upon closer inspection, Archie

107

realised it was his arm. It looked mechanical and had gears, cogs and flashing lights. He moved his arm up, and it bent at the elbow joint as an elbow should. Archie could not believe what he was seeing.

"Plundell was a renowned surgeon, like your father, until this accident. Without the efforts of these great men, he would no longer be able to assist our group. Now, he can continue as he did before, and still do more. The power he has in his left arm is incredible. Show him." Archie sat in amazement as the man, who did not look particularly strong or athletic, approached Archie's seat. He bent down and picked up the stone chair and Archie in one go, with no effort at all. Archie grabbed the arms of the chair in panic as the other men in the room laughed. What was this man or machine or monster before him?

"As you can appreciate boy," continued Marsden, "Plundell cannot return to normal life. People cannot see him like this. The country could not cope with this. So, he remains here; or in places like this, safe and able to do his work as and when he requires. Put him down now." The chair returned to the floor and Archie jumped as the stone hit the ground. Plundell returned to his original position and lifted his bent mechanical appendage again. Gears were turning and gusts of steam shooting from various joints of the arm.

"So, this is what we do Archie, and you are now part of it. It may be unusual, it may appear strange, but if you embrace this life, you will be rewarded beyond your wildest dreams. You will not believe the power you can harness and use. What do you say?" In truth, Archie felt there was only one answer he could give. Whether it was the right one, he knew what he had to say.

"I'm in."

"Excellent boy, you will need to prepare for your next visit. To Romani Grove."

Chapter 9
Romani Grove

A few more days passed in the hotel by the coast. Archie could see from his window a fantastic view of the seafront: lavish hotels, set out neatly like a set of highly polished teeth; a wide paved promenade, the strolling section for people to exercise and feel the sunshine on their faces; the long pier, extending out from the foot of the hotel and disappearing into the blue sea to his left. He could see children playing on the pier, on marvellous mechanical merry-go-rounds and Ferris wheels, but these seemed to lack the attraction they once had. After all, he had seen, how his life had changed, and what the future may hold for him, Archie just sat and gazed at the world as it passed him by. The only comforting thing at these times was the sporadic appearance of Abe; never directly, but a brief presentation, only to Archie, to show he was watching.

His father had many more meetings during this time, and Archie did not spend as much time as he would have liked with him. His relationship had blossomed over the last few days, and he was glad, but he wanted to extend it further. He thought of home and Kat and Ms Buddington. That part of his life seemed so far away and so long ago. What would they make of all this? Having spent nearly every day with Ms Buddington, he found the void of her presence hard to fill. Yes, there were servants in the hotel who did everything he asked, but he felt like he needed her to talk to. After everything he had seen in his coastal visit with her, he felt so confused. Yes, Alium said his father was working for a secret society, but their interpretation of the organisation was not a pleasant picture. His father's perspective was not the most positive but a lot better than the landscape they had created. Archie felt he must explore this a little further before ultimately making his mind up. Could both sides be correct?

The day arrived for them to leave the hotel. Roker came into Archie's room with some packages. Inquisitively, Archie asked what they were.

"Do you remember our shopping trip; the one that was cut short," his father replied. Archie nodded. "Well, these are the things we purchased that day. Do you recall?" Archie remembered the jewellers, the bookstore, the milliners and the tailors before they were interrupted. "You will need to change accordingly before we depart. Here."

Archie's father handed him package contain a crisp white shirt. Archie placed it on the bed and stripped to his underwear. He put on the ice white garment and buttoned it up. It felt new, and the collar was overly stiff, but Archie did not want to appear to complain. Next, his father produced a suit bag and after unzipping the front Archie saw a black velvet suit. His father handed him the trousers, and he slipped into them comfortably. A perfect fit. A brown box was opened next and inside were the calf length, black leather boots; the distinctive smell of new leather was soft on the nostrils, but still smelt so primitive. He slid them on and like his collar they felt stiff and new. A good walk is what you need, Ms Buddington would say when he got a new pair of shoes, he recalled fondly.

His father now approached him with a red cravat and helped him fasten it around his neck, again a job usually saved for his ward. Next, came the velvet suit jacket; as black as the night - its distinctive soft weave giving a dense pile - deserving of the phrase 'smooth like velvet'. Archie recalled the list he had seen prior to his shopping trip, and it brought to mind the vulpes corvum lining. Upon closer inspection of the silken interior he was met with an over-enthusiastic repeating pattern: a large black feather was the most striking element of the design; a flock of black birds were making a hasty departure from the feather or perhaps it was the menacing skull that peered out with a sinister grin from its bony teeth or the fox head that scowled also; a selection of patterns and flowers completed the background aside from what appeared to be an obelisk with an ornate frame at the bottom containing a picture of what looked to be two characters from an Ancient Greek play. Archie liked it. The repeating pattern was fun to try and work out the start and where the next repetition began.

Archie was instructed to button up the jacket which he did obediently. Next came a cap. Not a towering top hat like all the other men (of which Archie was glad) but a flat, slightly oversized cap. This covered Archie's head quite comfortably, and he felt there was plenty of room to grow into it over the coming years.

"Excellent Archie, now you look the part," his father, "only a couple more things."

He produced a case with the letters A.R. on the top. "This is yours, Archie."

"Thank you," Archie replied gladly. Inside the box, he saw a large velvet piece of material; a deep red colour. On top of this was a leather-bound book. Upon the cover was a similar image to the lining of his jacket. There, in front of him, was a skull and upon it stood a raven with its wings outspread, ready to take flight. Both were embossed on the thick brown leather cover of the book. He picked it up and flicked through the pages; they were all blank. He turned and looked at his father.

"For you to write in. The things you have and will see you will want to make some notes." Finally, the small box Archie recollected from the jewellers. "You may wear this now, but when you put it on, you must promise me never to take it off. This ring will give you power beyond your imagination. Wearing this ring means you are somebody." The box was opened, and the ring faced Archie. Around his finger were two loops of, what can only be described as, industrial tubing, but so minute. These encased and held in place the fabulous centrepiece. Archie could have sworn it was an emerald eye staring at him. A bright and striking iris surrounded a deep black pupil. He slid it onto his finger.

"Perfect fit," his father announced. Archie smiled. He was a little overwhelmed by the presents he had been given. Not merely by the probable cost of them, but also their significance. Something important, but equally unknown to Archie at this moment.

These thoughts stayed with Archie as he and his father travelled in the carriage back to the train station. The journey back on the train was as equally elaborate as the arrival, but in his new attire, Archie felt much more meaningful. Arriving at another station, Archie departed the train and stood on the platform; personalised case in hand. Although it was similar to the one they had boarded the train from, this station was much smaller. The same iconic features of steel and glass still shone through as a station of the time, but there were only two platforms. And the number of people present were far fewer than previous. In fact, other than the guard, who was stood on the platform at the very rear of the train with his red flag and whistle, there were only Archie and his father; both holding matching leather cases, though one much bigger than the other.

Another carriage pulled up outside the limestone station, highlighted only further by the deep red paint on the woodwork. As they mounted the steps of the coach, Archie noticed the scarcity of other buildings in the vicinity. There were trees and fields, as far as the eye could see, but that was it. A barren green carpet set out in front of them. No industrial landscapes or the sight of steam of smoke. Foliage and, between that and the blue skies above, some hills in the distance. The familiar presence of a raven flew high in the air above. Although not sure, Archie was sure it would be Abe.

"That is where we are heading Archie," Roker stated, pointing to the hills.

"What is there?"

"That," came the reply, "is Romani Grove."

On the journey to the Grove, Archie occasionally glanced out of the window, interlaced with a discussion with his father. This was a good time. They talked about football, the hotel, Plundell's arm and many other things. Archie suddenly felt talking about these things felt normal. This is what he needed. The outside world passed them by: two farmers chatted and prepared to eat their lunch, waiting for their wives to bring them something. A hard morning in the fields was work enough for this day. An hour later, after a bumpy journey, the carriage suddenly moved onto what felt like smooth ground. Archie gazed out of the window. Suddenly, in front of him, the old country roads had disappeared, and a flat surface lay below them. Looking up, Archie could see what he assumed was a long driveway, and there, at the end and top of the drive stood a white house. It looked minuscule now as the drive was extensive in length, but as the smooth surface allowed for a swifter journey, the building soon came into sight. As they approached, the sun was beginning to set, disappearing behind the horizon, behind the house, making it almost impossible to see in the blinding light.

As the house came into sight, Archie noted its Greek/Italian architecture and was impressed. The grand entrance appeared to match the Parthenon in Greece with six great pillars stretching up to the tympanum, supported by the shafts, illustrating a story in the freeze that may have been there for generations. Again, the images of skulls, obelisks, foxes and birds dominated - a continuing pattern that Archie was becoming increasingly familiar with - in every element of his life. The carriage door was opened, and Archie and his father stepped out. There, in front of them, stood a gentleman in a suit matching that worn by Archie and his father.

"Archie, this is Mr Wesley Lillyvick. He is the guardian of Romani Grove. Anything that happens here only happens because he has allowed it to. He oversees everything: what you eat for dinner to security. Whatever you see here or what may happen you do not need worry because Lillyvick has it under control."

Archie smiled at the bald man in front of him but was more concerned with the words his father had used. Whatever you see? Whatever may happen? What was he going to see? What was going to happen?

"The sun has almost set sir. If you would like to meet on the rear veranda, I will ensure your bags are taken to your room," Lillyvick offered.

"Very well," Roker answered in a knowing voice. Archie moved his case towards the man. "No Archie, you will need your cape." Suddenly Archie realised what the red velvet material in his case was. He pulled it out and swung it over his shoulders. A stylish silver clasp joined the two collars together, and a hood hung behind him. His father repeated the same procedure, and they both handed their cases over. Lillyvick disappeared into the house, and the pair of robed beings moved themselves to the rear of the building.

A sea of red met Archie and his father as they turned the corner around the back of the house. Everyone present wore the same clothes: black velvet suit, leather boots and a thick red velvet cape. As Archie looked around, he noted some familiar faces from his recent excursions. Lord Burley Wilberforce - head of the asylums, Dr Borthwell - charity founder extraordinaire, Eligah Bilton - the specialist in disease prevention, Crowle - head of the police and the Crowlies. As Archie and his father continued to move around, more familiar faces appeared - Hudson Carbey Lowther, Floyd Williams Davis and Bertram Keiler; all from his recent seaside visit. As he looked at these gentlemen, they gave him a nod or

116

gesture of recognition. Archie felt - now that he was dressed the part - that his levels of respect would increase and this seemed the case.

All these gentlemen stood with silver goblets in their hands. Archie wondered what they were drinking and could he have some. He looked to his father.

"Sorry Archie, red wine. You're still not old enough," Roker remarked as a goblet was passed to him and he took a large mouthful. As the silver chalice moved away from his mouth, Archie noticed the remnants of wine around his mouth. Roker rubbed it away, almost embarrassed by his manners.

"Time to cure us of the Vermes," ordered a voice, whom upon closer inspection Archie realised was Eligah Bilton (at the forefront of disease prevention). Archie watched carefully and noted a selection of the robed gentlemen - some he knew, some he did not - pick up ornate rifles and point them towards the woods.

"What are they shooting at father?" enquired Archie.

"Foxes," replied his father. They normally shoot pheasant, but the foxes have had their fill this year Lillyvick was telling me. So, tonight, they shoot the fox."

Archie watched carefully. A group of men, at least ten of them, stood with rifles aimed across an open, green lawn, towards a selection of what, even Archie could tell from this distance where exotic trees. Suddenly, foxes appeared. One to start with but then, two, three - four, then five. All out in the open or at the edge of the woods. This seemed unusual behaviour for foxes thought Archie, but he was sure the poachers knew best. Shots rang out, and four of the five foxes ceased their movements, Permanently. The laughing and joking of the hooded,

117

velvet army was in sharp contrast to the silence that befell the battlefield. A little shocked by their response, what followed made Archie shudder even further.

A young adult appeared on the field, wearing next to nothing but rags. Archie was about to tell his father when a loud whining siren rang out, and the huntsmen calibrated their aim to the new target. The girl, seventeen at the most, stood like a startled rabbit. Archie did not know what was going to happen next and if he did, he undoubtedly would have looked away, as the girl - who was uncontrollably sobbing - took a bullet in the shoulder. This knocked her balance and made her sway. Next, one hit her chest, close but not direct to her heart. Finally, as she collapsed to her knees, a shot from the hooded assassins hit her in the temple. She slumped to the floor and moved no more.

"Do not worry gentleman. It was an intruder, no doubt trying to steal things from our rooms, Lillyvick explained. "Security was on their way to apprehend the thief, but you boys have done a sterling job. I feel the need for a glass of fresh red for everyone. Yes?"

There was raucous laughter and cheers; Archie was unsure of the feeling inside of him. Looking at his father, he could see an acceptance of this behaviour, but something did not sit right with Archie. Who was that girl? Why was she trying to steal items and why was she wearing rags?

The shooting ended, and the men (for Archie noticed they were all men) moved to a large marquee on the lawn. He could not help but stand in disgust as these men stood, laughed and joked, lighting up cigars, as a corpse lay blood splattered on the floor. Roker could see this in his son's eyes and gestured Lillyvick towards him. Within moments the body was being removed by two orderlies all in white.

"Archie, life may seem a little extreme here, but we live in an extreme world. These men here are some of the most powerful men in the country, if not the world. They work all the time, for the good of the country. But for one week a year they come here- a holiday- to relax and forget about the rest of the world. As I said, you may see things here you do not believe, and what you do see you must not share with the outside world. That is very important Archie. Privacy and secrets are what make this society what it is. Men may leave here after a week with their energy levels recharged and ready for work again. Some even continue work while they are here, having meetings and making deals for the good of the globe."

"Why was that person shot?" Archie questioned, seemingly unimpressed with his father's speech.

"Archie, try and understand this. What I have told you about these people; their power, their influence, some people see it negatively. That they are controlling, they think nothing of the common man only to make themselves richer. That the decisions they make are supposedly for the many but only benefit the few. But a lot of these people can't see the bigger picture. What these men do is what is best for everyone. Sometimes that may affect some people in a bad way, but suffering for a few outweighs the needs of all. Do you understand? Some individuals don't agree with this and will do anything to disrupt it; anything at all."

"But why would people want to stop it if it is for the good of others?" Archie asked confused now.

"Because they are anarchists. They don't like being told what to do even if it is for their best interests," came the reply. Archie nodded; pretending he understood it completely, but he did not. He did not understand any of this. Everything he knew had changed. Life was a lie, but who to believe. He found himself gazing around at the gentlemen in front of him. His father had explained many of them were businessmen: politicians and bankers, the corrupt part of society, but this secret group, so he claimed, controlled them all.

"These men think they have the power, but they are so arrogant, they cannot see they control nothing. We are the puppet masters," Roker had detailed further. "Take the gold they protect in their reserves; in their precious vaults in the Bank of England. See that man over there; he is called Calvin Coleman. He is responsible for the postal service in this country. By the age of thirty, he has set up a national system for delivering messages around the country. Fantastic - a real example of how someone can make something of themselves - not like those anarchists who try and disrupt everything. The bankers believe they are hoarding the gold of the country, but Coleman has used his underground postal service to collect the money from the Bank of England, and others, and now the society has control."

Suddenly, there was a minor disruption at the main house. Everyone turned to see what the cause of the commotion was. Archie could recognise from a distance the footballer, Shapter, whom he had met on the previous occasion. Next to him stood the giant figure of Ebenezer Dorrington, the 'celebrity' artist. He had a robust bearing, with a slightly overgrown beard and hair, but styled to perfection. He obviously took great pride in his appearance: careful and immaculately finished. A 'celebrity' of the time, few newspapers were published without him being mentioned or written about. With him was another man, as equally smart in appearance, but Archie did not recognise the face. Long silky, black hair hung over half of his face; a partial mask to the man's natural looks, a thin pencil moustache, sleeping on his top lip.

"This is my good friend and associate, Tillman Thompson: musician, artist, poet, actor. Where he goes, I follow, as he is talent." A polite applause and cheers of 'bravo' followed.

"Shall we go and introduce ourselves?" Roker suggested.

The two casually walked over. Archie felt very uneasy but watched his father who seemed to feel completely at ease in this experience. Like it was a typical, humdrum event, meeting a famous luminary. Archie knew his father was familiar with a lot of influential people, notably the Queen, but this somehow seemed different - as if his father were equally famous. Being the monarch's private surgeon obviously meant he knew her and the royal family. He was a regular at the palace, and one did not become the surgeon to the Queen by luck. Skill. Skill and reputation.

"Ebenezer, always a pleasure. How is the latest script coming along?" Roker enquired, knowing full well the current play Dorrington was working on had been anticipated for the last twelve months.

"That patient of yours keeps interfering with my time. Can you do a portrait of this? Can you write a speech about that? I don't know how you put up with her Mr Roker!" came the reply in a deep, masculine tone. "Tillman here has been helping me with the script, and he has some wonderful ideas, with some extraordinary detail, I can tell you."

"Really," responded Roker, shaking Thompson's hand firmly, "well, I shall look forward to reading about it when it is finally published. When will that be?"

"When you get that woman to cease badgering me!" They both laughed heartily, and Archie and his father moved on.

"What woman were you talking about?" quizzed Archie.

"Oh, I think even you can work that out Archie," Roker grinned back at him.

"The Queen!" Archie gasped. A nod was the reply from Roker.

The evening continued very much in the same vein, with Archie being introduced to many people, all from differing backgrounds and professions. He was particularly interested in meeting Enoch Howlett, the chocolate entrepreneur. A long conversation followed: the origins of Howlett's Chocolate, the process of it being manufactured in the enormous Howlett factory (one which employed thousands of people), how it is distributed around the country and the world and finally, what Archie's favourite flavour was. Howlett had promised Archie he would personally send a box direct to the house. But he had also warned (with a laugh and a joke) about the addictive element of the chocolate. That is why it sells so much, he had boasted to Archie. According to Howlett, other than the sugar and fat present, that makes the brown gold feel addictive, there were other chemicals introduced to heighten people's moods, causing feelings of excitement and attraction. This rung true with the information Ida had told him, but with a slightly different outcome.

The evening drew to a close, at least for Archie, and he was escorted to his tent. When he looked upon the camping facilities he could not believe, again, the excess that spilt out. This tent would be considered a luxury for a normal family and would dwarf the housing of many residents of the city. The initial impact was the porch area at the front on the canvas heaven - one on both sides of the doorway. Archie could see a comfortable table set for several people, if they chose to dine outside. On the other, an elaborate swing seat, covered in a long fur, the skin of which animal Archie was unsure of. As he was ushered past the porch, the two flaps at the entrance were lifted, and two suited gentlemen stood, holding the canvas doors ajar. Archie was met with a circular meeting room: a large fire pit, smouldering in the centre of the room; a selection of chairs, of varying sizes, covered again in exotic furs; an array of furniture holding lamps and interesting trinkets, plus a well-stocked drinks cabinet, bottle and glasses aplenty. From this circular den, three more passages led off like holes in a rabbit warren. The attendant, who had held open one of the doors, now gestured towards the passage on the left. Archie entered and found himself in another canvas dome, this one with a four-poster bed to the right, a set of wooden drawers next to them (upon which stood a porcelain bowl for washing and other such ablutions) and finally on the left, an x frame upon which Archie's case was placed and opened, clothes still neatly folded, suits and jackets hung up on a rail attached to the side of the case. Soft light glowed from a selection of lanterns around this snug abode, and the attendant left him to prepare for bed. Archie rapidly changed into a nightshirt and climbed into the cosy, soft bed.

Archie slept soundly, for what felt like a day, but was, in fact, little over ninety minutes. The soft lighting emitting from the candles around his room had all been extinguished bar one. The gentle glow created wild and wary images on the white canvas walls of the tent. Archie watched as he saw shapes dance through the darkness and he let his imagination run away with him in an attempt to drop off back to sleep. However, the change in slumber made Archie realise that the bedpan was more urgent than rest. He reached under the bed, but the porcelain pot was nowhere to be found. Archie got up from his bed and felt the warm furs under his feet. With arms out in front of him and eyes half closed, he set off to find the mobile privy. Eventually, he came across the chamber and set about the task in hand. When complete, he carefully placed it back on the floor, in a safe place that would not be stood on, either by himself, or someone else visiting in the morning. He now turned in the darkness and aimed for the drawers by his bed to wash his hands. He recalled some water was left in from the previous night, enough to rinse his hands. As he stood there, drying his hands on his nightshirt (no towel was apparently present, and he now wanted the comfort of bed again), Archie heard laughing. The sound of a few men laughing at something someone else had said. The words were unclear, but the laughing was clear. He thought it might be his father but who did the other voices belong to? One stood out above the others, and he recognised it as the unique tones of Hudson Carbey-Lowther. Archie, despite having acquired new findings almost daily, wanted to know more and concluded that he would get closer to hear clearer. He moved through the rabbit warren tunnels, so all that separated him from the circular meeting room was a canvas sheet. He could not move the barrier to see, but he listened intently to what was unfolding behind the canvas shield.

"Phase three can begin then." Archie recognised this voice as Marsden. "Is your model ready Keiler?"

"Ahhh, yes. She is ready to do as required when required," came the reply.

"Phase one should come into play soon, is that right Bilton?" Archie heard his father say.

"Why of course. Just as we planned," responded a voice. "I know Howlett has worked on phase two, so everything is coming into play perfectly."

"Excellent work, excellent," Roker responded.

"We can just blame the French, again. And start a war why not. I did very well out of it last time, especially from the cannons and heavy artillery," quipped Carbey-Lowther. Laughter again filled the tent. Then Archie heard the strangest thing. A peculiar mechanical voice, almost unearthly, something Archie had never heard before.

"And I shall tell them all about it. Precisely what we want them to know," came the mechanical, monotone modulation.

"Exactly Harrington, exactly," Marsden roared. Arnold Harrington, the newspaper publisher! Again, laughter filled the tent. Archie felt he had to look. Peering through an eyelet in the canvas, Archie could see a dimly lit room, flames dying in the fire pit and gentlemen smoking big cigars, drinking red wine from glasses. He recognised a few, but gasped when he saw the owner of the monotone voice. There, dressed equally smart as all the other gentlemen, was a machine. Black gloves covered the hands, but the head was copper, with blue ocular cavities. The skull reflected the fading light making further reflection upon the ceiling. Archie could see the right side of the skull was open and inside a series of cogs and gears whizzed around. A simple slit - five or six centimetres in length - was where the mouth should be, but it did not open or close. It stayed as it was. Archie held his breath and looked away. He was not sure of what he had just seen and did not know how to react to it. He gathered his thoughts and breath and heard the men leave the tent. He continued to hold his breath and edged back to his canvas shelter. As he did, he stumbled backwards over something on the floor - the chamber pot. He felt his feet wet as landed backwards on the floor. The canvas door swung back, and his father was stood there in front of him. Archie did not know what to say. What was phase one? Two? Three? Why does Harrington have a mechanical head? Why are you involved in all this? Why is Carbey-Lowther so creepy? Do you know that I heard all that? So many questions. Instead, he built up to the one he had dared not ask over the last few days, until now.

"So, Mr Marsden is the leader of this secret group?"

"Yes Archie, he is."

"And what is it called?"

"It is called Imperium."

Chapter 10
Maddie

Archie returned home; now more confused than ever before. Just when he seemed to find out something about his complicated life, another earth-shattering announcement was made, throwing the previous exclamation, and those before into chaos. His journey home was without his father, but two Crowlies sat in the carriage with him for the entire trip. Roker had explained that he needed to stay at Romani Grove one day further on business and then was required to see the Queen, so maybe a couple of days visiting the palace. Archie was glad of the relationship he had developed with his father but was relieved to have some space from everything that was going on in his world. The Crowlies sat there, motionless for the whole journey, like two angry statues that had just been involved in an intense argument, a snarl appearing over their hairy, bearded faces. Archie felt if he spoke, let alone say a crossword, and there would be severe repercussions. He dare not open his mouth, let alone mention the apparent guest that was following the carriage from the air. There was Abe again, watching.

As they arrived back home, Archie saw the familiar figure of Smetherly, waiting by the entrance to the front door. He looked as always, ready for work. Archie assumed Smetherly slept by the front door as any time any visitor arrived at the house he was perpetually there, ready.

"Good day Master Roker," he greeted the weary traveller.

"Good afternoon Smetherly," he replied. "Where is Ms Buddington?"

"She has been away for a few days young Sir, but she is due to return today." Archie wondered where she had gone. She never took a holiday, but he could imagine her destination. He felt sure it would have been the seaside and a visit to Ida. Since her visit to the coast with him, he had seen a different view of her, more specifically, knowing her first name and seeing a more personal side to her. Up until that point in his life, he was her job, and he never saw her in any other way than that. To see her relaxed and 'normal' with Ida only increased his feelings for her.

He passed Smetherly and started up the winding, snaking stairs, but as he did, noticed the pair of Crowlies entering, with their sour, miserable faces also. The smaller of the two spoke in hushed whispers to Smetherly, and there they stood, remaining at the entrance to the house. Up to the music room he ventured, and there he waited, closing the door behind him. He leant back on the doors and breathed a massive sigh of relief. Now he felt safe. He thought of this for a second: was it the room that made him feel safe? He enjoyed the music room and always felt at ease here, especially when playing the violin. Maybe it was the house in general, but upon further consideration, he realised it was neither; it was the presence of Ms Buddington that made him feel safe and now, it dawned on him, that she was not there, and suddenly he felt very alone.

He passed the next few hours, waiting for Ms Buddington, and regularly checking, within ten-minute intervals, whether the Crowlies were still downstairs. Looking over the bannister, he could see their presence was still evident. What was going on he thought to himself and why are they still here? Why was Ms Buddington not back? Surely she would have been told that he had returned and her services would be required. He just could not understand why she was not there.

After what seemed like an age, Archie heard the door handle rattle. In walked Ms Buddington. He ran and hugged her, overwhelmed with happiness. At first, there was little response, but eventually, a hand tapped Archie on the back; assuring him there was no disaster and the world was not about to end.

"Where have you been?" Archie questioned her.

"Just a short break away, some time to myself, while you were away with your father." The look on her face said something very different to the words she was delivering. From her oversized, knitted bag, she produced a notepad and pencil. As she continued to talk about the seaside and the temperature of the sea, she wrote - 'There is a Crowlie by the front door and one outside this door. We are being observed - closely. Do not tell me anything out of the unusual'. This overwhelmed Archie, and the look on his face must have said it all. Ms Buddington continued about the dinner she had eaten the previous night and how the prawns had not agreed with her very well while writing - 'Someone is coming to speak to you. I know it is hard, but it won't be for much longer. The truth is almost here. Meet Avem'.

She continued the talking; now about the weather, and how the sea air had been good for her chest but opened her bag and onto the handle hopped a tiny mechanical bird. This bird was much smaller than Abe and did not appear to have as many rusty cogs and levers. The finish was immaculate on the wings - with a coat so clear you could see your face in it. Its beak and a thin strip across its forehead, join the eye sockets, where a golden, but corroded metal, appearing to be unkempt in comparison to the pristine wings. This must be Ms Buddington's angelus custos here to serve and protect. One final message was written on the paper - 'stay here'. Avem flew back into the bag, and Ms Buddington picked it up, slid it onto her right forearm and headed for the door. As she closed the door, Archie tiptoed to the exit and listened carefully to what was being said.

"Master Roker is dreadfully tired after his long journey and is not to be disturbed. His father has said that he is thankful for you and your colleague's efforts and you should wait at the entrance; one at the front, one at the back - to prevent any intruders. I have errands to attend to and as I said Master Roker needs his sleep."

"But we was told we was to stay 'ere," came the low, droll reply.

"Very well, when Mr Roker returns with Mr Crowle and asks why there is not a guard at each entrance to the house, I will be sure to explain that I passed on the instructions."

"Err, right Missus," he panicked, "I'll go then."

"Good, and it is Ms, not missus I'll have you know."

Silence returned, though the sound of flapping wings interrupted it. Archie peered out of the door and he could see Avem, fluttering around from bookcase to grandfather clock and back again. He watched in amazement as this tiny bird - which he felt sure was a robin - like the one on Ms Buddington's broach - fizzed from one place to the next. This continued for several minutes until Avem stopped suddenly and froze to the spot, looking severely to the stairwell. Archie panicked and closed the door rapidly. He backed away from the door towards the piano with his hand out behind him to prevent any collision with a musical instrument but always keeping his eyes on the door. A presence could be heard at the door, and Archie contemplated who it could be: Ms Buddington? Smetherly? Kat? One of the Crowlies? Or someone else? The door opened.

"It's ok Archie, it's only me," came a familiar voice. It was Kat.

"Oh Kat, I'm glad to see you," he said as he gave her a great big hug. She returned the hug and Archie felt relaxed and safe, but not for long as suddenly he felt another hand on his back. He tried to work out if it were Kat's but it could not be. He opened his eyes and then he saw it - Milo. Archie leapt back in shock and fell to the floor. It took a moment for him to catch his breath. Kat was laughing at him, and Milo looked just as shocked as Archie did. If Milo was here, that could only mean one thing - Ida.

Sure enough, in walked Ida.

"What are you doing on the floor?" she questioned. Kat continued to laugh, but Archie answered.

"Don't ask!"

"Fair enough. Listen, Archie, we need to talk. We know you have been to Romani Grove, we know you have seen lots of the things, and you must have lots of questions. Am I right?"

"Yes, my father has told me everything. It doesn't necessarily make sense, but he has shown me things that make me believe Imperium want something good for this country," Archie replied.

"Archie, I cannot come between you and your father and I will not. That is not my job. However, what is my job is to make you realise the things you have seen and heard are not all as they seem. Let me speak to you and answer your questions, and if you are still not convinced, then I will go and turn in myself to the Crowlies downstairs. Is that fair?" Archie felt like he had little choice even if he did disagree.

"Archie, listen to me, you have seen the extravagant life that is being led at Romani Grove, but the rest of the country and the world are just slaves to the rich who control everything. These men are the counsellors and brokers to leaders around the world. These leaders are pawns in a game of chess they can never win. Why? Because they do not control the game, they are mere foot soldiers. And if these leaders do not follow Imperium, then they are surplus to requirements. Like the so called intruders at Romani Grove. The wealth of Imperium is more than the combined wealth of everyone else on the planet. And this hidden wealth is making a world government that the rest of the world's population cannot see."

"General people don't know what is going on and even worse they don't know that they don't know. What do Imperium do? Develop a society of people not worrying about the future only looking to blame each other for their current problems. Where do these problems come from? They are manufactured, then they are solved and then another is created. You met Howlett - drugging the population with an addictive substance. Coleman - delivering whatever message Imperium want to the masses, not to mention hoarding all the gold of this country and many others. Carbey-Lowther - the explorer? No gun for hire and gun seller. Wars have been created. Why? So Carbey-Lowther can sell weapons. Who to? Both sides. With the resources they have, Imperium could end poverty for the many. Imagine the technology you have seen but used for all. They introduce a minimum wage for all - enough for people to think they are getting something but not enough to escape the life they are stuck in. Why not use these machines and technology to do the job of the workforce? What would Imperium do with all these people if they were not working."

"I know, I know, you have told me this before," Archie responded, "but it depends upon the way you tell it. When my father told it, it sounded so different."

"Very well," Ida responded, "did you see someone being shot while you were there?"

"Err, yes as I arrived," Archie mumbled, "it as an intruder."

"Was it Archie, was it?" Ida answered in a quieter tone. "Archie, that person was probably the last of a much larger number of intruders. They are there to be shot, Archie. Imperium provides these men with a life unlike no other, and the rules and laws of the land do not apply to these men. You arrived at the end of the shoot. Those men will have been shooting others throughout the day. For sport. Not because they are intruders. People taken from their families, the homeless, orphans, it doesn't matter as no one will question Imperium." Archie slumped silently into a chair. Could this be right? Could the words that Ida was saying be the truth?

"But…" Archie did not know what to say.

"There is more Archie." Ida seemed unsure whether to continue or not, but she did. "Were the gentlemen drinking red wine Archie?"

"Yes." This did not seem an unusual thing to Archie.

"Archie, that wasn't just red wine. It also contained the blood of the victims from the hunt." The colour drained from Archie's face. He felt sick. He did not want to believe this; he would not believe this.

"But why?" Archie asked, almost disgusted to do so.

"Imperium believe it gives them more power and strength. They take on the vitality of those whose blood they drink. They are not vampires and do not sink their teeth into people's necks as Bram Stoker would have you believe. By drinking the blood of their prey, they cure their soul and steal their victim's spirit; making them more superior to other humans. More like the leader of Imperium. The one they all worship."

"You mean Marsden?"

"Marsden? Charlie Marsden? He is responsible for developing a new power source. You have met him?"

"Yes," replied Archie

"How do you know he is the leader?" she continued.

"He is definitely the man in charge."

"What makes you say that?" quizzed Ida.

"On my final night, I heard them talking about a plan, and he was obviously the man in command. That was apparent." Archie then proceeded to tell Ida the details of the different phases he had heard and who was there. She listened intently to all that was said, paused and pondered for a moment, composed herself and asked the question.

"How do you know Marsden is the leader of Imperium?" Calmly, Archie looked at her and truthfully answered.

"My father told me."

This information seemed to change Ida's whole attitude. She suddenly seemed apprehensive and unsure of her surroundings. As if someone may enter at any second. She looked around the room suspiciously and pressed a few buttons on her strapped wrist. Milo awoke into life, his abdomen glowing intently, and moved to the door. Ida followed and opened the door ever so slightly, to gain a view of the corridor, almost checking the security of the room. When she opened it further, Milo began to move his eight legs through the door, and Archie could hear the tapping of his footsteps fade away down the corridor. She turned back to Archie and said,

"I need to check this house is safe. What you have just told me is very important. You need to pass this information to Madeleine O'Reilly," and with that, she was gone.

Within less than a minute, Archie could hear the footsteps returning down the corridor. What did Ida want now? He opened the door, but was presently faced with the mask of Madeleine O'Reilly, the long bird-like beak, hood and lost black goggles. Although he had never formally met Madeleine (or Maddie as she was known), he felt he knew her due to her presence over the last few months. Like Abe, she had been there in the shadows, watching him. Protecting him? Ida followed behind and closed the door as she passed through it. Ida explained to Maddie the information Archie had passed on. Archie felt a little apprehensive: he did not know if his information was accurate for these women, if they believed him or if, in fact, he should have told them any of the information at all.

"Interesting. It seems like Imperium are planning something and soon. Time for a few more truths I think," Maddie offered.

The brown hood came down, and, cascading from it, long, ebony hair untangled from the back of the black, leather jacket. Her hands went up to the beak-shaped mask, and for a split-second, Archie wondered what lay underneath. He assumed and was unsure why, that Maddie would be pretty, but perhaps he could be wrong - maybe she may have a disfigured face, hence the reason it covered all the time. The excitement and anticipation took hold of him, but nothing could prepare him for the face that greeted him.

"Ms Buddington?" Archie was astounded and confounded at the figure in front of him. "But, how is this possible?"

"Archie, I am not Layla Buddington. She is my twin sister."

"Twin?" replied Archie, "you have to be kidding me!"

"It's true Archie," interjected Ida. "Madeleine and Layla are twins. Identical twins as you can see." Archie rubbed his eyes.

"That is amazing. You look so alike, but somehow, so different."

"That is certainly true Archie. We do look identical, but our personalities are very different. Layla is much stricter than I am. A disciplinarian, a surrogate mother, married to the job. Perfect for bringing up a small boy. Unlike me. I, on the other hand, am the kind of person who would disappear, hide in shadows, and join a secret society called Alium to battle against another secret society called Imperium, who are determined to crush society as we know it. Not Layla's kind of thing."

"No," said Archie grinning to himself happily. He thought fondly of his governess and all the things they had experienced, but to see her in this role; that would be something extraordinary.

"I'm just trying to imagine her out of her formal black clothes and with her hair down," Archie smirked.

"That's Layla. Prim and proper to the last," Maddie answered, rolling her eyes. "So, Archie, can you confirm that Marsden is the leader of Imperium?"

"Yes, my father told me," Archie replied.

"And are you certain of that? No one else seemed…" She paused. "More in control."

"No one as much as Marsden. Even my father seemed afraid of him."

"Really," considered Maddie. Her and Ida looked at each other with a knowing grin. This comment left Archie confused and about to ask a question when Maddie continued. "What are Imperium? Have you thought about that Archie? I know you believe your father when he says they are working to better the country, but you need to open your eyes and see what is really going on.

Look at the bigger picture. What are Imperium?" She paused again. "A slow poison that is killing people's souls. Imperium put across good and make people believe their lives are positive, but secretly they are killing them; turning them into lifeless beings. Imperium are filling people with fear. They turn people against themselves, turn people against each other and are keeping people ignorant - people exist, they don't live."

These seemed profound, thought-provoking words for Archie and he strived to tackle the points as they were raised. He knew what Maddie was trying to infer, but he was also trying to look at it from his father's point of view. She continued.

"What kind of world do we want to leave for our children and our children's children? Why are we still at war with each other when we do not know what the war is even about? How can we meet everyone's basic needs, while ensuring a common future? How can we protect our basic human culture that promotes equality for all, not just for the privileged?"

She pursued these points, like one of Roker's lectures in the surgery, inviting Ida to make points and share her thoughts and opinions.

"What did it say in Ephesians?" Ida added, "For we wrestle not against flesh and blood, but against principalities, against powers, against the rulers of the darkness of this world, against spiritual wickedness in high places."

"Indeed, well said Ida," Maddie replied.

"This is too much to take in," pleaded Archie, his head hurting. "I don't know what to believe anymore. I have no reason to doubt what you say, other than it contradicts what my father has told me, and vice versa. It feels like I should doubt everything."

"I understand Archie, I do." Maddie answered reassuringly," If you don't believe my words then maybe you will believe your own eyes. I think it's time to shift."

Chapter 11
Similis

"Shift?" repeated Archie, "what do you mean?"

"Don't worry Archie, you need to see this to believe it, and I do not blame you," replied Maddie. "Come with me." She moved towards the door, beckoning Archie to follow her. He turned and looked at Ida, and a nod of approval followed.

"What about Ms Buddington? I mean Layla, I mean… oh, I don't know what I mean," Archie sighed.

"Don't worry Archie, all in hand," Maddie responded in a manner which could have been Ms Buddington. They left the music room and almost glided down the stairs to where Roker's study was situated.

"We're not allowed in there," quivered Archie.

"Of course not," Maddie replied tongue in cheek, "what would your father say?" Archie moved his mouth to say something but nothing came out. What could he say?

Entering the room, Maddie headed straight for the bookcases on the right of the room. She knew exactly where she was going. Lower level, the third bookshelf along. On the far edge, before the next set of shelves was a very decorative but subtle design between the two sets of shelves. Fleur de Lis - a stylised lily that had been used throughout the ages as a decorative design or symbol. Whether it be on a coat of arms, flags, in architecture, or symbolism in religion and art, Archie recognised it from history and art lessons. The repeating flowers, one on top of the other, with an extensive carving on both sides echoing vertically from top to bottom, identical all the way down with one exception. Shoulder height was one flower, but rather than being convex when carved; this was concave.

"Off you go Archie," Maddie ordered confidently.

"What?" responded Archie, slightly flummoxed at what he was meant to be doing.

"Open the passageway please."

"How?" Archie was unsure if Maddie was playing a joke on him. He had not been in this room for a period of time before today, yet here was Maddie instructing Archie to open a secret entrance. He had no key. What on earth was he supposed to do?

"Oh, come Archie, you've been carrying the key around with you, and you don't even know. Hand!" Maddie put out her hand waiting for Archie's.

"Not that one the other one. The hand with a ring on your finger," Maddie responded, sounding a little annoyed in her tone. Archie gave the other hand and Maddie grabbed his wrist and pulled his hand towards the bookcase. "Make a fist please." Archie obeyed. She moved his fist toward the bookcase and Archie now realised what she was in fact doing. The emerald eye of his ring was placed into the concave flower design and, sure enough, the bookcase swung open, much like the doorway at The Grand Hotel. Another metal grill faced them which Maddie made light work of and swung to the side.

"In we get." Maddie enticed Archie and Ida into the lift and followed them. Archie had no idea there was a lift in his father's study. He foolishly thought at first, it must take them to the ground floor, but as soon as the carriage shot into life, he knew he was going elsewhere, not just down, but sideways also. This journey seemed much longer than the trip at the seaside and Archie imagined he must be travelling under the city centre. His imagination ran away with himself as he concocted several destinations: the park, Pinkerton's Sweet Shop, the square in town where he listened to music, Howlett's Chocolate Factory, the seaside. Imagine travelling to these places in an instant without worrying about others or waiting for trains. His thoughts stopped as he came back to reality.

"Where are we going?" he enquired with slight uncertainty in his tone.

"You'll see," Ida responded.

Suddenly, the lift stopped abruptly, and everyone stood shaken on their feet. The grill was pushed aside again, and a doorway appeared as the door slid to the left. Maddie peered through cautiously and then set off into the light. Ida followed and then Archie. To his amazement, he found himself in his father's study at the surgery. Upon leaving the doorway, Archie noticed it was another bookcase, and the same Fleur de Lis pattern marked the edge, again with one concave flower. Gazing around the study, he noted the variety of odd shaped bottles, flasks and test tubes stacked ever so neatly on the shelves; some empty, but some containing a selection of mysterious liquids and solutions.

A small window at the far side of the room allowed ample light in to illuminate the large mahogany desk, central to the office. Upon this table, lay a basket with some pieces of paper, full of jottings and technical drawings. There was also a human skull sat there - grinning inanely at patients as they entered. His father always joked it was from a patient the previous day who had been taken ill and had a disagreeable turn. Archie still laughed. Next to the desk, a wheelchair - metal framed, with wooden arms and backrest and a soft cushioned material seat and backrest. Sat on the seat, Archie recognised his father's medical bag. A dark brown leather holdall with the initials T.R. emblazed in gold. Many a time Archie had rooted around inside playing with the stethoscope and other peculiar looking items when he was younger.

"Why have I never been that way before? I've been to the surgery hundreds of times. Why would my father not show me this way?"

"Why indeed Archie!" responded Maddie, adding to, not solving Archie's question. They left the study and Archie already knew where they were heading; the doorway in the surgery. Sure enough, Ida led them to the mechanical barrier and gesticulated to Archie to open it.

"My father did this last time, I don't..." Ida interrupted him.

"Don't think, just do. Think of the lift." Archie looked at his hand and made a fist. He placed it towards the locked barricade and nothing happened.

"Look for the mark Archie," Maddie assured him. Again, he found a small concave dent in the door. He placed the emerald eye in, as if spying on the enemy through a peephole, and the door again swung into action.

Through the doorway they went, down the rusty staircase, onto the balcony with the expertly decorated

144

floor, past the array of pipes, cogs and gears. Through the next door, with Archie's assistance again, to the sea of drawers. They swam through, wave after wave, never seeming to reach the shore until finally, they reached the safety of the other side. Meredeth was not present, no longer guarding his samples. In fact, Archie had seen no one which, in itself, was a little unnerving. At the end of the ocean of woodwork lay another metal door. It seemed like a distant harbour or fort, waiting to be attacked, though possibly impenetrable to any foreign invader. The same procedure again and the door swung open. A tiny corridor, almost like an extended cupboard, lay in front of him. As the door opened, wall lights flickered into action and Archie could see another simple doorway at the end.

"Open it, open your eyes and believe," Maddie urged.

The door opened effortlessly, and again light flooded past him into the dark corridor. Of all the new and unusual things Archie had seen recently, this was by far the most astounding. He felt as if he were literally in another world. A second earlier, Archie thought he was underground, beneath the surgery, yet now, he stood outside in broad daylight in a world like no other. There was a hive of activity going on with people passing by, but no ordinary scene Archie was used to. Yes, he had become familiar with the clothing worn by Ida, Maddie and Krewler, but this was obviously where they felt at home.

Men wore smart suits and top hats, but everything was accessorised with leather or some form of mechanical contraption. Upon the top hats, many men wore a pair of goggles, as those Krewler had worn, but the designs were more intricate than ever and unique to every individual.

Some wore leather caps, more suitable for swimming, thought Archie. Others had, what looked like, breathing devices or an array of leather strapping, holding all sorts of accessories, ranging from weapons and bullets, vials or liquid, or documents rolled up neatly for storage. One gentleman walked past with his face completely covered in a mask and a conical hat wrapped in a veil over the top. The next had his grey hair shaved to the skull on both sides of his head, but down the centre of his skull it stood up straight and tall, over six inches tall. Another had, what could only be described as a glass bowl over his head, with a brass pipe emitting from the top into a dial covered backpack which had bellows pumping rhythmically as he walked.

The women too, perhaps more so than the men, gained looks as they passed. Back home, a lady would keep herself very plain and covered up if mobile, as Ms Buddington would, but not here. As one lady walked past in a full-length skirt, Archie noticed the front part was absent, except for the frame of the dress, looking like a giant bird's nest, he thought. Another wore a goggle type monocle and what Archie assumed was a witch's hat. Again, with leather strapping to match. The colours of the clothes were the most striking thing and the women's hair. Red, purple, blue and green. One lady wore what looked like a leather neck brace and matching sheath on her arm in which a long knife lived. The other striking element of the women were the number wearing trousers and long leather boots, again with various attachments.

If they were not walking, they were travelling in magnificent machines. One trundled past, with colossal caterpillar tracks either side of a beautiful leather

Chesterfield, accompanied by a small table, protruding from the right arm with a tall glass to drink from should the driver's thirst require it. A three-wheeled bike shot past, two at the front to steer and one at the rear again below a lavish seat. The driver was wearing a top hat with tails streaming behind in the breeze in a rainbow of colours. Another crawled across the floor like an insect on its six legs; the owner sat in a turret in the centre which could turn any direction allowing the driver a 360-degree view of all around. Perhaps the strangest was a large wheel inside which the operator sat; the large wheel spinning around as handler sat perfectly still in the centre. Behind him, on two much smaller wheels, lay a simple furnace, creating steam to power the considerable roller, with a funnel protruding from the rear emitting smoke as it progressed. Struggling to take it all in, Archie moved forward and looked past the men women and vehicles before him.

Beyond the hustle and bustle, stood a grand building, its roof and spires showing hints of gothic architecture, with tall steeples towering into the cloudy skies above. Two oversized towers were held up by two sculpted characters, shouldering the weight of the construction above them. In between them, a giant clock face, much larger than any other Archie had seen, loomed over the square before them, the clock face made up of a sea of cogs and gears, swirling like a torrential whirlpool; the vast hands bridging the depths of time from one side to the other. Below this, a stained-glass window, equal in size to the clock face, allowed a look into the heart of the building, and likewise, allowing to soul to peek out. However, the base of the building was the remarkable feat of this structure, for there, were three mechanical legs, emerging from a hive of wire and steam moving the building around. Archie blinked and blinked again. It was moving the building around! The entire building was moving from side to side at the current moment, with little or no regard for the effect of the people who may be inside.

To his left, Archie observed a jigsaw of buildings, angular and jagged in design, though ideally suited to sit on each other. Hundreds of dwellings, some with balconies, some with bridge attachments to other buildings, some with trees growing ten or twenty stories high. Huge towers inter-twinned with the smaller abodes and, like the first building, disappeared into the clouds above. Suddenly, the buildings appeared to be moving and Archie thought for a second they were collapsing, but, no. The apartments shifted position on the face of the building. Archie carefully watched as one particular home, with a balcony and family at the forefront gradually moved down the front of the building, as if it were a rat trapped in a laboratory maze. One way, then another - no set pattern - erratic and spontaneous. Eventually, the dwelling made it to the floor, and with a whoosh of steam, Archie could see the family disembark their balcony onto a wooden jetty at the base. Without hesitation, as soon as the last young child stepped from the balcony, the whole process started again, and it was the turn of another home to move.

At the base, a series of interlock waterways connected the buildings. He watched as the family boarded a simple looking boat, not much bigger than Archie had seen in the local park he had visited numerous times with Ms

Buddington, but this boat appeared to have no oars or another form of propulsion, only a large box in the middle of the central seating area. Suddenly without warning, a train emerged from the steam behind the boat, but this was like no train Archie had boarded before. The carriages resembled those he had visited the seaside previously, but the track did not exist as the coaches hung from a rail above. Again, a series of mechanical mysteries made the machine move, and Archie could see the carriage stop next to a balcony further up on the moving building. A lady in a white dress with a parasol entered one of the carriages, and in a flurry of steam it set off on the hanging rail again.

As the steam disappeared, Archie returned to the family in the boat on the still waters below. He suddenly felt sorry for them - all this marvellous technology around them, and they were stuck in a dull rowing boat - but not for long. Archie observed as the father of the family stood and inserted a handle into the side of the box at the centre of the boat. He began turning the handle anti-clockwise as if in charge of a tremendous Jack-in-the-box, but Jack did not come out of this box. Instead, a large chimney began to emerge from the centre of the boat. As it progressed to fifteen feet high, a small platform developed at the top, as if a crow's nest was growing from the peak of the steeple. Then in a fabulous explosion of colour, a balloon erupted from the end of the funnel and began inflating. As it grew in stature, the boat began to rise from the water. He noticed a ship's wheel had emerged from the box at the centre of the boat and the youngest child was behind this wheel preparing to set sail through the air.

As incredible and unbelievable as this contraption seemed, it dwarfed into comparison to the beasts that lay to Archie's right. There, as part of a vast cliff face were more than twenty 'boats' mooring in the air to structures on the fascia of the hill. These airships, as Archie assumed they must be, were in all shapes and sizes. Some similar to the simple rowing boat he had seen below, tiny and able to slip into any space; some like the galleons that pirates travelled upon when they terrorised the seas, an array of colourful sails to power it through the air; others with large zeppelin type balloons above them, enabling them to travel high and vast distances; others like junks, oriental in design but fitting perfectly well into this world with mechanical adaptations. Archie noticed one with three large circular balloons above it, but rather than a boat below, this appeared to be a house, simply floating in mid-air. To its rear, an eight-sailed windmill provided propulsion, along with the steam engine which had a long, snake-like exhaust port emitting smoke below the graceful sails. What was this place? Where was he?

An array of capacitors and Tesla coils; everything in front of him could easily have been found in Shelley's mind and Dr Frankenstein's laboratory. Steam engines and hydraulics powered everything from the giant clock above his head to the machine that dispensed a newspaper called The Daily Verum; excessively oversized and very impractical looking but, nevertheless, a thing of beauty to look at. Everything around had defined edges, rivets and dials; finely crafted and visually appealing; functional with a hint of luxury attached. Maddie explained that the idea to build a fantastical machine that took up a vast amount of space and time to do a task that one man could do in a tenth of the time seemed madness in the ordinary world, but here it was encouraged. There was no embarrassment, no downtrodden workforce feeling repressed or left to starve homelessly. Here optimism was the key. One person helping another for no other purpose than to make someone else's life a little better. If something needed doing, then a steam-powered machine with superfluous routine could solve the problem. Ida went on to explain that people did not work as Archie had seen at home. There was not the subdued and crushed look on people's faces. Everyone seemed genuinely happy as there appeared to be no frontiers to stop anyone. The technology was available to help anyone, and if it is not, then someone would create a machine that could do it for you. From what he could see, this seemed to Archie to be a utopian society, what did anyone here need? Life was simple, everyone was treated the same, and everyone was happy to help each other.

In Archie's standard world, steam played a part: the train engines were driven by steam and revolutionised transportation not only in the country but the whole world. The steam engine was also beginning to be introduced into manufacturing and farming. Archie's father had discussed the benefits of steam in medicine as a way of cleansing materials. The more Archie thought about it, the more he realised steam was increasingly present in the everyday world, but not to benefit everyone; only the wealthy elite. Flywheels and pistons were the power lines of the new world: they allowed one component to move with another and create the magic.

"What is this place?" Archie questioned.

"We are nowhere new, but merely have shifted. Shifted through Similis. This is where it takes us," Maddie replied with a wry grin on her face.

"This is unbelievable," Archie gasped open-mouthed.

"I know, I felt the same when I first came through. To be honest, I still do every time I shift," Ida added.

"But why has nobody been here before from ..." Archie paused. He did not know what to call the place he had come from and the place he was now.

"We are still in the city; we are still on Earth. We call here the same as you would home, but we call your home Volgaris," Ida continued.

"Volgaris," Archie scratched his head and pondered for a moment. "But why doesn't anyone in Volgaris talk about this place? Do they not know?"

"Archie, as we have tried to explain to you what you have heard from your father is not entirely truthful." Maddie continued. "Imperium knows about this place, but they make it their utmost priority that no one else in Volgaris knows about it."

"But why?"

"Why do you think?" Maddie responded abruptly to Archie's question. "If everyone you knew found out about this place, what would happen?"

"People would be scared," considered Archie.

"Initially, yes," replied Maddie, "but when they realise there is no threat from here, then what? Would people want to come here? Would people want to stay here?" Archie nodded in agreement. "Then the power Imperium has over the city, the country, the entire world - it would be gone. No more. They rule through fear, and by making people fear their futures and each other. Imagine if people knew they could live in a place where machines did everything, where everyone is happy, and most importantly, everyone is treated equally. They would all want this."

"Therefore," Ida added, "Imperium will stop at nothing to prevent us coming through to Volgaris and letting everyone know. We have tried, many times, but they are too powerful in Volgaris. They hold all the cards there, and we are left empty-handed, struggling to help people who do not realise they need to be helped by a group of people they don't even believe exist."

Chapter 12
The Power of Steam

The next morning was spent looking around the new world Archie was part of. He was being taken by Maddie and Ida to meet someone called The Colonel. That is all he was told about the mystery person. Excitedly, he followed his guides through the narrow streets. There were many similarities to the world he knew; there were still shops, houses and such like but they were all different in ways he could not imagine.

The immense housing complex he had seen the previous day was only one example. As he strolled down the street, he noted boat homes – like the ones he had seen on the industrial canals - but these would put those to shame. All had at least two stories, some three or four, decorated in an array of flags and drapes as if supporting their local football team. Huge chimneys sprouted from them, bending acutely and obtusely as they ventured skyward. Some appeared to have arms protruding from the sides, perhaps to assist with propulsion, or even lift out of the water if required. If there was an issue with moving a boat, Archie observed a sky tug, hovering above – a boat with a huge balloon inflated above, enabling it to drift where required – able to move any home if needed.

Mobile homes were prevalent also, ranging from floating ships moored to the pavement, to what Ida explained, trike homes. Passing an open-doored example,

Archie noted its humble setting - a one-roomed house, primarily a bedroom and bathroom, but, as he observed, with the pull of a lever, the bed and utilities disappeared into the walls, and a simple kitchen and table and chairs appeared. The room you required at the time. On the exterior, at either side, two enormous wheels sat there, protecting the home – at the front (like a child's tricycle) a much smaller wheel and a steering device. As the occupant had finished her morning ablutions, she decided to take her house for a drive: she sat upon the saddle, and with the flick of a lever the vast wheels spun into action and she set off in front of them, searching for a new home.

A pyramid tent was a popular option for some residents; the example Archie was stood in front of was a bold red and white striped design. White bunting decorated the entrance and inside, the attention to detail and facilities, were outstanding. Archie noticed a freestanding bath, an exquisitely carved hat stand and a roll top dresser. Another, a two-tiered wooden house on wheels, with staircase, balcony and turrets.

People did have static homes, but again the eccentricity of them was something to behold. A row of terraced houses at home would involve thirty to fifty houses all identical: door and window downstairs, a window on the first floor, roof, chimney. All made in the same red brick. Here, no two houses looked the same. Yes, in a terraced row, they all were roughly the same height, but that was it. The houses were narrow, very narrow, but they were at least five stories high. Each had a grand entrance at the front, with a door, but in a multitude of mind-blowing colours, shapes and sizes. Archie felt as each house had a personality, perhaps that matched the occupant. Some had balconies, but not like the one that Archie had at home. These terraces moved – extending outwards and upwards – depending on the occasion. It was not only the balconies that changed. Windows had large pistons surrounding them, and Archie noticed, with a gust of steam, the shape of the windows would transform into the most irregular asymmetrical shapes possible.

Then there were the houses that stood on their own. In the space of one street, Archie saw a windmill with an elaborate pair of mechanical arms spinning the blades of the mill when required. He was unsure if the windmill was producing anything but thought of the efficiency as these blades needed no wind – only power of steam to drive the large fans. Next, he watched as a young lady came out of the top of her lighthouse. A lighthouse! In the middle of the street. Red and white striped like a barber's pole but only guiding passers-by away from her door. Following this was the glass house. Archie had seen many glass houses before and, with his father, stood in awe at the architectural design, but this was a colossal fishbowl. The entirety of this home was see through. Quite simply you could see everything that was going on inside this house. The children were playing in an upstairs room, the father making breakfast and the mother sat at a desk writing (Maddie informed Archie that this was Dottie Kirkham's residence – the writer of The Daily Verum, the Alium newspaper). And so, it continued residence after residence – no two the same.

The shops were just the same, but different – the clothing stores sold the same things jackets, suits, dresses, but everything was much more extravagant. There were live models parading around outside the shops, showing potential customers what they could purchase. Colourful jackets and suits to match any occasion and any accessory in any colour to match. Not to mention all the other accessories to go with it, ranging from leather strapping and bronzed armour to an extensive selection of goggles and a top hat for any occasion. With the amount of differing fashion Archie had seen so far, he was sure the tailors and milliners would never be short of a trade.

He noticed a public house selling alcohol; a place for men to frequent, as in Volgaris. Not here. Here, drinkers sat on stools at a long, mechanical bar at the front of the establishment. Drinks came by on a rail track, and they helped themselves to their favourite tipple. Empty glasses were then returned to the rail and disappeared into a metal mouth, clamping down on glass anywhere in its vicinity. Women too sat at the bar with the men, all laughing and joking, and children also had their own mini bar, below the adult level where they spoke into a square speaker, and a mechanical arm produced the drink of their choice.

At the butcher's, there was plenty of meat – but the difference here was all of it was alive. People were leaving the shop with animals in tow – sheep, pigs, even a cow, on leads. More like a pet shop than butchers. And the pet shop was equally strange. Like Milo and Abe, the pets were all mechanical creatures – again, all composed of delicate, mechanical workings, but moving so eloquently, like the real things. Ida explained to Archie that you would find children receiving their Angelus custos, when they reached the age of shifting.

Much to Archie's excitement, he gazed in wonder at a magic shop – Napoleon Gordon's Magic Emporium, the name read above the door as the sign was cut in half and then lifted and travelled through a hoop, like magic shows Archie had seen with Ms Buddington. In the window, Archie saw a picture of young man: white shirt and white cravat; a pale blue waistcoat with a black silk trim; a leather belt with a selection of keys and handcuffs (for his world-famous escapology act Maddie informed him). His right arm had a mechanical covering, matching that Krewler had been wearing on Archie's first encounter with him. Maddie went on to explain he used this mechanical device in many of his illusions as it had many appendages to it, including his rip saw, used for his trick - cutting a man in half – lengthways.

Lem Footter's Technology Store was next in the street. Here, Archie saw many things; things he would find at home, but they had some mechanical extension to them. Typewriters, clocks or chess sets, all modified in some way. But also, there were many, new items of technology Archie was unsure of. A wooden hand, wires attached to the knuckles and a large key emitting from the wrist. When wound up, the hand began to move around the shop. A variety of backpacks for various purposes and exciting looking appendages to be attached to legs enabling people to spring around. Perhaps even more surprising, was Lem Footter himself: a sizeable red cravat, a thin, tired ancient face, a large leather top hat and a pair of golden goggles with similar ear covers - piping leading to two large amplifying speakers protruding from either side of the top hat.

Apart from the standard shops, there were many mobile outlets also. Sellers on steam-powered vehicles, with the ability to follow their customers, if they were so inclined. One gentleman travelled around on a tricycle. He shuttled the contraption around from the front, a large funnel, billowing smoke was in the centre, and at the rear were three seats facing backwards. When passers-by hailed him, he would stop, and they would climb on board at the back. There, they would be treated to a shoe cleaning experience by a mechanical wonder. Arms would appear from underneath the seat, first with polish, then a brush to apply it. When fully covered, a rotating brush would buff the shoes until they were as shiny as new, and finally, a cloth would appear to wipe them down. If the recipient required any other leather products cleaning, such as a bag or hat, they merely presented them, and the same would happen again. And not only did they get a clean and polish, but they would also get a ride through the town while it was being done – cleaned and chauffeured.

Another magnificent machine was Chuzzlewit's Body Art. This mobile tattoo parlour was impressive to see in action. Based on a simple platform with two large wheels either side and two much smaller ones at the front and rear, the recipient of the tattoo sat in a chair in the centre of a huge metal-framed sphere. As impressive as this looked, it was Leta Chuzzlewit who made the show. With her thigh length leather boots, black leather jacket and matching top hat and goggles, she sat on a chair that rotated to every possible position within the sphere, enabling to tattoo at any angle. Ida explained that if anybody wanted a tattoo, then Leta was the person to do it. Wherever she stopped, crowds would gather to watch the artist at work and often, applause would break out spontaneously when a recipient had been completed.

Similar applause followed the buskers as they performed in the streets: some reading poetry about the demise of Volgaris, others playing magical instruments solo - one particularly playing a lute with great skill but Archie was unsure of the complete talent of the musician, as a mechanical hand was also performing with the two human hands. The highlight for Archie was the group of musicians who entertained the crowd with their traditional sounding folk tunes that excited and intoxicated the audience with slight sinister overtones. Again, the instruments fitted the mood with an array of stringed instruments ranging from embossed violins to tin double basses, euphoniums with lights attached to them and a stringed instrument made from a cigar box but amplified through a large velvet box with a dirty sound that intoxicated Archie.

Leaving the musicians behind, the trio continued their trip through the town. The tight, narrow streets were not as confining as those at home. Everything felt much more open and free. There was no feeling of uncertainty or worry that something may happen. This really did feel like a utopian society. As they passed down the street, Archie noticed it began to widen at the end. A fork appeared in the road, with a small humble looking church in between either path. Wondering which direction they would go, Archie was shocked when he saw Ida walking up the steps to the church door. He looked up the steep steps and took in the fascia of the pretty white church. Although it had been painted recently with blue woodwork around the window and on the sills, this building had certainly been there a long time. It stood out from all the other fancy buildings he had seen already as the most normal looking building. From the outside, it looked tiny, especially for a church. Not many people would be able to fit in here, Archie thought. He climbed the steep incline to the front door of the church and followed Maddie inside.

"Welcome to Alium headquarters," Maddie announced. Archie was unsure what to find inside, and through the door he was greeted by a spiral staircase, leading downwards, below the ground.

"More underground," he muttered to himself.

"What was that?" questioned Maddie.

"Oh nothing, it just seems I've spent most of the last week underground in one place or another. I have enjoyed my morning in the sunlight."

"I know, but The Colonel wishes to make your acquaintance – and we don't say no to The Colonel."

"Ok then," and Archie headed for the staircase.

"Where are you going?" Ida asked with a smirk on her face.

"Well, there is only a staircase, so I assume it is down here."

"That," replied Maddie, "is for coming out. We are going in." She moved over to the right of the staircase and carefully tapped the wall with the edge of her elbow. A flap dropped down, and a black circle appeared in front of Archie.

"A black hole. Where does that lead?"

"Oh sorry," Maddie apologised and gently tapped the wall again. Suddenly, the tunnel lit up with a kaleidoscope of colours. "First go to me!" With that, she dived into the illuminated tunnel and disappeared.

"Come on Archie, keep up," added Ida and she followed also. Archie was left alone at the top of the staircase, his two friends disappearing down a rabbit hole. For a second, he felt like Alice, having read about her trip to Wonderland. It certainly felt like this to him and, like Alice, he tumbled head first, straight into the rabbit hole.

Down the smooth spiral slide, Archie slid. The dazzling colours whizzed past him and, what he assumed were mirrored sides, only heightened the effect, creating an infinite image - making him feel almost sick as he reached the end. There, at the base, stood Ida, Maddie and an enormous man Archie had never seen before, and looking at him, he was quite glad. The man must have been at least seven feet tall, with broad shoulders, much like a rugby player. He had all the usual accessories about his body: mechanical arm piece, golden trim and leather strapping but his head made him stand out much more than anyone Archie had seen.

A snow-white beard adorned his chin, but surrounding the neatly trimmed beard, his flesh appeared a rusty orange and heavily scarred, as if attacked by fire or a flesh-eating bug. Around his eyes, there seemed to be little flesh at all, just two poignant eyeballs, moving in their ocular cavities, into positions an average human could not, due to the constraints of skin. Upon the top of his skull the man had what appeared to be a golden crown, but upon closer inspection, Archie could see it was protecting the man's head, for underneath, there was no skull, but pulsating red human tissue, with tiny fragments of brain edging through. A copper tube left the golden cage from the back of the head and wound round into a chest piece on the giant's chest.

"Archie, this is The Colonel," introduced Ida.

"A pleasure to meet you Archie," he boomed in a strong North American twang, "I have heard lots about you and look forward to hearing what you have to say."

Archie shuffled his feet a little and glanced warily at the Colonel.

"I'm not sure what I have to say that will interest you, but it's a pleasure to meet you too." The colonel roared with laughter; Maddie and Ida both joined in.

"Not sure what I have to say will interest you," he repeated, "good one Archie." Ida continued to laugh, but Maddie, aware of Archie's increasing look of bewilderment, stopped and put a hand on his shoulder. She guided him through into a room which, to Archie, seemed like a Wild West saloon he had read about in comics. They sat around a table on simple wooden chairs. A waiter came from behind a bar to the table with a tray full of drinks. Archie found himself continually staring at The Colonel's skull. At the third occurrence, The Colonel spoke up.

"Something you wanna ask me, boy?"

"Your head, how did it happen?"

"Perfect time for a whiskey," sighed The Colonel. He then proceeded to tell Archie about an encounter he had as a soldier in the early days of Alium. He and another soldier, Private Vernon Caulfield (a new cadet, aged only sixteen) had been on a reconnaissance mission to Romani Grove. While there, observing from a distance, they noted many hedonistic activities, with Imperium believing they were the gods. There was torture and the shooting of slaves on the hunt and the drinking of the blood of the innocent - the usual things. But on this occasion, something new was happening. He and Caulfield observed a young Imperium member performing surgery on a man in rags, someone who looked homeless or as if he was not going to be missed if he did not return.

"What I witnessed at that moment changed my life forever," The Colonel sighed, taking a large drink from his whiskey. "Can someone get me another one? Anyway..." He continued his tale, intermittently gulping a mouthful, followed by barking for another. "That young doctor strapped that man down to a chair and tied his head to the backrest. Then, without any sedative, he peeled back the skin on his scalp, like peeling a banana. He then took a hand drill and made three holes on the skull, making a triangle. Do you know what he did then?" Archie shook his head, almost afraid to ask. "He took out a hammer and small chisel and chipped away between those holes. The position of them and the angle he hit the skull made it crack like an egg. We were looking through a spyglass from a distance, but we could hear the screams of the man. And when the screams stopped we knew what had happened. The man had died. Caulfield and I were a little unsure as to exactly what the purpose was, but that became clear in the hours that followed. Caulfield had gone to take higher ground to observe another part of the grove, and unbeknownst to me, I had a pack of Crowlies on my position. Anyway, next thing you know I was in that chair for the same procedure, except now I know why. The latest thing of Imperium is eating the live human brain. They said it would give the knowledge of a thousand men, but it was to be alive. This young doctor,

164

he was trying his best, but he couldn't keep the patient alive long enough. They had a go at me, they cracked open my skull and nearly succeeded, but Caulfield came to my rescue. A few shots from his rifle; one into the neck of the guard, caused panic and they all fled. He got me out of there that day and with the help of some clever folk, I get my crown to protect my skull."

"What happened to Vernon Caulfield?" pondered Archie.

"Not sure, the last I heard he was in Volgaris. I'd sure like to meet up with him someday." He took a long drink from his glass, and he and Archie sat thoughtfully in silence for a minute. Maddie cut the silence.

"Archie, you need to tell The Colonel what you told me about Imperium. Can you do that? Tell him about the phases and what you told us about Marsden."

"Marsden, you gotta be kidding me," The colonel complained. "I knew that man years ago; we fought together in colonial wars, side by side. What's he done now?"

"He is the leader of Imperium," returned Archie.

"Son of a gun, I knew it."

"You didn't know it, Colonel, none of us did, until now," Ida stated, putting the Colonel in his place.

"Goddammit! Marsden? Are you sure?"

"I am," answered Archie, "I have seen him discussing the plans, and seen how the others behave in his presence. My father confirmed it for me."

"Your father? How is he involved in all this?" questioned The Colonel.

"He has been doing things for Imperium, under duress, or they would hurt me. I have asked him what but he said it was too complicated. I have been followed and spied upon, I have been taken to secret underground bunkers and Romani Grove. My father has shown all this. Are they after taking over this world?"

"Here?" answered The Colonel, "No Archie. They have no power here. Look at life here, you've seen what it is like. No one controls anyone. We are all free to do as we please and help each other at the same time. What happens here does not affect Volgaris as the gates are controlled from the other side. We cannot get through unless we enter when they come here, and that doesn't happen very often. Imperium have a wonderful life in Volgaris, living off the hard work of millions. They have everything they need."

"Opening a doorway to here would only cause trouble." added Ida, "If anything, they'd seal us off forever. The gate you shifted through, and many others like it, are guarded by Imperium; well those Crowlies. But people in Volgaris don't know we exist; they have no reason to come here. Why would they? Imperium have made sure of that. Anyone who has gotten through from here and started telling the truth in Volgaris is locked up in Wilberforce's asylum, or worst still dealt with by the Crowlies." She gestured a throat-slitting action causing Archie to gulp.

"And people here overall, other than Alium, have no desire to go there," Maddie concluded. "Imperium would cause trouble for our world, and we are at peace. Only Alium believe we should help the people of Volgaris to make everyone's lives better."

"Now, tell me Archie, about this plan," pleaded The Colonel. Archie proceeded to retell, again, the story of how he had overheard the different phases. Phase one - something to do with Eligah Bilton. Phase two - Howlett and his chocolate and phase three, Keiler with his model - ready when required. None of this made particular sense to Archie, but the look on The Colonel's face told a different story.

"Are you thinking what I'm thinking ladies?" he asked the others.

"Probably," they answered.

"What?" questioned Archie.

"Well, we know Bilton is heavily involved in disease manipulation on a grand scale. Howlett has the easiest way to distribute a disease through chocolate. But this with Keiler - a model ready when required? Did he say anything else?" quizzed The Colonel.

"He said she would be ready, as and when..." The three of them sat and thought for a moment, sipping their drinks, concocting plans in their heads then sighing as they realised they were no good. Suddenly, Maddie whispered something to Ida. A furious hushed discussion took place.

"You don't think they would..."Maddie pondered.

"Could Keiler pull that off?" Ida asked.

"We've all seen Keiler's work first hand. He's a genius and if anyone can do it, it's him," Maddie replied.

"And what better person," added The Colonel, obviously becoming aware of the ladies' plot, "think of the power!"

"What's going on? Can someone please explain?" Archie interrupted.

"Keiler is a mechanical mastermind." The Colonel explained. "We have all seen first-hand over the years what he is capable of. If what you have told us is correct, along with other bits of info we have picked up over the last few shifts; then it appears Imperium are going for the top. Archie, who is the most powerful person in the country?"

"Imperium?" he guessed.

"No Archie, Volgaris do not know about Imperium. As a normal man on the street, who is the most powerful person in the country?" The colonel questioned.

"The Prime Minister?"

"No, who does he answer to?" Suddenly, it dawned on Archie, and the look of realisation spread over his face. "Your father has had to do certain tasks for Imperium or something would happen to you or him. Your father, the surgeon. And who is his most important client?"

"No!"

"Yup," replied The Colonel, "they're going after the Queen!"

Chapter 13
The Asylum

Things moved very quickly from this point. Archie, still unsure of Roker's role in all of this, felt he had to speak to his father to get his side of the story. Plans were afoot for members of Alium to travel through the gates to Volgaris, not just through his father's surgery, but through the many portals he learnt about. There was no order to the position of gates. As people did not travel through them regularly or with necessity, they were just there. Doors that could not be opened. However, back home, Archie realised that wherever a gate was then, Imperium would have some control over it. It appeared that important, symbolic buildings or monuments were built at the sites of the gates. The person in charge of this monument or building would be a member of Imperium.

Maddie felt it better if Archie remained safe away from his father, but The Colonel, and indeed Archie, thought it would be more helpful if he were to find out further information.

"You cannot be serious," Maddie replied. "He is in great danger, and you're asking him to head straight back into it."

"Maddie, he has seen Marsden, learnt the plan and been to Romani Grove; straight into the belly of the beast. He is, potentially, Alium's greatest asset ever," The Colonel replied.

"And it's my decision," butted in Archie, "I'm going back."

"Very well," replied Maddie, "but I'm sending someone to keep an eye on you."

"Who?"

"The less you know, the better!"

Maddie escorted Archie back to the plain, simple door on the hectic, chaotic street. They both stood and looked at the door when it suddenly dawned on Archie.

"How do I get back through if you cannot open the door from this side?"

"I wondered how long it would take for you to realise that," Maddie answered. "That is what we have a phantasma for."

"A what?" came the reply.

"Think of this. Many years ago, when people first started shifting through the gates, a problem soon became apparent. How do we get through? Long ago, explorers from Volgaris came through but could not get back, so people had to be ready at the gates. That was their job, to stand at the gate and wait for it to open. Once it opened and a phantasma went through, the other phantasma, on this side had exactly one hour to alert the authorities and prepare whatever team or equipment was necessary for the next time the gate opened, as I said, exactly one hour later. This however developed over time to a more elaborate system, but the basic principle is the same. Someone is waiting on the other side, perhaps in mortal danger, but ready and waiting to open the gate."

"So, we are waiting for the door to open?" Archie questioned.

"Exactly. Try it now, and it will not open. Go on." Archie moved forward and turned the handle. As Maddie had said, the door would not move. "However, in exactly 367 seconds (and counting) someone will open the door from the other side."

"Who?" Archie asked.

"Ha," Maddie replied, "that you will see, very soon." They both stood there watching the clock countdown. The flaps were falling every second to reveal the next number below. What was just over six minutes seemed to take thirty. Each second seemed like five. After what seemed like an age, the numbers finally dropped to zero. Sure enough, with a soft click, the door opened.

"Take care Archie, I'll see you soon," Maddie promised.

Archie walked through the door, and he moved towards the next door. As he was about to open it, a familiar voice spoke behind him.

"You might wanna wait a minute if I were you." Archie spun around and there he saw his friend.

"Kat! What are you doing here?"

"Oh, you know, just another one of my jobs," she replied in her usual dry tone. "Listen, Archie, we haven't much time, and we certainly can't stand around chatting. We've got to get back before you are missed." And that was it as far as the conversation went. No small talk, or realisations of the enormous events that had unfolded, just silence. Silence until they stepped out of the lift in Roker's study.

"Right, go back to the music room and wait there, I'll see you later," Kat instructed him.

"Kat..." She turned and faced him. "Thanks." She just smiled and turned away.

Archie ran up the stairs and down the corridor. He flew down the hallway and into the music room. He did not know who to expect in there, but his father was the last person he thought would be waiting for him. Except maybe for Marsden, who was stood looking through the window.

"Archie, is the house on fire?" Roker exclaimed, laughing as he said it.

"No, I was just excited to see you," Archie improvised. He wanted to talk to his father, about a great many things, but unquestionably not with Marsden present.

"And how was your trip with Ms Buddington?" lied Roker, winking at Archie as he spoke.

"Oh, it was great," improvised Archie, "we did lots of things."

"That's wonderful Archie," Marsden interjected, "Now, Roker, you need to be leaving and paying a visit to the asylum. Phase three is nearly upon us."

"Yes of course." He turned to Archie. "Now son, we are going on a little trip, is that ok?"

"Err, yes father. Of course." He found this little strange as his father never spoke like this.

"Then I'll be on my way," Marsden bellowed, "I will see you later Roker." With that, he was gone, and Archie and his father remained in the music room.

"Father I..."

"Archie, not now. First, we must do as Marsden says and go to the asylum."

Archie did not like the asylum. He had only been once before as a small child, and he made his father promise he would never retake him. Yet, here he was, preparing for another visit.

The afternoon was drawing on as the carriage drove through the high metal gates of the asylum and up the long drive. The input Wilberforce had on the asylum system was well known throughout society, and Archie was keen to have his views changed from those he kept now. He was soon to be disappointed. The building looked derelict, dilapidated and downtrodden. Like an old dog that no one wanted anymore but was still there. It had turned evil and ill-tempered in its last few years, and no one wanted to be close to it. Because of this, it's fur was unkempt, it had an unpleasant aroma, and people were scared to go near. Like The Wilberforce Asylum for the Insane. From the outside, the building looked unused with boarded up windows, an inferior paint job and a roof containing several holes of various size. Staring at the outside walls, Archie could see tremendous portions of plaster that had fallen away, leaving strange, ominous shapes on the walls, some that looked like hideous faces, protecting the people inside - or perhaps warning the people outside to stay away.

At the gatehouse and the front door were Crowlies on duty. Not the best form of security Archie thought, but, as his father explained in the past, that was it. Crowlies were guarding the outer gate and walls and the main entrance. Roker had revealed that when you went through the front door, you were on your own with the inmates. Some people were in for mild lunacy. Archie had been told the days of being locked up for jealousy or fighting fires had gone and, looking at the conditions, he prayed this was the case for the inmates. Roker calmly informed him that he would be perfectly safe. Serious offenders would be locked up, and mild offenders would usually be in straitjackets. This did little to soothe Archie's fears, but he held them back and bravely followed his father in.

A smart gentleman met them at the door: a fashionable three-piece suit, slicked back, short hair and round spectacles. A door that looked as if it were hanging on rusty hinges and would not close even if Archie tried. A lattice of glasswork was above the door, but some panes were cracked or shattered, others missing completely. The amount of dirt and dust around them made Archie think a maid had not visited the place in months.

"Mr Roker, what a surprise! What brings you here?"

"Lord Wilberforce, we are here at the request of Mr Marsden," Roker replied.

"I see, then you had better come in, come, Master Archie, come and see our guests."

Archie felt as if he were present at some freak show; walking down a corridor, gazing through wire gauze at individuals, most either restrained or drugged so incapable of any form of movement. Again, bare walls greeted them either side, covered in markings and stains. The ceiling appeared to be made from stone, arched to support the weight of the stone next to it, like a cavernous cellar, some seemed to be partly charred as if a fire had spread through part of the building. The floor had no covering and, like the walls, appeared marked and worn. They came to an office, and the three of them entered and sat down.

"So, what is Marsden's plan now?" Wilberforce asked.

"We are about to set phase three into action," Roker replied, "I will need to visit a certain lady soon. I have come to check that her accommodation is prepared."

"Indeed," Wilberforce agreed. "Shall we go and check?" Roker nodded.

"Archie, you stay here." The look on Archie's face must have said a thousand words. "You will be perfectly safe here."

Archie nodded very unconvincingly but decided staying in a locked room was better than seeing all the inmates. Roker and Wilberforce set off, and Archie bolted the door securely behind them. He sat down on a worn leather chair, the stuffing oozing out from several places and wondered how many people would be residents here for knowing about shifting and the other world. His question would be answered much sooner than he realised as Archie heard a tapping at the door. He stood and edged away from the door. He could see a silhouette of a man with a beard through the glass as the reverse of Wilberforce's name rainbowed across the translucent pane. The tapping stopped, and the man seemed to disappear, leading to a sigh of relief from Archie, but this soon changed to panic as the door was now being rammed. Suddenly he heard a shout,

"Archie, let me in please, I'm friends with The Colonel." Unsure of what to do Archie panicked. He went to the door and questioned the man.

"How do I know I can trust you?" he asked.

"How do you know you can't?" came the reply. "I know you have shifted, I know where you have been and what you have seen, and I know it isn't safe for you here. Wilberforce will change. Change who he is. And the leader - the leader is here." Archie did not know what any of this meant and was not sure if he really wanted to. "Please Archie, there isn't much time." Archie closed his eyes and opened the door. In walked a man in very modest clothes, a white cotton, collarless shirt, simple brown trousers with black braces and he was barefoot. His face, however, was very angular. A long pointy nose, led down to a long pointy chin, which was covered with a long-pointed beard.

"Thank you Archie; you haven't much time. You must get out of here before they return."

"But where would I go?" Archie asked.

"Outside," the man replied, "get outside and you'll be safe."

"Who are you?"

"My name is Vernon Caulfield, and I am a friend."

"I know who you are, The Colonel has told me about you."

"Then please, trust me. You must go. Now!"

Archie heard noises at the entrance. He hid behind the door, and Caulfield started screaming and shouting across the room. After an initial panic, Archie realised he was causing a distraction, and it worked. The door opened and other inmates charged in. Once they had passed, Archie left the room and ran. Even though it was light when they entered the asylum the corridors were very dark and dim. He could hear moans and screams as he moved down the hallway. He had come a different way than he had entered so had no clues of which way to go. As he edged down the walls, the flickering lights played tricks on him, and he was sure inmates were surrounding him. Shadows loomed higher and higher until he could take no more. He entered the nearest room and slammed the door behind him. He stood there breathless, gulping for air but trying to remain silent. He noted in the very dark room a window as tiny strips of light bled through gaps in the crisscross carpentry over the panes. He moved towards them and tried pulling the planks away. After much tugging, Archie managed to realise one, but upon looking around the now light-flooded room, he panicked as he saw several inmates waking from drug-induced slumbers.

The comatose characters staggered, almost zombified towards Archie, with their arms, grabbing for him. He continued to pull at the wooden planks over the window frame but to no avail. They were stuck. He felt the hands of the inmates grabbing at him in desperation, and he helplessly tried to fight them off. The next thing he knew he was hoisted into the air, like a lamb being taken to slaughter. All his limbs were being pawed at as if he were the last piece of meat for a pack of ravenous dogs. He tried to release himself from their jaws but fear overtook him, and his limbs seized up in panic. The next thing he knew, he was being strapped into a chair with thick brown, padded leather straps with the hands of the insane grabbing, stroking and pulling at him.

"Enough!" Archie recognised the slightly muffled sound of Lord Wilberforce, as did the inmates but, what he saw in front of him was completely different.

The new look Wilberforce returned and sent the fear of God into those present. Gone had the mild-mannered gentleman in a smart suit and, in his place, a beast, a vision of nightmares. Wilberforce now wore a dark brown hessian jacket - matching an inmate's straight jacket, but without the oversized arms. Over the forearms where black leather strappings but alarmingly, underneath on the left hand, were old, soiled bandages, and more worryingly, on the right, a series of tubes connected to syringes that were strapped to each finger. These, in turn, led to a control device installed into the black leather straps. As if these would not incite fear enough, over his face he wore a terrifying mask, that of a skull, but with deep black sunken eyes, the jaw and upper mouth piece wired together with steel pins and two breathing chambers emerging like silver turrets from each cheek. To top off the whole look, he wore a hangman's noose around his neck like some form of macabre jewellery. Archie was unsure who was mad - the patients or the man in charge.

The inmates cowered back into their corners, averting their eyes from the terror before them.

"Do you want to know how I reformed the state of mental health in this country?" he called in a much more sinister time than before, "Fear. Fear of me, fear of a new world order, fear of Imperium. Do not worry yourself Archie; I am not here to hurt you, only protect you. But first, you must know some truths. Your father has told you he works for Imperium and that he is being forced to do tasks for them. If he doesn't, then he will be punished by Imperium hurting you, is that correct?"

"Yes, let me out of here."

"Well, I'm here to tell you that that is not the truth. The truth is - your father is a member of Imperium, and he is willingly working for them to allow them to take over the world."

"That's not true," Archie cried, "he wouldn't lie to me."

"Would he not?" cackled Wilberforce in response, "take him down!"

One of the inmates, his head covered in a wooden box with a metal grill at the front, pulled a large lever by the wall. Archie heard machinery sluggishly waking up and starting to work. Wilberforce stood there, laughing menacingly at his victim as suddenly, the chair upon which Archie was sat, dropped underground and the light disappeared. As he travelled into the depths of the asylum, machinery whizzed by, being tended to by inmates; steam and smoke emitting from funnels and valves, screams of inmates, piercing the pitch-black abyss. Suddenly, the chair came to an abrupt halt. Silence and darkness were all around. Archie had no idea where he was and what was around him.

"Hello," he shouted hopefully into the darkness.

"Archie, is that you?" Archie heard his father's voice.

"Yes, where are you?"

"I'm here, next to you."

"What's going on? Why is this happening?"

"There are a lot of things taking place Archie, as I have told you all along, you need to believe me."

"I do," Archie replied, still sat in the darkness. He had so many answerless questions rushing through his head. "What about Wilberforce - the way he was dressed?"

"Archie, what you saw was Wilberforce controlling the inmates. He is a member of Imperium."

"He said you are too," Archie blurted out.

"Archie, listen to me - it is true. I am a member of Imperium." Archie was overcome with confusion. Everything Maddie and Ida had said about his father was correct.

"Archie, I know you have shifted, I know you have seen the other world, met people and been told things.

You have been told many things, some true some very untrue. But I am here now, telling you the truth. I am a member of Imperium - not necessarily through my own choice - but I am a member. Imperium also wants you to become a member. I have tried and tried to prevent this; I have done what they have asked to stop this from happening, but I have my hands tied now. You're a clever lad Archie; I'm sure you know what's going on. Imperium want to get to the Queen. I don't know why, but I think they want to assert their control over the whole country. They want a meeting with her, and that is where I come in. Can you see that Archie?"

"Yes, I can."

"Everything will be sorted after that, and we can carry on with our normal lives. Is that what you want?"

"Yes, it is," Archie replied, relieved at his father's response. Could life go back to normal? Archie wished it would, but he was not sure how now with the things he knew. Perhaps if things were as they were before, he would be able to talk to his father about shifting and the others. Roker's voice rang out from the darkness.

"We need to get away from here, that's the first thing we have to do." A deep, echoing laugh boomed around the black abyss as if present at every angle. "Who's there?" Roker commanded. The darkness lifted and a cavernous rock face confronted Archie. He looked around and saw his father sat next to him strapped into a chair identical to his. Around the edge of the cave, stood a barricade of men, or part men as Archie thought. Their masked faces looked like paintings or sculptures, from another time in history, stony white and emotionless. Beneath this skin, their heads appeared to be covered in a brown cloth bag with rough, uneven stitching prevalent. The remainder of their heads seemed mechanical with a series of resistors and dials joined by copper wiring. Black tubing spread out from the creatures' heads and hung either side of the skull like dreadlocked hair. On the right of the face, a golden eyepiece of some sort draped down, easily moved to and fro in front of the eye - like a telescope or sight for a rifle. This matched the much larger appendage on the right shoulder; some type of weapon, like a short rifle, able to pivot to any position. Metal piping protruding to a backpack each one carried. All of them alike, bar one.

This one dressed much smarter: a full length, black leather coat, stretching down to the owner's knees, decorated from collar to hem in pairs of dulled silver buttons; long leather gloves protected the hands, firmly holding an ebony stick, straining under the tension applied by the owner; finally, knee-length boots, so shiny they looked almost wet. These items made the individual look authoritarian, but the mask being worn made the individual look inhuman. The entire skull was covered in some type of metal mask. There was no mouthpiece or nasal passage, just one large monocle over the right eye and a black hole where the left should be. The ornate skull appeared military green with brown markings and etchings covering the crown. The top portion of the casing seemed to rotate if required, changing the sockets over the eyes. This, Archie assumed, was the man in control. Although all the men were masked, this appeared to be the dominant force. Archie was incorrect.

The next moment, another presence appeared in the subterranean hollow. The one that Archie had feared all his life, the one that had haunted his dreams and nightmares. From a darkened passage, the hooded figure with a skeletal mouthpiece emerged. Tall and foreboding, his presence caused an immediate reaction with the identical characters in the chamber; all of them turning in the direction of their cloaked superior. Archie panicked, unsure who was beneath the mask, but his father had no doubts.

"Marsden!" The menacing laughter returned.

"You will continue with the mission, you will meet with the Queen, and phase three will commence."

"I will do as you ask, but leave Archie out of this. It has nothing to do with him."

"If you complete your task you will be able to return to your normal life; fail in your task and Archie will become bait at Romani Grove. Do you understand?" Marsden roared.

"We're not afraid of you," Archie shouted, "I know what you're up to and I know your plans. You can't threaten us."

"Oh, I can and I will. Look what happens to those who disobey. Crowle!" The man with the metallic skull turned to Marsden. So that was Crowle, and these soldiers must be his Crowlies.

"Get the Persona to bring our latest victim." Crowle made a series of hand gestures, and two of the Persona Soldiers moved into action. From another darkened tunnel, they emerged dragging a body between them. In the centre of the room, they flung the corpse to the floor. Like a sack of potatoes, it landed with a thud and Archie instantly recognised it as Wilberforce.

"He didn't follow the rules, and he has paid the price. Roker, you will do as you are told, or, Archie will pay the price." Reluctantly, Roker agreed and was untied from his bindings; he was then led away by the two Persona who had brought Wilberforce in. Archie was left, still bound to the chair. Marsden turned to him.

"Now then Archie, it is time you and I had a little chat."

Chapter 14
Imperium's Plan

"Archie Roker, you think you know it all, don't you? You have learnt of Similis and met your new friends. Now you think you can come here, save your father and return your life to normal," Marsden barked. As he spoke, he removed a weapon from a holster upon his belt and waved it in the air. The gun, with a dark red studded handle, appeared to have several barrels, all stacked up upon each other. Each had a purpose: to fire a bullet, to fire steam, to fire a dart and a set of sights to ensure accuracy. As he moved it through the air, a strange purple glow emitted from the rear of the weapon, as if it were to set alight any second in protest of its treatment.

"But Alium know your plan. They know what you are planning to do and you will soon see that they will stop you," responded Archie. He was confident in his thoughts and responses to Marsden. Now he knew the plan he felt sure he would release his father.

"Know my plan? Know my plan?" Marsden was almost laughing now like a maniacal hyena. "Archie, they know what I want them to know, they do what I let them do, they see what I let them see. The plan? Does it involve disease? Chocolate? And the queen?"

"Yes," Archie shouted back, "and The Colonel is coming, everyone is coming. You will be stopped."

"They are coming are they Archie? Well, I positively hope so," Marsden growled in a low murmur. Archie was now a little confused. "What do you think my plan is Archie? Please tell me what you and your sorry gang of fighters think Imperium have planned."

"You want to control everyone here in Volgaris. You are going to poison people with the disease Bilton has developed and spread it using chocolate that Howlett provides. Give the poor something they desire and use it to kill them. And you are planning something with the queen, perhaps kidnapping, or holding her to ransom. That's where my father fits in. It doesn't matter, Alium know this and are sending their full force," Archie answered confidently.

"Then my plan has worked perfectly," Marsden smirked.

"You just want control."

"Control? Control? I have control of this world now. I make the people do and think as I wish. If there are too many, I merely inflict a disease and terminate some. I need them to think something, I control the press, and as for religion, you don't know the half of it. There is nothing that happens in this world without me knowing it or approving it. You and Alium have no idea."

"But..."

"But nothing. Take him away. He needs to be kept secure until his father has completed his task." Archie was approached by two more Persona and Crowle. The faceless monster waved his hands again, and the Persona followed Crowle and Archie out of the cavern. The cave he had confronted Marsden in was more like a courtroom, with Marsden sat upon his high throne passing judgment. Judge, jury and executioner thought Archie. He now moved down a dark, narrow candlelit corridor, led by Crowle and flanked either side by the two Persona.

Upon exiting the confined corridor, they emerged into a long, rectangular room, flanked by cells, two stories with wrought iron bars. The prison smelt damp and unclean - no toileting facilities were visible. The floor, uneven earth - mud in places - was littered with stone and what looked like human bones. It appeared that it might have been used for something else at some point - perhaps a wing of the asylum - or even a prison from some distant period. The dull, dirty walls, painted many years earlier, were covered in scratch marks - perhaps from memories of an insane patient or prisoner, drawing closer to their punishment. The light flickered as torches lapped the air as they walked by. Crowle stopped abruptly and turned to the cell on his left. He turned, and Archie could see him flexing his ebony cane in front of him. He swiftly swung the baton to the cell door with a clang. The Persona opened the cell and Archie roughly pushed inside. He fell to the floor. There he sat, unsure for how long - alone in the darkness, with only screams and cries for company - wondering what was happening to his father.

Gazing around his new quarters, strange shapes appeared on the walls as shadows danced in the flame light with fluttering moths as they sought the light at the end of their tunnel. Upon the wall, Archie saw further scratch marks - a tally to show the days an inmate had lodged here. Day by day passing, the chipped pain telling past stories. There were no windows, no escape to natural light and the outside world. The revolting smells overpowered the cell with the lack of oxygen around, and

186

Archie found himself sat with his hand over his mouth and nose the whole time.

After what seemed like hours, when the cells appeared to quieten down, Archie moved to the metal, lattice door of his cell. He could see the cells opposite, but not into those either side of him. The opposing cells seemed to be empty, but the noises he had heard earlier must have emanated from somewhere. Archie strained at the edge of the cage for a look down the long corridor but to no avail.

"It's no use, Archie, you won't be able to see," a voice called out of the night. "What you need is something like this." A hand appeared around the edge of the cell holding something in the outstretched palm.

"Who are you? How do you know my name?" questioned Archie, looking at the piece of mirror he had been handed.

"Well, you're Roker's son. Everyone knows who you are now. And do you think I'm friend or foe locked up in here?" the female voice returned.

"I don't know, with all the things I have seen recently I have no idea what is going on."

"The name's Abberton, Minta Abberton. Perhaps you've heard of me?"

"Err, sorry no. Should I have?" Archie replied almost apologetically.

"Should you have? Of course you should have. Minta Abberton! The greatest spy Alium has ever seen."

If you are the greatest spy ever seen," Archie questioned, "then why are you locked up in prison?"

"What? Locked up? All part of the plan Archie. I'm gathering intel and passing it onto my contact."

187

"Really," Archie responded, slightly dubious and unenthusiastic towards his new friend. "I can't see how you can do that in here! Who is your contact?"

"The less you know, the better. If you don't know who he is, he's not likely to be given up, but he is in the inner circle of Imperium."

Archie picked up the mirror and positioned it so he could see down the corridor. No one about, or no one he could see in the dimly lit dungeon. "Where are the guards?"

"There won't be any here now; we are well and truly stuck here. If we did get out of the cell, we'd have to get out of this corridor. And if we did get out of this corridor, we'd be in…"

"…the asylum."

"Exactly. Sometimes Archie, it is best to observe the actions of others. Not everything is as it seems."

"So why are you here?" Archie asked trying to change the subject.

"I was captured, by the Persona. I was working as a phantasma. One of my many jobs!"

"What else do you do?"

"As I said, I am a spy, so I do what is required. Put it this way, there is no other person in all Alium who can match me and my skills with a bow and arrow. I have been known as the silent assassin. The female Robin Hood."

Minta, even though Archie had not seen her, sounded like someone who liked it the sound of her own voice. Not a silent assassin at all. Archie felt she seemed very righteous and all-knowing, like Ms Buddington. He felt confident they would get on very well: discussing the state of the day, what they had done that day and, more importantly, what they needed to do next. Archie felt sure she would love the sound of her own voice but dare not even think about that regarding Ms Buddington. He valued his life too much. He sat and smiled, thinking of her and his ordinary life beforehand; perhaps even laughing out loud as Minta started to question him.

"So, what is Roker up to now?"

"Secret plan for Imperium. Something to do with the queen. I'm not sure what though. Once they have released their disease through the chocolate."

"That's an old plan with the chocolate; they have controlled your life all the time for years. That's not the current plan. One of my contacts has informed me of some details that led me to think there is something far more sinister afoot. "

"More sinister than poisoning the population?"

"I agree with you Archie, but they have done that before - it won't be done again."

"Again?" Archie exclaimed. Minta proceeded to explain: whenever there was a need to do something to a portion of the population; if people needed to be made ill, subdued or sacrificed; if people need to feel happy of elated - Imperium had the means through its vast network to do something.

"Do you recall a few months back there was an outbreak of Scarlet Fever - lots of children with aches, pains, loss of appetite and vomiting? Well, caused by Bilton infecting chocolate supply to the areas Imperium felt needed purging."

"Why?" Archie asked, confused at the motives for such a barbaric act.

"I hear from my informant that that area of the city had developed an excellent community spirit. People were helping each other out, covering each other at work to enable people to spend time with their families. Some even tried to take holidays to the coast. Imagine that... a holiday - people not working. So, what's the best solution? Kill some children, lower everyone's morale and make them come back to work. People were even taxed in their wage to cover treatment for the illness. Treatment that Imperium knew wouldn't work as only Bilton had the cure. When enough children had died, or people were desperate again, then the antibody would be introduced, and credit could be given to someone for curing it or reforming conditions to aid people. People like your father."

"My father is being forced to do it."

"Is he Archie?"

"What do you mean? Of course he is. He is a surgeon. It's his job to help people, not kill them."

"But think of the bigger picture, think of the glory he would get for saving all those lives. All controlled by Imperium."

"But that is madness."

"For most people, yes, but they don't know any better - the way Imperium like it." Minta then went on to explain how she and Maddie were friends from an early age. "I have known Maddie for a long, long time; since we were younger than you. We grew up together. She wanted to change the world, and she's still trying now. You may not believe this but many years ago Maddie and I, your father and Marsden were all friends. We talked about how we would make the world a better place. Marsden was a different man then. I can't believe he is the leader of Imperium now. The four of us together basically started Alium. We thought as a group and came up with many plans and ideals when we studied at university together. Through numerous meetings at that time, we shared thoughts and feelings about how the country was falling to pieces. When we discovered Similis, that's when things started to change. Marsden's work was vital to developing the link to the other world. He became obsessed with that place. As we left university, we went our separate ways: your father to medical school, Marsden left to develop a new source of energy and Maddie and I continued our struggle with Imperium in the other world."

"So, you know my father?"

"Yes, Archie. Your father did a lot of research on Imperium, and he shared his findings with us. As I said, we had such high hopes of changing things. Your father found out about the history of Imperium and began to unlock many secrets as to its control."

"Did Imperium start then?"

"No, not at all. Imperium has been around in some form or another for centuries."

"That long... really!"

"Archie, the beauty of Imperium is that they control everything, but no one knows that they are doing it. There is no visible sign; the general public doesn't know they exist - let alone who is a member. If you think back through time to great eras - Roman, Egyptian, Viking, Renaissance. The seat of power was provided by that day's equivalent of Imperium. Over the centuries, they have developed and adapted to the trials and tribulations of the society in question, making it great and crushing it when they have finished with it and taken what they want. Now they are poised with a cunning plan when the world is at its most technologically advanced. Remember Archie, whatever you think of Imperium, it is likely they are two steps ahead. There only purpose is to benefit them. By mutual assistance of its members for the reformation of the world for Imperium."

Suddenly, they heard a gate open, keys rattle and footsteps approaching. The expressionless face of a Persona opened Archie's cell and beckoned him out. As Archie took his first glimpse at Minta, sat wrapped in a long black cloak a straight cut fringe and piercing blues eyes, she offered one final piece of advice.

"Trust nothing!"

Archie re-entered the cavernous court, again finding himself surrounded by Persona, with Crowle, the conductor of this sinister orchestra. In his hands, Crowle held, not a baton, but a weapon - a cross between a rifle and a bow, with two embossed handles and projectiles from the top and bottom, joined with a stiff, taut wire. Next to him, on the floor was, what looked like a bench with something upon it, draped in a black silk cloth. Crowle stood over the bench, holding his weapon; protecting or guarding whatever was under the fabric. Marsden emerged into the chamber again wearing his silver, skeletal face mask - sending a chill down Archie's spine every time he saw it. As a judge, he sat above everyone else at his bench, peering down dominantly, with his faceless jury awaiting his every command.

"Now Archie, it is time for you to decide," he ordered from the dock.

"Decide what?" questioned Archie.

"Whether you are going to join Imperium."

"I won't join Imperium, ever!"

"We will see about that. Crowle!" came the order.

Archie turned around to see Crowle lean over and pull the cloth away. Underneath, Archie saw his father strapped to the bench below, unable to move. A gag covered his mouth, and Archie could see his father was desperately trying to speak. Crowle removed the dirty rag from his mouth.

"Archie, are you ok?"

"Yes, are you?"

"Archie, don't worry about me. Listen, don't do anything they say."

"Silence traitor," boomed Marsden, "you have shown your worth or lack of it. You had your chance; now it is Archie's." He turned to Archie and looked down at him menacingly. "So, I ask again Archie, are you going to join Imperium?"

"No!" came Archie's defiant response.

"Oh, I think you will." He gestured with his arm in a grand downward movement. Crowle moved towards Roker and pulled a lever on the side of the bench. In a second, the bench leapt into life, like it was possessed, and moved into different parts like limbs, enabling Roker to be moved upright into a crucifixion pose. The gears and levers that had moved Roker now hissed and groaned as they held up its captive. "If you please, Mr Crowle." Crowle now raised the crossbow, aiming it directly at Roker's chest and heart.

"Archie, don't," implored Roker, "just don't, no matter what."

"So Archie, will you join Imperium?"

"I... I..."

"You what? Archie, your next answer will result in one of two things," Marsden inferred.

"Archie, don't listen to them," Roker shouted.

"Gag that man," Marsden commanded. Crowle removed the gag from his top pocket and stuffed it into Roker's mouth. The muffled sounds of Roker gradually reduced as his attempts at speaking proved fruitless. "I shall now continue. Archie, say yes and your father will be freed; say no, and you will watch your father die moments before you are killed."

Archie stood there, knowing what his father wanted him to do, and knowing what he had to do. Reluctantly he replied,

"I'll join, I'll do as you ask."

"Of course you will, now take that Roker away to do his job. Archie and I need to pay a visit to Romani Grove."

Chapter 15
Return to Romani Grove

The journey to Romani Grove was in silence. Archie had no desire to talk to anyone. Even though inside, he felt nothing but hate for Marsden, he admitted to himself that this was the best thing to do in the current situation. If he joined Imperium, his father would be freed, and life could return to normal. Roker had been taken elsewhere by the Persona and Crowle. Archie was in a carriage with two Persona, Marsden following in another he assumed. It was dark outside and none of the things Archie had seen on his trip last time were visible. He recalled the long driveway and the house at the end, and when the carriage came to a final halt, he assumed he was there. As he exited the vehicle, he noticed far in the distance upon a hill, a flaming beacon - a cube brick structure set alight in the jet-black night - offering a dancing orange glow to a cold evening.

Archie noticed Wesley Lillyvick again at the entrance. He approached Archie with his hand extended in front of him.

"Master Roker, what a pleasure to see you. I believe you have fully joined us now?"

"Yes, that is correct."

"Well, may I suggest you stay here for a few minutes and observe the beacons."

Archie turned to him, "I can only see one."

"Ahhh, one at the moment, but keep watching. Our beacon upon the Pike has only just been lit. See what happens now."

Sure enough, as Archie stood there and the beacon upon the Pike grew taller, another orange dot appeared to the right - small at first, but growing rapidly into the moonless sky. Then another. Another. Soon, Archie counted at least fifteen beacons surrounding him plus another five or six further off into the distance.

"The quickest way to signal the other members. In days of old these beacons were used to warn kings and queens of imminent threats from foreign invaders. Now Imperium uses it as a call to members for meetings here at the Grove."

"Where do they come from?" Archie asked. Lillyvick smiled.

"From all over Archie, you can maybe see ones from five miles away but this message will be sent all over the country and soon - they will arrive."

"How?"

"Airship, carriage, underground tunnel or even Similis. We have our private gateway at the Grove. I'm sure now you are a member you will be able to use it."

Sure enough, within the next five minutes, the distant sound of steam - a train and an airship could be heard. The train could be heard but not see in the darkness, but the airship could be seen heading towards the Pike, one at first then three more. Soon there were several, all travelling for the beacon on the Pike.

"How do they know where they are going?" questioned Archie.

"They head for the beacon, and then they will rendezvous with us in the oriental gardens on the side of the Pike. Basic members will stay above ground and join in the hunt. But, for the inner circle, like you and your father, you will enter the Pike through the pigeon tower."

"Pigeon tower?"

"A simple building that opens up Romani Groves secrets. The only entrance into the Pike and our gateway."

"What is the hunt?" Archie had been told what it was but did not want to know really - desperately seeking a different answer.

"You will see the hunt when the others arrive. Now relax." Archie sat on a veranda at the rear of the Athenian detailed building, gazing at the airships in the sky as they approached, one after the other. He wondered where his father was and what the task he had to do. Archie assumed the vital person must be the Queen but what was Roker charged to do. Archie was unsure. He thought of the others he had met over the last few weeks. Where was Maddie? With Ida, Krewler and The Colonel? Were they coming to stop the plan as they said? What happened to Minta in the asylum? Did she escape with the aid of her contact? And Archie thought of home. Ms Buddington! It felt like an age since he had seen her and he tried to imagine her worrying over his safety. And Kat - he missed his friend - his best friend. So much had happened and how he longed for a regular life -how it used to be. He just had to wait here till his father had finished his task and then he could go back home to them. The nightmare would be over.

The evening sky seemed to be lighter and lighter with the entrance of further steam trains and airships. Archie could see a path developing up the side of the Pike to what he assumed were the oriental gardens Lillyvick had told him about. Looking into the sky, the light of the airships glowed softly like light bugs around a flickering candle. Two of the lights appeared to be growing. Soon, they were much larger than any of the others, growing by the second. Archie could begin to see the magnitude of the airship in front of him. The zeppelins were gigantic and would have dwarfed a football pitch. Two enormous balloons parallel to each other were joined at the front and rear by two perpendicular metal frames. At the back, thick black smoke coughed from numerous chimneys, powering the thunderous beast through the skies. The ship was heavily fortified with an array of weapons ready poised at every angle. Perhaps most impressive were the two landing strips that sat upon the zeppelin's backs. The first, running the full length of the left-hand side with a command station at the front; the second running from the front left corner of the ship diagonally to the rear right where a second command station was situated. A hive of other modules and compartments were barely visible, but every possible space upon the ship was used for some fiendish purpose of Imperium. Lillyvick approached.

"Ahhh, Volantem Mortem has arrived."

"Volantem Mortem?" Archie asked in awe, still gaping at the sheer scale of the vessel in front of him.

"Yes, the head of the Imperium fleet."

"How does it not get seen?"

"That depends upon when it is flown, and if someone said they saw an enormous vessel flying through the sky with the largest balloons ever seen above it, what people say?"

"They wouldn't believe it."

"Exactly," Lillyvick continued. "Now you must make your way to the oriental gardens. We will be met there." Archie gazed at the vast ship above him and noticed, protruding from one side, a zigzag joist was extending out into the space beside. Cabling and wires could be seen hanging from the arm and next, a box emerged from the side of the craft.

"What is that?" asked Archie.

"That is how you disembark Volantem Mortem. It does not land; it always stays afloat in the air. That box is larger than an average slum house. That gives you some idea of how big Volantem Mortem is." Archie hated the word slum house used to describe the poor accommodation people lived in most of the country. Quite often these homes had two families living in them - one upstairs, one down. Terrible, squalid conditions, but nevertheless, a large size for a lift from an airship. The magnitude of Volantem Mortem had grown even more.

Archie now left the veranda he was sat upon and was escorted to what seemed to be a little railway platform. The next thing he knew, a machine, identical to that he had experienced at The Grand hotel at the seaside approached and stopped in front of him. Lillyvick gestured his arm towards the carriage, and Archie sat down. Lillyvick followed him. The cogs and gears whirred into life and the contraption set of toward the flaming beacon, still burning brightly on top of the Pike. Although Archie could not see into the distance, the entire route was lit using torchlight every few metres. He could see elaborate stonework, ornate passageways, highly engineered archways and geometrically designed flooring - a stone mason's dream. As speed decreased as they began to climb the side of the Pike on a uniquely developed part of the track, Archie noticed a tower approaching. He was now moving diagonally on a platform - keeping the carriage horizontal at all times.

"What is that?"

"That is the pigeon tower I was telling you about," responded Lillyvick. Archie gazed at the doorway to the Pike - the side approaching him rounded with steep steps leading to the foot of the tower, then split either side of the structure. As he passed, he turned and looked at the reverse of the tower. He smiled to himself as the chimney breast appeared like a nose with two narrow window eyes either side. Below, two other windows looked like an expressionless mouth, as if holding the secret of the Pike. The carriage continued through the lavish gardens and in the flickering torchlight, Archie felt as if he was travelling through a distant rainforest with exotic unknown trees and shrubberies - a sensory overload. He would not be surprised if a tiger would emerge from the undergrowth at any second. The thought of a predator increased as Archie noticed many Persona, fully armed, surrounding a magnificent pagoda.

The metallic box that had emerged from Volantem Mortem was now visible next to the lavish Chinese structure, and Archie could now fully appreciate its size. The mechanical cube looked like it was from another world, quite literally, and steam was still emerging from it. The carriage pulled to a halt, and Lillyvick disembarked and then offered Archie a hand to follow him. He exited but refused the hand, instead pushing himself out on an array of gears. Looking up at the tiers of the pagoda, Archie noticed a platoon of Persona, with firearms pointing out into the darkness. Archie followed Lillyvick up several flights of stairs, and they entered a large room with what looked like a red, velvet throne at one end. To the right was a set of sliding bamboo doors which were opened as they approached. This took them out onto a balcony where Archie found the masked presence of Marsden, the silver skull covering his face. With him were Plundell, Bilton and Dorrington.

"Just in time for the hunt," he cackled.

"Hunting what?" He laughed maniacally,

"My favourite, traitors!" Suddenly, a bright light emerged from the darkness in front of them. There, in the distance, Archie could see a wire cage full of people. Some of the occupants looked malnourished and unkempt, but, to his utter shock, he started to recognise some of the people. Minta was captive in the cage. Her excessive ego seemed crushed as she stood helplessly in the cage. Then, next to her another face appeared, the one Archie dreaded - Kat.

"What are they doing there? Let them out!"

"But Archie, you are Imperium, and they are traitors."

"No, I don't want anything else to do with this. My father would not want this to happen."

"Your father is still performing his mission, and you have a job to do also. I have it on good authority - mainly from you - that Alium are planning a raid tonight. They will enter through the gate in the Pike. All of them. They intend to overthrow the Grove and Imperium. But I know what is going on, and I will not take this. You wish to save your little girlfriend? Easy. You will enter the Pike, act as phantasma and lead Alium into a cage like this. If you do not, your pathetic friend will be the first to suffer in the hunt. A simple choice Archie."

"You said if my father did as he was told, you would let us leave and return to normal."

"And you will Archie, all you need do is follow the instructions. Your father will return from his mission soon, and after you have completed this, you will be free to leave."

"But what about all those innocent people?"

"Innocent? Innocent? They have caused nothing but trouble for this organisation. We have tried to increase our power and make the world a better place, but their interference has set us back."

"But you were once with them. All those years ago. You wanted good, didn't you? You were friends with Maddie, my father and Minta." Marsden moved forward seemingly angered by this trip down memory lane. He shifted into a position to confront Archie.

"Silence boy," he bellowed and struck Archie across the face sending him to the floor. Archie landed in a heap, and he felt the anger building in him. He launched to his feet and aimed to attack the silver faced fiend, but received another strike, sending him back to the ground.

"Seize him, NOW!" Marsden ordered. "Roker, this is simple, lead Alium into my trap or your girl will be executed now." He waved his hand and the sound of Persona preparing to fire rung in Archie's ears. "Take aim. Ffff…."

"Stop," a voice came out. Everyone in the room turned and there, like a lighthouse on the dark ocean, stood Roker, his father. Marsden stopped, stood like stone. A pause filled the room as if no one dared speak. Archie turned to his father. There he stood, proud and dominant like he always was, but now he had a comprehensive, black monocle, spinning on cogs and strapped on with a leather binding. Over his left shoulder, a large tan strap with golden metal work, all linked to a series of straps and mechanical devices upon his arm. On the forearm, a similar looking device, with an array of controls, bulbs and dials - even his father's pipe - ready for action at a moment's notice.

"Roker?" stuttered Marsden. Archie was confused. The whole attitude of Marsden had changed. He spoke as if he were in fear of Roker, almost cowering in anticipation of his next words.

"You do not touch my son," came the words.

"I'm sorry, I lost my nerve, please forgive me Dominus."

"You will not touch my son," he replied. Marsden was now dropping to his knees.

"I'm...I'm… sorry," he grovelled in response.

"Too late." With that, Roker raised left arm and pointed it towards Marsden. Archie stared in disbelief at what was happening. What had caused this to happen? Archie noticed the dials on his father's arm spinning almost uncontrollable and slowly, a syringe rose from the elbow joint. Roker aimed and with the clench of a fist, a dart fired from the needle, piercing Marsden in his neck. The look of fear was frozen on to his face as he grabbed his neck. Marsden fell to his knees and, as his breathing slowed, he first fell to his knees, then his whole body slumped to the floor. Archie did not know what to think, but instinct took over him, and he ran to his father. In his presence, he felt safe and secure, maybe now more than ever. But suddenly, a feeling of uncertainty crept over him. What would the Persona do now? Would they fire upon them both? But nothing. The selection of troops in the room stood as statues - no movement at all.

"What's happening? Have you done your task? He has Kat and was going to hunt her. What is going on?" Archie asked.

"Don't worry Archie," his father responded, "everything is different now." He walked over to Marsden, perhaps to check his condition Archie thought, as he is a surgeon, but no. Roker bent down and removed the silver skull mask. What was he doing? Why hadn't the Persona responded?

"Why did he call you Dominus? What does that mean?"

"Archie, listen to me carefully. He called me Dominus because I am the master. I oversee Imperium." With this, he placed the silver mask upon his face. Archie stood in silence dumbfounded by Roker's actions.

"But… but…"

"No Archie, listen. You need to see what is happening here. You are a member of Imperium now. We can make the world a better place, and I am going to do this with you by my side."

"No, this can't be right."

"Archie, you have given Imperium the information needed. You have been a double agent without even realising. You made Alium believe a plot that never existed. You made them plan an attack that was not needed or will never succeed, and you have risen to your true position as the rightful Heir of Imperium. I am so proud of you." Archie did not know what to say or think.

204

"But what about Kat, why is she in that cage. Ready for the hunt?"

"That is Marsden's work. He has done that."

"But why did you pretend he was in charge?" I don't understand."

"I needed to sort out Alium, and you were perfect to do that for me. Can you not see the great duty you have done for your country?"

"But I won't act as a phantasma. I won't betray my friends."

"Friends?" Roker pleaded, "Friends? I have arranged all this. I knew you have shifted. I know about Abe, Ida, Maddie, everything."

"But I won't betray them!"

"You don't have too. Lights!" Suddenly, Archie knew the outside was lit up again. He moved to the bamboo shutters and looked out into what once was darkness. The cage with Kat and Minta still glowed in the night, but now another enclosure was illuminated. Inside, Archie could see a sea of familiar faces: Ida, The Colonel, Krewler and Maddie to name a few. He sighed in disbelief.

"Why are they here?"

"They are the enemy. Fugitives. I have worked hard to build this world into the society it is, and they want to destroy it all. How is that fair?"

"But is it fair what you have done to this world?"

"People know where they stand and I have control over them all through Imperium. They live in a world with no rules, no order. They are free. People have no control. But that will end soon."

"What do you mean?"

"Archie, the plan was never to infect the population with a new disease via chocolate. That has been done many times before. No, now Imperium will move into the new world, and when we are there, we will seal the gates bar one. No one will be able to enter, and Imperium will control the new world, as we have done here."

"But how will you do that, the world is different there. They know all about you, they live in a utopian society. It won't work."

"It will work Archie, as we have planned it here. Would you like to know the key?" Archie apprehensively nodded. "Steam!"

"Steam?" Archie questioned. He had no idea what was going on.

"Archie, you have been to the new world have you not?" Again, he nodded. "Then you will know everything is powered by steam. From the biggest wheels of industry to the smallest shop on a street corner, they love steam to power their crazy lifestyle. Over the last few years, in Volgaris, I have, with my close circle of acquaintances, tested various strategies to control the population through steam. Where do you think the invention of steam technology came from? It was introduced from the other world and developed to suit Imperium's need. We let them progress as much as we needed them to. We tested our solution throughout the steam in factories, on trains, everywhere you may find steam. We have bided our time to find the perfect solution for an airborne particle that will infect the steam. All people need to do is breathe it in. Simple."

"But why? We have everything we want at home."

"But we don't have complete power, complete control. That is what Imperium stand for - control."

"But this is the wrong way to go about it."

"No, it isn't. This way we have perfected a specific manner of control, and now we can implement it straight away."

"But I don't agree with it."

"You don't have a choice Archie. This is your destiny. I have planned it out since you were younger. Everything I have done is to lead to you being the next leader of Imperium." Archie sat there confused. Roker told him he was the next in line to control the most powerful organisation in the world and he felt nothing. He did not want this, and he certainly didn't want people he knew getting hurt.

"I can't agree with this."

"You don't have a choice. You are a mere pawn in the huge organisation of Imperium. Archie, you are my son, you have joined Imperium, you know your destiny, and now you will be part of the next plan." Roker proceeded to tell Archie how the members of Alium would be left in Volgaris. All the doors around the country would be sealed apart from the one in the Pike. The key players in Imperium would move to a life in the new world and take control there - for a better life for those people in Imperium. Take total control. He then proceeded to tell Archie of the final part of his plan.

"We need to take a visit to the palace."

Roker now swept out of the room, and Archie was ushered after him. As they returned to the lower floor and entrance of the pagoda, Crowle met them at the door, again in his hideous skull mask.

"Tell Dorrington and Thompson we are going to the palace." Crowle nodded obediently, and Roker exit passed him and sat back in the carriage in which Archie had arrived. "Get in Archie, the new world of Imperium awaits you." Knowing anything other than obeying would result in the death of his friends, he sat down opposite Roker. The carriage juddered into action and Archie could tell they were moving back down the Pike. The face of the pigeon tower that had made Archie smile earlier now smugly looked upon him as the carriage pulled up in front of it. A simple doorway was the only entrance to the tower and Roker moved a dial upon his left forearm, and the old wooden door swung open. Inside, they were met by two Persona guarding a lift shaft - like the one he had experienced in the hotel. There was ample room for Archie, Roker, Crowle and now, Dorrington and Thompson joined them. Archie pondered on the journey ahead. Would it be a long and twisty affair, or sharp and sudden as he had experienced before? The door to the lift slammed shut, and Archie could see nothing. He felt the lift drop, and suddenly lights whirred past his eyes. After a couple of seconds, they stopped, and Archie realised he was in a glass lift. In front a tunnel with what looked like the smallest train track he had ever seen. Surely a train on this route would only be suitable for a child. He soon realised his mode of transportation. As they entered the platform, Archie noticed a long, sleek carriage sat upon the track. The entire roof of the vessel was glass and Archie could see inside the angelic, white upholstery of the cushions. Crowle walked past the first single-seated carriage to the second which had two seats, one behind the other. The entire glass door lifted and Roker sat in the front seat.

"Archie, you get in behind me." Archie did as he was told, unsure of what else to do but mainly due to the menacing silent glare Crowle was miming from behind his ominous mask. Now sat, or almost lying as it felt, in the carriage, he saw the other two gentlemen pass, presumably to another carriage, and Crowle entered the first one. The glass doors of the vehicles slowly closed and Archie worried if he were to be sealed in it forever, like a funeral nightmare. "You may wish to hold onto the sides. This can be a little fast." As the carriage started to move, Archie notice on the far side of the track two Persona stood at a magnificent metal doorway. "Recognise that?"

"It's like the one in the surgery," answered Archie.

"Correct and it will take you to the same destination. Very soon, the only way you will be able to shift via Similis will be through that doorway. Always guarded, on both sides, set in the heart of the Pike in Romani Grove. A place that people in this world do not even know exists."

Archie took one last glance at the doorway before he heard a sound like a rocket being set off. The carriage he was in propelled forward at a tremendous speed, and he grabbed the sides tightly. Roker sensed his panic and reassured him.

"It's perfectly safe Archie, I have used this many a time. Sit back and enjoy the ride." Archie gazed in wonder as the carriage rolled side to side as he went through tunnels. He imagined it like the new roller coasters he had heard of in other countries, mainly

America. Thrill-seeking rides on wooden tracks in tiny carriages. He believed one was being built in the seaside town he had visited with Ms Buddington - though she would never let him go on something like that! He turned around and, looking beyond the array of machinery in front of him, he could see the next carriage with Tillman Thompson at the front. He did not know much about Thompson other than that he was always with Dorrington. A tall, slender man, he always wore black and grey suits with a waistcoat to match. He had long black silky hair, continuously hanging down the right side of his face but pushed behind the ear on the left-hand side. A finely trimmed pencil moustache and little stubble upon his chin matched the dark eyes. Archie felt sure he must be wearing makeup of some sort.

He returned his gaze forwards and noticed Roker rotating dials on his forearm and instantaneously, the bullet carriage began to slow. As it drew to a standstill, Archie saw another platform like the one he had seen before embarking on the journey. A Persona approached the carriage and opened the glass roof. Roker stepped out and held his hand to Archie. He took it and exited the platform. Now, Roker led the way again, through a maze of tunnels and staircases. As they went higher, foundations of buildings became apparent, and Archie noticed the grandeur of the design. Surely this must be the palace. Suddenly Roker stopped. It appeared they were at a dead end.

"Not to worry," Roker grinned. He raised his hand high to the top of the door frame and pulled a lever. The door uneasily popped open, and when emerging, Archie saw they were coming out of a panel in the wall. A white wooden door with an internal silver trim and external golden trim. He looked around to see an ornate golden stair rail, exquisitely finished with various emblems and designs. As they walked up the red velvet steps in front of them, Archie noticed the staircase split into two. In front was a tremendous dominating door which was ignored. Roker set off to the right up winding steps, almost pulling himself up with the rail. Archie followed and could see paintings of monarchs from the past recognising some from history lessons, but no time to stop and gaze at the artwork now. Past priceless Ming vases to a grand doorway at the top. Archie felt sure they would have to wait to enter, but Roker just opened the door and walked straight in. A man approached them as they entered.

"Ahhh, Cairns. I assume Her Majesty knows we are here. If not, please tell her."

"She is aware of your arrival and is waiting in the throne room for you."

"Excellent." Down a long corridor they walked, the same white walls and silver and gold trim. Another set of doors approached with two footmen guarding the way. They merely moved aside opening the doors for Roker as if he were the monarch himself.

They now entered the throne room. How did Archie know this? Apart from the grandeur of the chamber, at the far end, sat on a simplistic throne, in front of plush red velvet curtains, sat Queen Mathilda I of England. Archie was unsure of how to behave in the presence of a royal, but as Roker was the Queen's surgeon, he felt if he followed his lead then all would be ok. He could not be further from the truth.

Roker walked straight up to the Queen, up the three steps in front of her and sat down next to her, upon a matching throne next to her. The throne of her dead husband. Archie did not know what to do but the Queen looked as worried as he felt.

"Mathilda. How are you?"

"At your service, Dominus." Archie was lost for words. This was how Roker spoke to the Queen and how she spoke to him. Her sour face, a face the Queen was well known for, seemed slightly intimidated by Roker's presence. A tall woman she sat on her throne in a black leather dress. A red corset was worn over the top attached to a shoulder and neck piece. The stone of Mathilda hung around her neck, gleaming red in the bright throne room lights. Her hair tied up in two circular plaits either side of her head and the golden veil crown nestled upon them, covering her forehead. Her deathly white face accentuated all the other features of her face, primarily her blood red lips. All Archie had heard of her, her dominance, her influence, all now gone as she cowered in front of Roker.

"Excellent," replied Roker in a blasé manner. "I assume Keiler has been with his delivery?"

"Indeed he has," a voice from behind answered. Archie spun round to see - Queen Mathilda walking into the room with an entourage behind her. Archie did a double take, looking at the lady stood next to Roker and then to the lady approaching the throne.

"Well, he has surpassed himself this time hasn't he," Roker exclaimed turning to Crowle and the others. They nodded obediently. "Well done Keiler." Archie noticed him entering the room, still with goggles upon his forehead, menacingly stroking his twirling moustache.

"I serve to please," were his words to Roker.

"And please you have done. Now it is time to take our plan to the next level. We have the key figures of Alium captured. We have Bilton's disease to distribute via steam, and we will have a world we can develop and take to the next level. A good day's work if I say so myself. There are a few final plans we need to discuss and a few loose ends to sort out, namely your first model, but I think within the next forty-eight hours we will have little problem implementing our masterpiece."

"But what about the others. Maddie Ida, The Colonel. What about Kat?"

"What about them? They will be stuck here, living the life of everyone else. The same humdrum controllable life. We will crush the resistance in them and purge the world of their ideas."

"But..." Archie intervened.

"No buts Archie. I have had all your things brought to the palace. Thompson will you take my son to his room, sorry, the Prince's room and let him sort his things. A change of clothes is in order I think."

"But you can't do this!" Archie pleaded.

"I have and I will. And together Archie Roker, you and I will rule the world. Thompson, take him."

Thompson grabbed Archie's arm, firmly but gently and led him from the throne room. Archie's mind was a whirlwind. What was going to happen next? He had agreed to Imperium's plans to save his friends but what of their future. Stuck here. And Imperium to take over the other world. This was not right.

"Why is he doing this?" Archie begged of Thompson.

"Come to the Prince's room, and I'll tell you more."

"No, I won't I need to get out of here." They arrived at another set of grand doors - the Prince's chambers. Two Persona stood outside, expressionless as ever.

"No Archie, come in here with me." They entered the room. Thompson grabbed Archie by both hands and whispered into his ear. "Trust nothing; open your mind to everything. We will protect you from those who wish you misfortune."

Chapter 16
Tilman Thompson

Archie stared at Thompson, unsure of what to make of what he had just heard.

"Why did you say that to me?" he questioned. Thompson smiled at him.

"Archie, I am Alium. I have been working deep undercover in Imperium for years. I have been passing information to my contact, but she has now been captured and is being held at the Grove."

"Minta?"

"Yes, and as you saw, they are all trapped there now waiting. My hand has been forced, and I need to get you to safety. You cannot stay here with your father; it's too dangerous. We are getting out of here."

"But how, there are Persona on the door, and the whole place is teeming with Imperium," questioned Archie.

"I'm not a spy for nothing, "grinned Thompson as he set off across the room. The Prince's bedroom was a circular room of grandeur. A large bed was opposite the door - potentially the grandest bed Archie had ever seen. A sumptuous curtain hung above the bed meeting in the centre below the golden cornice that surrounded every section of the room. To either side of the bed, were two plain wall panels with bedside tables in front of them. Then, moving around the edge of the room, large multi-paned windows looked over the palace gardens,

215

intermittently separated by chairs or dressing tables. Another door to the right led to what Archie could only assume was the escape route. Archie set off towards the door.

"That will get you nowhere other than the toilet," Thompson implied slightly embarrassed."

"But where…" before he could finish his sentence, Thompson was dragging a chair across the circular rug that almost covered the entire floor. As he crossed the centre, he lowered his head, fearing he may clash with the chandelier but it was too high in the ceiling to interfere with his head. At the left-hand side of the bed, Thompson positioned the chair and stood upon it. Grabbing the candlestick by the bed, he gave a sharp tug on it and twisted it left to right rapidly. The plain panel now popped out of its ornate frame and swung to the side.

"In case the Prince needs to escape quickly. This whole palace is full of secret passages. Follow me." With that, he disappeared through the doorway and was gone. Archie could feel a draft coming through the gap and stood on the chair. He seemed to be becoming more and more accustomed to these dark, mysterious passages. He stepped to the edge and suddenly found himself sliding down a long spiral tube. Now in the pitch black, the sensation mirrored that of a helter-skelter. He approached the bottom as he could see the light and Thompson was waiting for him. As he stood, he saw to his right a platform, like that he had arrived at the palace on. To the left a long tunnel that led into darkness, the flickering of candlelight the only source of comfort.

"Sorry, we're on foot tonight. We need to travel to places that would not be expected. Tonight, they will assume you will have gone home, to the surgery or through a gate. We must do none of these. I will take you to a safe house for tonight while a plan can be formulated to rescue the others. It is a bit of a trek, but you will be safe."

Down the endless tunnel they set off, for what seemed like a good hours walk. Archie surmised in his head to get out from under the grounds of the palace would take at least half an hour. After twisting and turning at the end of the long passage, and passing through barricades and boarded up doorways, they eventually reached a door that was locked.

"May I borrow your ring?" Archie leant forward and obliged. Thompson pushed the door slightly to peer through. The cold night air blew in, and Thompson appeared nervous for the first time in the plan. "Wait here a second, I'll check the coast is clear," and with that, he was gone. Moments later, he returned and ushered Archie out of the doorway. Looking around, he could see he was stood under a dimly lit archway. Peering up and down the street he could see a cobbled road, leading down into a dark, deserted warehouse. The other way, the way Thompson was leading him, was slightly better lit with street lanterns offering modest warmth as they moved up the street, hugging doorways and alleyways as they went. As they approached the brow of the hill, Archie could see a public house on the corner. He looked up at the hanging signboard, swaying gently in the night air and smiled to himself at the name of the pub - The Raven - a picture of the bird with a cane and top hat next to the title.

Archer led them to the establishment, and upon entry, Archie could see a very dark, dismal looking place. The wooden floors creaked with aches and pains as Archer strode across in his expensive leather boots. Furniture was sparse: a couple of tables, one stool and a couple of beer barrels- so punters could have something to lean against. The bar, if it could be called a bar, was a small gap in the wall. Archie thought the landlord might have a gun pointing through at any customers or unwanted visitors. The low ceiling was dripping with a liquid Archie could smell but had no idea what it was. The occasional drop would splatter onto his head and, if unlucky, would dribble past his nose or worst still, into his mouth. Archie hoped it was not the beer dripping through the ceiling from a leaky keg as he were sure it was some manner of poison. Terrible stains covered the walls and ceiling, and Archie was not in the least surprised to see there was no one in this evening.

"What are we doing here?" he questioned Archer.

"Quiet Archie," came the abrupt reply. "Now then my good man, can I possibly have a gin?" From the small gap in the wall, a face appeared. Long thin greasy hair hanging over a dirty stubbly face greeted them.

"Have ye got some money? No drink without money."

"Of course I have." Archer reached into his pocket and pulled out a golden sovereign.

"Hmm, I'll have that now," grunted the man. Times must have been hard if customer service was like this. The sale was important but having the money was imperative. Too many thieves and looters around. Archer flicked the coin through the gap in the wall and watched as the man caught it with his grubby hands and grunted to himself as he inspected it closely. He placed the coin between the few remaining teeth he had in his mouth and bit down hard. "It'll do, but I have no change."

"Then I'll take the bottle," Archer replied. Begrudgingly, the barman handed over the bottle, an oddly misshapen vessel with a cork in the top. Archer placed the cork between his teeth and pulled out the stopper with a pleasurable pop. He spat the cork onto the floor and took a large mouthful of the clear liquid. "Terrible," came the verdict as he offered Archie a drink. Shocked, Archie said no. He had never had an alcoholic drink, except for the one occasion he had opened the brandy decanter in his father's study and had a sip. A sip in front of Smetherly. Something that did not go unpunished. "Suit yourself,' he replied as he took another mouthful.

"What are we doing here?" Archie demanded.

"You will see very shortly." He moved away from the bar and ventured past into the side room. Often kept for meeting places or a quiet snug, Archer walked through a low, narrow passageway into a smaller room with just a beer barrel in the centre. He passed the barrel and stood behind it. Archie entered the minuscule room and was about to give up hope.

"What's going on?" Archer only smiled in return. Placing the now half empty bottle in his deep jacket pocket, he put both hands on the top rim of the barrel table. With a loud screech, Archer spun the metal trim around the edge as if he were unscrewing a jar. The lid rose slightly, and he flipped it up on its hinge. Archie could only see the very top of Archer's head now, and he wondered if he were going to climb into the barrel.

"Are you coming?" he asked Archie. Unsure of exactly where Archer meant Archie walked around the edge of the barrel. Archer now had his hands on the inside rim of the barrel, and he grasped inside as if he were desperate for a pint. Archie heard a clicking mechanism, as if cogs were moving and the barrel opened in two sections like a doorway. Archer stepped back as the doors spread out exposing a staircase. "This is the emergency exit normally, but now it's our entrance. On a night like this beggars can't be choosers." He disappeared down the staircase and Archie eagerly followed. The spiral steps led into a much brighter and stylish place. Pictures and glowing panels covered the curved, cavernous walls, framed by pipes snaking around with gauges and valves. Comfortable but straightforward furniture was set out neatly with a wide selection of people sat socialising: some chatting with friends, some drinking marvellous coloured liquids from equally uncommon vessels, some sat alone focused on small glowing devices in their hands.

Archer moved through the crowds of people towards the main bar. Archie gazed at his surroundings. On the wall a stag's head mounted with huge antlers reaching out; a mechanical eye-piece over one eye, identical to that worn by the Persona. Looking again at the pictures on the wall he saw flashing lights blinking repeatedly, and he recognised it as a Vigilate, matching the one he had seen at Ida's house. Where the dots representing people in the bar or elsewhere? The bar stood out like a beacon on a dark night. Green strip lights highlighted the base of the bar and underneath every shelf. High above top hats made light shades hanging from the ceiling as if every man at the bar had put their top hat there for safe keeping. The copper bar surface was held up by large coils that glowed as people approached. On top, a large pipe rose from one end, travelled across the bar and disappeared into the bar at the far end. Spaced out across the duct, various pumps ready to be pulled for a refreshing pint. Light fittings around the room consisted of old bottles, no longer in use, or taps and pumps pointing out from various positions with different implements ready to use.

Archie turned to see an old sea mine in the corner of the room now being used as a wood burner. A controlled source of power providing heat, not destruction. As he stood in awe of all these things he had to step back as a gentleman sat inside a giant wheel travelled through the building squeezing his horn as he passed, much to the annoyance of the locals drinking. A band played in the corner and he noticed an old man sat at a table with a pug across from him. The dog, wearing a bowler hat, was grunting to itself, licking his nose. He appeared to look at the timepiece hanging from his collar and abruptly stood up and shook the silver canister on his back. Two wings spread out either side and, following a short bark to the old man, he ran down the table and took off out of the bar. A variety of other Angelus custos were present also, and Archie gazed in amazement. Mechanical creatures: a fierce scorpion - the size of a cat, an owl and parrot, a hare and a snake. Likewise, there were living animals, but with the attire Archie had become used to. A pug wearing a leather cap and goggles; an eagle with leather strapping and an artificial wing - finished off with a top hat.

Archie suddenly realised he could no longer see Archer and he began to panic. Fighting his way through the crowd, he found himself in the middle of a dance as the band played. People whizzed around him dancing in formation, and he felt trapped on the dance floor.

"You never were much of a dancer," a familiar voice called out from behind him. He spun around instantly as he recognised the tone of his governess. He smiled and hugged her which was warmly returned. "Goodness me Archie, you have grown. I can only imagine the things you now know and the things you have seen. I have tried to contact you - myself, and through Abe, but you have been too well guarded. Well, at least you are safe now." Archie did not know what to say.

"Ms Buddington…" he stammered.

"I think we're a little past that now don't you. Layla will suffice from now on." She smiled warmly, and he felt relaxed, the most relaxed he had done in a long, long time.

"What are you doing here?"

"Well, I knew Tilman was going to bring you from the palace so I thought you'd like a friendly face. You know I have always been here for you Archie. Always."

"So, what happens now? What about my father?"

"Roker has no idea where you are. He could explore all over the city tonight, and he will never find you down here," Archer added as he beckoned the pair towards him. They passed away from the busier music side of the pub and found a small room in an offshoot from the main cavern. As they followed Archer into the snug, Archie saw three strangers he had never set eyes on before. "Allow me to introduce, Dewey Philpot, Florida Curtis and Captain Buster Harrison."

The first, Dewey Philpot, was a young man, perhaps only a few years older than Archie. He wore an oversized floppy hat with the customary goggle worn by most folk now. A burgundy waistcoat covered a traditional but filthy white shirt. So dirty in fact, it had almost turned brown. He wore deep green, knee-length velvet trousers though they, like the shirt, had seen better days, as the knee area was covered in rips and patches. Below this, black and white stripy socks, though one leg the stripes were much thicker than the other, creating a compelling optical illusion when staring for as long as Archie was. From one of his belts around his waist (for he wore two), many keys hung, not in a bunch but individually, equally spaced, perhaps for someone who struggled to find them in a bundle. The other belt, Archie assumed was for the technical task of stopping his trousers from falling down. Dewey was a very slender man with large ginger sideburns escaping from either side of the colossal hat.

Next to Dewey stood Florida Curtis. This lady looked very grand, and the rotating monocle over her left eye was the most striking feature about her. It spun around as it zoomed in and out, perhaps allowing her to see things more clearly. A telescope, attached to her eye. Her hair was all tied up, looking a little messy, but perched on top was the smallest top hat Archie had ever seen. It seemed as though she had stolen it from a child. Around her was she wore a tight, dark brown leather corset. The straps on the reverse must have been pulled extremely tight as the ornate clasps on the front looked close to bursting open any second. A long skirt cascaded from behind her with pleat after pleat of brown material, gushing like a chocolate waterfall. Her laced knee-length leather boots

223

were topped off with black and brown vertically striped stockings, accompanied by a golden sextant, hanging from a hook on the leather constraint around her torso. Suddenly, something jumped onto her shoulder - a tiny monkey. Archie thought it must be her Angelus custos, but upon closer inspection, he realised it was a real-life living monkey, perched happily, inspecting the new visitors.

Finally, Captain Buster Harrison, the most daunting of the three. Captain of what, Archie was unsure, but upon his head, he wore a military dress hat - tan brown, dark trim and a foreboding emblem on the crest. A winged skull with a pair of crossed swords underneath; the words Caeli Pirata embroidered below. Harrison, a handsome chap with rough stubble around his chin, wore a white silk scarf and a long, thick woollen jacket. Despite looking well worn, the grey garment still added a hint of charm and panache to this rugged character, matching the black shirt and silk waistcoat below. The points of the collar glistened in the light - silver and sharp - like an outlaw from the old west. Harrington had an air about him, not just his clothing, but an aura around him. The others seemed in awe and subdued by his presence. A definite leader. This, Archie felt, was the real reason he was the captain.

"Captain Harrison, at your disposal Archie," a dominant voice boomed. He extended a shovel hand and firmly grasped Archie's and shook it sending a ripple effect through his entire body. "If possible, can you update my crew and me on the current situation at the palace and Romani Grove."

"We need to save the people there. They are being held captive by Roker - my father. We need to do something."

"We know that Archie but you have the best insight into what is happening. Archer's inside info has been tremendous, but now we have you. Are you on our side?"

"Of course!"

"Then tell us what you know." Archie proceeded to tell all of what had happened - from the asylum, right up to the moment of leaving the palace. Harrison rubbed his hand across his coarse chin, thought for a moment and turned to the others. "We need to assemble the crew. Dewey, contact Fizkin and tell her to prepare the ship. Florida, send a message to Alium and tell them we need to get as many members as we can. The moment has come. We need the two worlds to collide."

"There's more, "Archie interrupted. "It's about the Queen. There's a machine. That looks just like her. The same. Why have they got a mechanical version of the queen?" The crew suddenly went silent - gazing at each other with knowing looks.

"Keiler's been at it again," Dewey surmised, breaking the silence.

"That's what my father said. So, there are more of them?" Layla, who had been very quiet up to this point suddenly interjected.

"Archie, I think I can answer this. Come with me." The others seemed to busy themselves with tasks or mumbling between themselves as Layla took Archie by the hand and led him out of the room.

"There's something you need to know." They had now entered a small room and were alone. "Sit down Archie. This information I am about to give you was not meant to

225

happen yet. It was thought that your life would be in danger if you knew the truth, that you'd run off and do something stupid. Something your father would not allow. Circumstances have changed, and you are now able to know the truth. This will come as a shock to you Archie, a big shock, but I want you to know something before I tell you."

"What is it?"

"Archie, I have looked after you from an early age. I have tried my best for you, and I have always put you first. Your happiness and safety are the utmost priority in my life." Even though Archie knew this, he felt overwhelmed, and a tear welled in the corner of his eye. "There's no easy way to say this."

"Say what?"

"My programming was to look after you, and with a few tweaks I have been able to adapt and, shall we say, keep secrets from my master."

"Programming? Master? You mean Roker?"

"Archie, I am not Maddie's twin sister."

"But you must be. You look identical."

"Archie, listen to me carefully. I am not Maddie's twin sister as I am not real. I am Keiler's first model." Archie looked at her. First model? Programming? It could not mean that, could it? "Archie, I am…" She paused with a look of sadness coming over her face.

"No, it's not true." Archie gasped. Layla removed her long black gloves. The gloves she always wore, and Archie could see a mechanical forearm, full of wires, gears and mechanical moving parts. "I am not alive. I was built by your father to protect you and look after you. And that is all I have done. I'm sorry now to cause you

226

disappointment, but that is the case. I am a machine." Inside Archie was turning upside down. After everything he had been through, after spending most of his life with this woman, he now knew the truth. However, something suddenly came over him. He sat and looked at the woman in front of him and for the first time in his life, he thought of her first. He stood, walked up to her and hugged her. He could feel in the response that this was the kindest thing he had ever done for his governess.

"You may be a machine Layla, but you're my machine, and I wouldn't change a thing."

"Thank you Archie, but there is more."

"More?" What else could there be.

"Your father decided to create me - with Keiler's assistance obviously - to replace your mother. Your father wanted someone who would be there for you always. Someone who he thought he could control. But Archie - he didn't create me to just replace your mother. He created me in the exact image of your mother."

"But that means…"

"Yes Archie, Maddie is your mother." Archie slumped back into his chair. He was lost for words. One second he felt he had lost the closest thing to a mother he had ever had, and now Archie learnt his mother was alive and he had already met her.

"But why didn't she say?"

"There are a lot of reasons I'm sure, your safety being the main one but that is for her to explain - when we rescue her."

"Then that's what we…" A deafening explosion rocked the building. Brick fragments and mortar fell from the rounded ceiling. Layla and Archie both fell to the floor. The blast was so loud, Archie was deafened. He saw Layla stand and pull him from the rubble. Her face blackened by the explosion, skin torn and the inner mechanics showing through. In his silent state, he observed Harrison enter the room and gesture them out. A muffled sound repeated a phrase over and over but Archie felt like his head was under water. He could not make out the sentence. He was dragged out of the room by his mechanical governess, and as they ventured down a dark corridor with sparks flying and flames licking the walls, the muted phrase became so apparent as his hearing returned.

"They've found us!" Archie's eyes closed as he lost consciousness.

Chapter 17
The Ducis

As he opened his eyes, Archie was unsure where he was. He tried to recall the last thing he could remember - the explosion in the pub. Now, Archie lay on a small bunk bed, covered in a thick woollen blanket, with a strange creaking sound coming from outside the wooden walls, as if groaning in discomfort. Archie gingerly swung his legs over the edge of the bunk and, rubbing his head; he felt a bandage over his crown. He pulled the dressing from his forehead, touched a rare piece of skin and felt alarmed as he stroked something mechanical on his head. Getting to his feet, he saw a mirror hanging on a chain, swinging from side to side and he grabbed it to view his injury. A heavily grazed and swollen patch was covered in a small metal clamp. Upon closer inspection, Archie could see it had many prongs on either side which appeared to be grabbing his flesh and pulling it tightly together. However it looked, it seemed to be working very well.

He now decided to investigate his surroundings further and turned towards the door. As he walked in that direction, he found himself swaying from side to side. Initially, he thought his injury had perhaps caused him to stagger, but as he looked around, he noticed all the furniture and accompaniments were attached to the wall or ceiling and were equally visible in their movement from side to side. He reached the door and peered

229

through the circular window. A cloudy mist was all he could see, so, raising his hand, he wiped the glass in case it was steamed up. No change. Lifting the latch on the door, he pulled it open. A strong gust of air blew into the room along with the mist, and he cautiously walked outside.

Archie could see nothing in front of him, barely being able to view his own hands outstretched before him. Still on a creaking wooden floor, he slowly ventured further forward until he came across a large wooden pole, so large he felt it was a tree trunk. Heading to the right, he shuffled onwards again, still with minimal vision. Slowly, the mist began to clear and Archie could see a barrier in front of him. He continued with the aim of grabbing the wall when suddenly, a large gust of wind almost blew him off his feet. The air cleared and before him, he saw blue sky and an enormous drop down to the ground below. Suddenly, he felt a hand grab him from behind.

"Careful Archie, don't go too close to the edge." He turned abruptly to recognise the face of Maria Fizkin, the lady he had seen at the train station what felt like years ago, after all that had happened in the last few weeks.

"Where are we?"

"You are on board Ducis, the lead ship of Caeli Pirata," Fizkin replied. "After what happened at The Raven, this is now the safest place for you. Roker is obviously after you and will stop at nothing to get you."

"But where are we?" continued Archie.

"I think the captain can explain that better." She pulled him away from the edge and, upon turning around, Archie could see he was on what looked like the deck of a ship, but up above a large zeppelin balloon was keeping them afloat in the, now bright, air. The unobstructed view enabled him to look at the deck, and he could see other crew members, resting, sat on the floor or on crates. The wooden pole he had nearly walked into was near the bow of the ship and, upon turning around, he could see the deck disappearing far into the distance. A selection of buildings and chimneys raised to various levels; the funnels emitting vast plumes of smoke. From multiple points of the hull, heavy cables sprung out, firmly attached and leading to the vast ribbed balloon above. Overhead, a small cabin appeared to be directly connected to the rubberised cotton shell, and a large barrel of a weapon protruded from the front. As he followed Fizkin to the stern of the ship, he finally got some real perspective on the size of the zeppelin. The vast blimp must have been over two hundred metres in length with three ample fins escaping from the rear, providing balance and stability. The array of various flues emitting from engine rooms or control stations eventually led to the bridge of the ship, and after climbing a spiral staircase, Archie found himself once again in the presence of Captain Harrington and other members of Caeli Pirata.

"Welcome aboard Archie," he announced in a booming voice. "How are you feeling after your injury?"

"Better thanks, but I don't remember much after the explosion."

"We had to evacuate The Raven as quick as possible. It was swarming with Persona within minutes of the blast. Luckily, we had a small ship nearby, and we were able to get you to safety."

"What about Layla?" Archie inquired in a concerned manner.

231

"She's fine; she's on board - somewhere. She is fixing herself shall we say." Archie thought back to the immense revelation and the news that Layla was mechanical and Maddie was his mother.

"Are we going for the others? Maddie? I mean my mother?"

"Yes Archie, the fleet is being assembled, and we are planning a rescue mission. At the same time, other ships in the fleet are going to destroy the gates meaning Similis will be available for all. It is time the two worlds collided and both worlds unite against Imperium. Once the population know about and can use our technology; once they know what Imperium have planned they will rise against them and Imperium will be powerless. They have control, but we plan to take that control away. The power of the few will be overrun by the might of the masses." Suddenly there was an interruption. Dewey Philpot rushed in with news.

"Captain, it has started."

"What do you mean?" Harrison replied.

"Persona have begun to infiltrate the normal world and are looking to seal the gates. I've had numerous reports of squadrons attacking towns across the country. It appears Roker has changed his plan. He is going to destroy this world and leave it in ruin as he, and Imperium, shift. There is a town not too far away that needs help. It is en route to the Grove. Shall we intercept?"

"Let's see what they are up to. Give the coordinates to the helm and let's take a look," came the order. A flurry of orders was passed down the chain of command, and suddenly, Archie felt the ship banking heavily to the right or starboard, and he felt he had to, once again, grip on for dear life. The ship was now increasing in speed, and Archie felt the wind rushing through his hair at a faster rate. "Let's go to the control room."

Again, down the plentiful deck they marched, but this time with a little more urgency than before. They ventured into a building, but Archie was amazed to see a grand staircase - one that would be at home in a five-star hotel - in front of him. The stairs spiralled up with splendid, ornate features all around, leading up to a room with many windows. In the centre of the room was a large map of the country, but with a touch or flick of the hand the map zoomed into specific areas, and Archie could see, as he passed, small sips moving around on the surface. Eight large windows - four per side - allowed sunlight to flood onto the bridge of the ship and Archie smiled to himself as smaller ornate windows with tiny latches and curtains allowed a view high up into the sky. A series of consoles were passed on either side, and Archie noted different crew members performing various tasks at each: navigation, defence, weather monitoring, engineering and so on. Each console was as technical as the last - a maze of dials and levers - some moving independently with no input from the operator. Archie felt he was in another world but then looked up and noted a magnificent chandelier hanging above as if he were in the dining room back at home. The grandness of a mansion met with the technology of a machine. Moving to the front of the bridge, Archie saw a vast window, an eye to the sky, made up of many smaller panes, and there, in prime position, was the ship's wheel. Dewey was manning the wheel as Archie approached and he turned and smiled.

"That'll do Philpot; we're on a mission." He turned back to face the glass panes and skies in front of him, but when Harrison turned, he gave a smile and a wink in Archie's direction, and then pulled a face behind the captain's back.

"We're approaching the town," called the person in front of the large map central to the room.

"Full speed ahead," ordered Captain Harrison, pointing to the horizon. "Hold nothing back. The target is dead centre." From the elevated position they were in, even at this distance, Archie could see huge plumes of smoke, rising into the air, like charred columns holding up the sky.

"What's happened?" Archie asked.

"Imperium. They have attacked. Not only are they using their full force, but they will be using machinery that most people will never have seen before. They will be terrified." The captain moved to the window on the left that faced downwards to the ground. "I can see them now. It looks like some Firewalkers and some Prodigium. Still on the outskirts of town, but causing devastation where they roam. We can take these out." He reached for a long funnel close to the helm of the ship, pulled it from its holster and placed it over his mouth. With the flick of a switch, he spoke, and the whole ship could hear. "Prepare the incendiary devices. Steady now. We are almost upon them."

Archie felt the ship suddenly lunge downwards, creating a strange sensation in his stomach, as if he had left it behind, further up in the clouds. Through the clouds they pierced until suddenly, the ground appeared, rushing towards them with such ferocity. Archie noticed the crew had now taken positions at the edge of the ship and were hanging over the sides with incendiaries at the ready.

"Fire!" came the command from the captain.

There was an eerie silence for several seconds as the bombs dropped to their final resting place. Then, like an orchestra tuning up, a chaotic noise from an array of locations, building to a crescendo of deafening noise. The ship shook with the after effect of the explosions, rocking from side to side like a baby at bedtime. As the sound echoed into the distance, the Ducis began to turn, and as it banked and swirled one hundred and eighty degrees, Archie could start to see the effect of the drop. Where the Prodigium had dominated the landscape, leaving destruction in its wake; now remained a crater and remnants of the cold machine strewn all over. The Firewalkers, permanently extinguished, left only individual plumes of oil-fuelled smoke, thick and acrid in bright sunshine.

"Excellent work, a successful mission," Harrison exclaimed. "Now onto Romani Grove." Archie felt himself take a huge sigh of relief, but this did not last long. A crew member rushed to where they were stood.

"Sir, there is news coming in from all over the country. The main gate in the east has been destroyed. There is now an open link between the worlds. We have found some people are leaving this world and shifting. It's causing chaos back home. But some further member of Alium have come through to Volgaris and are joining in the fight."

235

"That's good news," Harrison replied, "people fighting back. Together."

"Sir, there's more. That is the only piece of good news. Persona have taken control of most of the cities in the country. Thousands of them on the streets. Normal people going about their daily business are now terrified."

"Imagine seeing the Persona for the first time, never mind the Firewalkers or Prodigium. Technology is taking over their lives." Harrison added.

"What can we do?" Archie questioned. Harrison sighed and rubbed his rough chin.

"We need to continue the battle and move on Romani Grove. We must set the others free." Another crew member approached.

"Captain, more news. The main gate by the south coast has been sealed. Apparently, over half of the south has been overrun by Persona. Many people have lost their lives or have been rounded up. Sir, they are being burnt alive by the Firewalkers."

"We must do something," Archie cried, "we can't leave people to die."

"We won't Archie, but our priority is to free the remaining members of Alium at Romani Grove - including your mother." Archie agreed, nodding as positively as he could.

The journey to Romani Grove would be at least an hour and in that time, further news, both good and bad, came through to the Ducis. Messages were being sent in all manner of ways: some via Angelus custos, others by the Vigilate on board the ship and even via smaller vessels approaching and either docking with the Ducis mid-flight, sending encoded details via steam-powered flags or by some vessels flying parallel and a crew member shouting. Archie heard stories of towns being destroyed by a vast influx of Persona. Apparently, hordes of them had entered through the gates and platoons were roaming the towns and villages, killing and destroying everything in their way. Some brave folk had decided to fight back and used makeshift weapons and tools to attack. Against a Persona, one and one, an average man may stand a chance.

Further north though, the problem was much worse. Here, from a vast storage point in the hills, many Prodigium and Firewalkers were leaving the average man little hope. Notwithstanding the immense firepower of each of these fiendish devices, the sheer size and number of them meant they readily out armed the normal population. Reports on ingenious attacks upon these mechanical beasts did, however, bring some comfort. Through the Midlands, following intel about the Firewalkers, the residents decided to cover the ground with paraffin, regularly used in the mining industry. They then enticed a Firewalker in their direction and waited for the operator to ignite his weapon. He did not stand a chance with that much flammable liquid around and burnt himself to death. Other ships in the Caeli Pirata fought gallantly, destroying Imperium ships and protecting people in their towns and villages.

"Archie, try not to worry," Layla whispered to him as she approached the group on the bridge. "All's not lost yet. There are still a lot of people out there fighting for the good cause."

"I just wish there was more I could do," sighed Archie in response.

"But Archie, look at what you have done already. You have informed us of your father's plans, you have told us more about Romani Grove than we ever knew, who the real leader of Imperium is and you are now a member of Alium."

"I suppose so."

"But now you are shifting more regularly; I think it time you dressed a little more appropriately, don't you?" Archie looked down at his clothes and, the once smart and height of fashion items he wore, now looked tired, ripped and worn. "Come with me."

He followed Layla off the bridge and along the deck towards the centre of the ship. There, he found a vast staircase with moving platforms, gradually getting lower and lower. Layla stepped onto one and beckoned Archie to follow her. He uneasily hopped onto the next moving platform, and it followed the exact route Layla's had taken. The light disappeared, and he found himself in the belly of the ship where huge pistons drove in and out emitting vast amounts of steam and an array of strange noises. Down a corridor they went until they passed through a door with a porthole in it. Suddenly the sounds melted into the background, and they found themselves in a long hallway with numerous doors leading off.

"Crew quarters," Layla announced. "Dewey said he might have some clothes that fit you." An uncomfortable ten minutes followed with Archie trying a selection of, as he initially felt, uncomfortable clothes. Up until this point, he had always worn the best, but the wardrobe in front of him would have left his tailor in despair. Initially, he chose a smart black silk shirt with equally dark marching trousers. Nothing out of the ordinary there. The waistcoat he put on was, again silk, but interwoven with an elaborate, intricate pattern. The main difference was the scarlet red material that shone like a beacon from the dull, ordinary room he inhabited. As smart as he always looked, avant-garde colours like this were frowned upon by his father as risqué. This, along with the double set of silver buttons which gleamed as if being presented to loyalty, made Archie feel uneasy. Next, he chose a long, three-quarter length leather jacket: double-breasted, fur interior, assorted ebony buttons, adding to the decoration on the front of the jacket.

Archie turned to show his new attire to Layla, in a lame attempt to gain approval. As he did, she presented him with an oversized cap, proudly boasting a pair of goggles, the kind all the new visitors Archie had met wore. He placed it upon his head.

"Perfect," Layla approved, grinning knowingly.

"I'm not so sure," Archie questioned, unconvinced with his new look.

"You need some accessories," she added. She proceeded to open a wooden box and inside, Archie saw a leather hand strap, adorned with straps, rivets, buttons and dials. "Now you're a member of Alium; you can now be contacted or contact command when you need to."

"Thanks," Archie responded gratefully.

"And you can contact Abe, whenever you need! I think that will be the most useful thing you will gain from all of this." A sturdy pair of leather boots were the final piece of the clothing jigsaw, and Archie now felt ready, or as ready as he could to face his crewmates and the battle ahead. "Now listen carefully, I need to leave. I have been given a mission by your mother, and I must complete it. I will take a small craft from here, but I will meet you at Romani Grove."

"But..."

"No buts Archie, you must do as I say and follow Harrington's orders." Archie reluctantly agreed and hugged Layla. She was his governess, his protector, but now, more than ever, his friend. Following her onto the deck, Archie gazed in wonder as a smaller zeppelin docked by the side of the Ducis. The pilot climbed on board, and Layla proceeded to exchange places, sitting in the single seat in front of a whirring propeller. With a wink and a wave, the craft edged away from the bow of the ship and disappeared into the cloud.

Stepping away from the edge, he was greeted by a mixture of gasps, whistles and sarcastic comments. Gingerly, Archie decided to ignore them all and made his way back to the bridge. Once there, Harrison made him feel at home by reporting back on the latest news he had. The country was in disarray. Yes, people had been fighting back, against an unknown enemy, but overall, people were scared and left with nothing. The power and might of Imperium had been too dominant. Archie grimaced with a feeling of hated running through his veins. He must help. He must do something. But what? He tried collating his thoughts, but so many were running through his head. He felt he must say something, but before he could, upon the bridge, the order came.

"Romani Grove approaching. Target dead ahead."

Chapter 18
Terror at The Pike

Romani Grove seemed deserted as the Ducis entered the airspace above the vast expanse. As the ship moved over the grounds, crew members swung into action: abseiling to the ground via rope and high tech hooks, mini escape pods resembling minute submarines dropped into the darkness or via parachute with mechanical backpacks, enabling the parachutist to move both horizontally and vertically.

"A ship this big is impossible to land in a place like this. We need somewhere to dock," Harrison quizzed, again scratching his rugged chin.

"I know just the place," Archie replied. "The beacon, on top of the hill." He moved to the edge of the ship and scanned the horizon for the beacon. Sure enough, in the distance, glowing like hot coals in a blown fire pit, the beacon gave Harrison what he needed.

"What else is around there Archie? We can't risk running aground."

"You should be fine there Captain, that is the highest point around by far." The numbers on board Ducis had now dropped rapidly due to the evacuating crew, so now, a skeleton crew remained.

"Archie, back on the bridge, follow the stairs down, and you'll find a gantry. This will enable you to get to the ground quickly. I will send a platoon with you." Archie set off for the lower recess of the bridge, and sure enough, as Harrison had promised, Archie found the gantry. He stood at the end of the long metal bridge, either side, decorated with an ornate black iron meshwork, below his feet, a simple grid lattice, diagonally weaving out in front of him. But what now?

Looking around, he saw a large lever on the wall with a round button next to it. Which would it be, he thought to himself. Unsure, he decided to push and pull at the same time. A decision that he was about to regret. The lever lowered the gantry, and it slid out like a telescope, heading to the ground, but the button turned the criss-cross lattice he stood on into a toboggan- a toboggan that set off at high speed down the gantry.

Clinging on for dear life, the metallic slide brought Archie to ground level and as he had set off on his journey, his platoon he had been promised appeared at the top of the gantry. As they prepared to follow Archie down the gantry, Crowle appeared from the Pike and confronted Archie. He withdrew an oversized revolver and pointed it towards the beacon. Initially unsure of the following plan, Archie soon sighed with great dread as he began concocting what he thought Imperium had planned. The Ducis had managed to dock very quickly, and now Archie was on the ground, alone with only Crowle for company. And Crowle had a weapon to hand. He fired the revolver towards the beacon.

At first, nothing happened, but soon the reason was apparent. The anchor and tow rope that held Ducis in place docked to the Pike swayed. In an instant, the beacon erupted into flames, flames that now lapped up the tow rope. If the fire were to reach the ship, disaster would follow. Archie waved his arms in desperation. The flames crawled further up the line and Archie could tell the Ducis was now in emergency stations. As the ship pulled up and severed the fiery tie with the ground, the gantry, upon which the platoon had started to progress creaked and moaned under the strain of the ship. Pieces of metal fell like ash following a volcano, the cries and screams of platoon members falling to their deaths high above. The sudden realisation dawned upon Archie. He had led Ducis to Romani Grove, he was alone on the ground, and the ship was in terrible danger. It was a trap.

From the ground, Archie could see the sails and propellers moving frantically in the opposite direction, enabling greater manoeuvrability from the colossal ship. Part of the tether still hung from the bow and, although most flames had passed, some again teased their way up to the rope to certain doom for the ship. Like a long fuse on a stick of dynamite, Archie watched helplessly. Surely Captain Harrison would be able to see this through. Suddenly a figure appeared at the top of the tether and, upon closer inspection with his magnifying goggles, Archie could see it was Dewey. Taking a mechanical clamp from his belt, he gripped it onto the rope. Powerful claws, like mechanical fingers, grasped the line and holding tight, Dewey swung out into the air and slid down the tow rope. As he dropped vertically, his velocity increased, and Archie began to fear for his friend. Not only were flames licking the long-gone link, but the rope was cut short. If Dewey could not stop before the end of the cable, he would inevitably succumb to the flames.

Acrobatically, Dewey swung himself upside down while moving at high speed. Now, from the clamp, a large shape emerged, like an umbrella, but shiny, as if made from silver. Dewey now reverted to his original stance and, through Archie's binocular goggles, it appeared Dewey was stood on top of a falling umbrella. A fantastic sight from the ground was only made more spectacular by the next feet. As the cover reached the fire, it extinguished it as quick as the umbrella moved down the rope. At the foot of the tether, the umbrella abruptly halted. Now, it turned from an umbrella into a sizeable spear-like harpoon. Dewey's clamp now fizzed into action and shot upwards, with Dewey stood upon it, back towards the Ducis. The battered and bruised ship withdrew slightly to regain its position and steady itself.

Archie sighed with relief but this soon dissipated when he felt Crowle's revolver attachment from his hand-piece press against his head. The faceless monster beckoned Archie towards the blazing beacon with the barrel of the gun and Archie reluctantly heeded the beast's command. As he plodded towards the inferno, almost pushing his skull back into the revolver, Archie noticed large doors sliding open across the floor on either side of the beacon. Then, like a flower protecting itself as it closes for night time, four large petals lifted from below the dark ground and rose to meet at a point above the blaze. As they did, the oxygen was extinguished from the fire, and the flames died down. Through one of the sliding doors on the ground, Archie saw a flight of stairs leading into darkness - the path that Crowle was now telling him to follow. Into the gloom he stepped, and as he placed a foot on the first step, the edge sparkled into life guiding him down - down to the unknown. This repeated on each level as the pair moved down - leading them one step at a time.

Archie gazed around him as he slowly moved further down the staircase, but nothing could be seen. Above him, the little light that came from the outside ended as the sliding doors rolled back into place. As soon as the grinding mechanism dragging the shutters ceased, the darkness was suddenly illuminated. Archie could see the steps illuminating, one at a time in front of him, slowly first, but then rapidly increasing. The view before him became more spectacular as the lights progressed, for Archie could see the steps spiralling down the inside of the summit with a vast abyss in the centre. Further and further the lights went until the spiral ended and a circular base now came into focus. As Archie and Crowle moved further down to the base, now fully illuminated, Archie saw Roker stood waiting for him.

Archie was unsure how he felt at this moment. His father had let him down, disappointed him and betrayed him. Archie considered charging at him and attacking the monster, but he then remembered the other beast with a gun at his head, following him step by step. He did not want to speak to his father, but he had so many questions. As Archie and his captor stepped onto the base, he could see Roker smiling at him, but he was unsure of how to take the smile.

"Hello Archie; impressive isn't it," he arrogantly stated. "The headquarters of Imperium. This is our sacred meeting place where members come to worship their master."

"You, I suppose you mean?" Archie responded sarcastically.

"Yes Archie, I have the power. The world as you knew it, I control. There is nothing Imperium cannot govern.

We have taken what we want, what we desire. We have left people in ruin and left them with no hope, and they have little idea what or who has caused it."

"But why? You have the power to do so much good; why ruin this world?"

"Why? Because I can. I once thought of changing the world for a better place but where was my appreciation? As soon as I had some ideas of grandeur, for you and your mother, then things changed. She didn't want that. She just wanted to think of others. The good of society over the wealth of individuals. There are so many people in this world who do nothing yet demand everything in return. Why should I work hard to provide for them? So, I decided that things needed to change. This world had to be cleansed - made right. People who did not perform would perish as there is no place for dead weight. Why should I work every hour possible while some man sits at home expecting handouts from the state? I tried to tell your mother it would not work but she wouldn't listen. So, I took up the mantle of Imperium. As you now know, Imperium has always been here, in one form or another, but I have now brought it up to date. I control everything. And now I have taken all I can from this world, I am now going to watch it burn. Then, when there is nothing left, I will do the same in that other world your mother calls home. Imperium will dominate there, infiltrate their society and, using tried and tested methods, dominate again. They have used steam to advance their technology; we will use it to control them. We have done it here. A simple inoculation in the past for Imperium and we are immune. It is that simple."

"That is your plan?" Archie questioned.

"Yes. Destroy here - now we have taken all we want. Then, move onto the next place, leaving the dead wood trapped here."

"You're the plague. The disease. Like locusts. Think of the people you will hurt and kill."

"It's what they deserve. The world will be purged, and a new order can start." Archie watched on in horror as he saw the crazed look in his Roker's eyes. Never had he seen him like this before. A madman - suitable only for Wilberforce's asylum.

"You're insane, a megalomaniac!" Archie blurted, unsure of what else to say.

"No, I am in control. And you could have it all. All of this could be yours, Archie. All you have to do is join me."

"Never!"

"Well, I thought you'd say that. Therefore, I have asked Bilton to develop a new kind of medicine. A mind control potion. You are my son and, whether you like it or not, you will join me. I'd rather it was through free will, but if not then I'll take it in any way I can. And if the mind control doesn't work, there is always another option. Tonight, will be the greatest night in Imperium's grand history. All members will congregate in this great hall and witness the pinnacle of human evolution. Led by myself of course." Roker now turned as if he were addressing a vast audience, but emptiness was all that surrounded him, and his calls echoed around the vast space."

"What about Maddie? My mother? Your wife?" Archie pleaded, trying to change Roker's view. "What will happen to her?"

"She showed her true colours many years ago. She picked her side."

"Why did you never tell me about her? Why did I find it out from others? And Layla too. Why did you make her? Why did you make her look like Maddie?"

"Archie, do you remember many years ago the day you were out with Ms Buddington and you were attacked?"

"How can I forget? I still have nightmares about it." He shuddered to himself at the thought of the events of that day and the continued effect it had on him.

"Tell me, Archie, how do you recall the events of that day?"

"We were walking back from town, and we were attacked by some men. One of them wore a mask like the one Marsden wore - the silver skull mask. Layla told me to run. I did, but I fell and banged my head. The last thing I remember seeing was that silver skull staring down at me before I blacked out. Was that Marsden? It would make sense that it was him."

"Interesting thoughts Archie, interesting. And what do you remember before that?"

"Before that? Not very much. You have made it so I can't remember much before that. No pictures of us as a family. No baby pictures. No memories for me to think of as a young child. It feels like my life started that day."

"That's because it did Archie. Have you not put the pieces together yet?"

"What do you mean?" Archie questioned. What did Roker mean by that? His life started that day? Now Archie desperately tried to remember anything from before that date. The more he thought about it, the more he realised he couldn't. What had happened? What had Roker done?

"Archie, the events of that day have shaped your life. That is why you are destined to be a member of Imperium. You joined that day. You became one of us. You haven't realised it since then, but now the truth is ready to speak to you, and you must listen carefully. Shall I fill in the details of what happened that day?" Archie nodded with a degree of trepidation. What could Roker possibly tell him? "Prepare for the truth, Archie. Yes, that day you were attacked by a group of men, but I feel attacked is a little strong, especially when one of them was me." The realisation began to dawn on Archie's face.

"You... but... why?"

"Think Archie, think," he whispered sinisterly with eyes wide, glaring into Archie's soul.

"Why would you attack Layla and try and kidnap me. Why didn't you just wait until I got home? Why wear the mask? What had Layla done...?" He broke off, and the realisation hit him like a steam locomotive at full speed. "It wasn't Layla, was it? It was Maddie! You took me from my mother. You attacked my mother and me and kidnapped me."

"Now the penny drops." Roker walked towards Archie clapping his hands in a slow, sarcastic manner. "Now you see. That fool of a mother kept you from me. When you were younger, we agreed on nothing. You lived with her most of the time, and I had only minimal contact with you. I had such great plans and told your mother that you would live with me. In our house, a state suitable for a child of mine. Not in some commune in a steam-filled world. That is what your mother had wanted.

To take you there, away from me and your destiny. So, I said I wouldn't allow it. Your mother planned to leave and never let me see you again, claiming I was insane, but I had planned your future from the day you were born. So Crowle, Marsden and I came for you. A simple plan. As you were so young, you wouldn't remember much before that, especially if you had no reference points for it for the rest of your life. So, we disguised ourselves and attacked your mother."

"I cannot believe this." Archie stood dumbfounded. His childhood had been a lie.

"Your mother tried gallantly to protect you, but we soon put an end to that. You managed to stop yourself by falling and banging your head. We had time to put things in place then, and you would never know any different."

"Know any different?" Archie was disgusted with Roker now. "What do you mean?"

"Well Archie, it's quite simple. Once we had your mother, we took her to the asylum and kept her locked up. You had, how shall we call it, a little memory-erasing potion and you were kept unconscious for a few months. In that time, I had Keiler build Ms Buddington. She was magnificent. It put any of those steam-powered contraptions to shame. She learnt behaviour and her strict manner made it easy for her to be a governess. The perfect cover. Your mother escaped back where she belonged and Crowle was put in charge of ensuring the security of the gates; you were never to know. However, as it turned out, some members of Alium could bypass his security and infiltrate certain members of your inner circle. Ms Buddington was made aware of her position and, even that scullery maid, was told. I had to see how

250

much you knew and which side your loyalties lay with. Unfortunately, you have let me down Archie, and now you will be made to follow. As so many others before have."

He became even more animated as he spoke, moving around the room like a crazed politician, stating his latest manifesto. Archie was amazed that Roker believed all this nonsense and was willing to sacrifice so much for his own gain. Suddenly, there was loud chiming noise. A repetitive droning bell, ringing over and over. As it echoed around the chamber Archie noticed more people entering the vast cavity.

"Ah, my friends, you have finally come." Archie gazed around the room and shuddered at the presence of so many evil characters in one place. All wore the Imperium clothing, as Archie had once worn, but they wore a multitude of masks covering their faces. Many had a skeletal feel to them, with hideous accessories as appendages. One, a black skull, had a faded gold trim around the ocular and nasal cavities. Spikes protruded from the top and a mixture of cogs and jigsaw pieces covered the forehead. Another appeared to, like Crowle's mask, cover the complete skull. Rivets came from the temple and met between the eyes leading to a mouth that could only be described as a mechanical metal squid. The tentacles, though industrial in nature, squirmed and moved as if alive. Others wore simple leather face straps covering mouth and nose, with goggles to complete their disguise. Some of these appeared to have sewn up mouthpieces or spikes emanating from where the mouth should be.

The mass entrance ended as soon as it had started and Archie panicked at the thought of the number of Imperium members around him. Perhaps even more than that, he wondered what Roker would do to him next. Roker raised his arms and a sudden worried hush came over the crowd.

"So Archie, the time has come. Are you going to join us of your own free will? Or shall we use other methods?" Roker began to roar with laughter and nervous chortles followed from the baying masses around.

"I will never follow you. I am no son of yours. You have made my life a lie and I will never be your son."

"As you wish. Bilton?" From the crowds, the mechanical squid-faced character moved forward. As he edged towards Archie, the tentacles on the face rose and pulled apart the mask, revealing Bilton's slightly psychotic face.

"You won't get away with this. The Ducis is here - and its crew," Archie threatened.

"Ahhh yes, the ever-dependable Captain Harrington. Archie, as you saw before your precious Ducis was nearly destroyed. It won't be long before Imperium's fleet destroy that and all the other Alium ships. As we speak, a battle is taking place above us in the sky. I have it on good authority from Crowle that Imperium outnumber Alium by at least ten to one. It is only a matter of time before that become ten to none." Roker turned and raised his arms to the assembled crowd and acknowledged them all. A slow, murmur developed in the spectators until Archie could make out the chant, a slow drone,

"Dominus, Dominus, Dominus!" As they chanted, vast plumes of steam vented from the floor and walls. The temperature was high and sweat ran down his face. He looked around for an exit, but nothing made itself clear. The hideous, masked faces were all around, some flickering in the flame lit room, others covered in condensation, making them appear even more ghastly than before. All of Imperium here in one room, all wanting Archie. Everything seemed lost.

"Bilton, the potion please." Roker was handed the potion and Bilton moved behind Archie. He felt overwhelmed by the presence of so many crazed individuals and stepped back into the path of Bilton. Suddenly, something grabbed his head and he felt he was unable to move. Realising what held him, Archie could see the tentacles of Bilton's mask holding his skull and shoulders.

"Now then Archie, you have had this potion before. Right at the time you left your mother and joined me. Now you will join me again. When you awake, all this will be over and you will be at my side as the heir of Imperium." Roker's eyes widened with a horrific joy as he opened the potion and poured it into Archie's prised open mouth. His mouth was then clamped shut and his nose held tight. The potion was swallowed, Archie was released and he fell to the floor. He closed his eyes, anticipating the worst and listened as Roker's laugh and the audience's chants became louder and louder.

Chapter 19
Battle in The Skies

The potion had a sickly taste and made Archie feel queasy, but that was the only feeling he had. He had expected to black out, forget where he was and be panic-stricken. However, none of these symptoms appeared. He remained on the floor, unsure of what Roker would do if he stood. The feelings of confusion ran wild in Archie's mind. The man he had looked up to all his life had let him down - Archie felt he could never recover. He tried to think back to the day he had been attacked as a small boy but the image was distorted now. He had spent so long trying to forget the image and now he could no longer recall it. The flashbacks had been a curse, but now he knew the truth, he could not remember all the facts. He thought about his mother, Maddie and his missed relationship with her. He thought about the lies and plans Roker had put in place throughout much of his life and how he now felt that his life was a lie - a facade that he had no control over - and now Roker was planning to control it even more. Yet it did not seem to be working.

Archie felt sure he must feel different, drowsy at least, but the fact he lay on the floor still completely in control of his senses, he was sure something must have gone wrong from Roker's point of view - fortune must have been on his side. The chanting of Dominus lingered in the air along the vast jets of steam and Archie felt the audience had grown and was consuming the room, suffocating the freedom from him. Roker stood in the centre of the cavernous hall arms outstretched, receiving the adoring chants from the masses.

"He is mine, the world is mine and Imperium will take what they wish." Roker looked like an inmate of the asylum, taking accreditation for a dastardly deed - perhaps an escape, or inflicting pain and torture on another inmate. Roker was certainly taking pleasure in his ability to control Archie, Imperium and, in his head, the world.

"I'm not yours," Archie responded as he took to his feet and confronted Roker.

"Well, this is a little surprising I must say," came the reply. Roker now looked a little uneasy and glanced at Bilton, who was now edging away from the spotlight. "I see that if I want something doing I must do it myself!" Bilton now melted into the crowds at the sides. Archie and Roker stood facing each other and began pacing slowly in circles, as a boxer would at the start of a bout - watching each other's moves, anticipating the next jab. The sweat dribbled down their faces - either from the pressure of the situation or the pressure of the steam in the vault.

"You cannot do this," Archie pleaded, "it's not right, can't you see?"

"No Archie, I have explained, I have done all this for you. I only wanted the best for you, for you to live a life of a king."

"But I haven't lived my life, you have controlled it all. You have taken away my freedom, my choice."

"I did it all for you and look at the thanks I get. If you won't join me Archie, I cannot let you continue. You will have to stay here as this world tears itself to pieces. Is that what you want? A world with no order? A world taken back a couple of hundred years?"

"Never mind a couple of hundred years, I would like to go back to my childhood and live again. I want to live a normal life - nothing fancy or grand - just a childhood with my mother. The thing you have taken away from me. My life has been a lie, I have lived it for you, not for me. You have taken away my very soul and I am now left with nothing. I am struggling with what to believe. You have robbed me of that and Alium have filled the void. That is your doing."

"Look around Archie, where are Alium now? You are surrounded by Imperium. You were born for Imperium, you are destined to be Imperium, I have made sure of that." Archie stared in horror at the covered hoards around him. Even if he escaped Roker in the ring he would have hundreds of other loyal Imperium members to pass. Another blast of steam filled the air; the temperature rising constantly.

"It doesn't matter, you have taken what was mine and I will never forgive you for that."

"Then Archie, here you will stay."

The call from the crowd had silenced as they spoke: the loyal dogs were eager to hear their master's words. However, their salutation began again. Quiet to start with but building, in a divergent manner. The low rumble and murmur changed and Archie could clearly hear something else.

"Alium, Alium, Alium!" Roker heard the same thing too and looked around bemused at what was happening.

Why were his loyal followers now chanting the name of their sworn enemy?

Even though the chant for Alium was rising, Archie could see the uneasiness of the masked characters at the base of the crowd. Disguised appearances worryingly glancing in all directions to account for what was happening. No answer was becoming apparent and a masked character approached the pair in the spotlight. The cloaked figure had its face obscured by the oversized hood, worn by many, but as it entered the light of the main arena, the features became more apparent. The blackened eyes were surrounded by an orangey red colour which emphasized the eyes even more so; the nose-piece protruded slightly, shining and flickering in the flame lit hall with a thin layer of condensation; and upon closer inspection, as the robes were opened, a silver heart with a robin engraved into the shiny surface. Archie could not help but smile at the masked character in front of him, for he now knew this was no stranger.

"Layla," Archie muttered under his breath - as if saying it any louder would put his protector into harm's way - despite the fact she was surrounded by hundreds of Imperium members.

"Step away from my boy," she commanded as her hood was lowered. There she stood, with her familiar ice-white face and blood red lips, but no longer the long black dress, now trousers and a velvet jacket. Around her neck, she wore a pair of goggles, and in her hand, an ebony cane with the familiar site of Avem perched upon the end. Around her waist, she wore a belt with an array of trinkets and gadgets attached. Some appeared to be cogs, others, precious jewels.

"Your boy? He has never been your boy, you mechanical menace."

"He has been more my boy than yours through his life. What have you done for him? Nothing."

"Silence," bellowed Roker, "I am your master and creator and you will obey me."

"No, not anymore. I haven't been your slave for many years, merely pretended. Maddie made sure of that. Having been reprogrammed all that time ago, I was given the assignment to protect Archie - from you. I was to watch over him until contact was made. We have been one step ahead of you all this time Roker. Now - now is Alium's time. We have overcome the struggle and we will take back what's ours." Roker laughed out loud. He could not believe what he was hearing.

"Are you insane? I think your programming has gone a little off track. You are alone in the stronghold of the most powerful force that has existed in society now or in our past. You are outnumbered and have no possible chance of escape. However, I am intrigued, please tell me how you intend to stop me."

"Well Mr Roker, you are correct, my programming has changed from when I was created but my primary goal still stands. To protect Archie, and I will do that with my life."

"But very soon Ms Buddington, you will be terminated and who will protect him then?"

"I haven't finished yet. You may have your chemists in Imperium to provide your steam induced diseases but Alium also have the same. And Roker… who said I was alone?" Behind her back, Layla opened a small satchel and a glass canister was presented. At this signal, many members of the crowd revealed themselves around the inner circle: Ida Redgrave, Randall Krewler, Minta Abberton, the Colonel. Then a face that filled him with joy. There stood Kat, grinning. Archie let out a sigh of relief as the prisoners had been released. If they had all been released then that would mean...

"It's over Roker," called out a recognisable voice from the crowd. From the shadows behind Roker emerged another hooded figure, and when the character revealed themselves, the gasps of surprise filled the room. There, opposite Layla on the other side of the ring, stood Maddie. Identical in looks with the same pale face minus the lipstick. Her hair flowed down freely over her shoulders and her clothing looked like she had spent a few days in questionable circumstances but Archie did not care. His mother was free.

"Archie, you ok?" Archie nodded. "Roker, as you can see, you are surrounded. Layla, would you like to tell everyone what is in the canister in your hand?"

"It would be a pleasure." Layla walked forward and circled the position in which Roker stood. The circular tiled floor of the chamber (similar in width to a boxing ring), was wet from the moisture in the air and this made the fox emblem in the centre of the floor reflect in the light. "As you are all aware, Imperium are terrorising this world and plan to do so on the other side. One of their primary means is a poison which is spread through steam. Some of you may not be aware that Imperium's chemist, Bilton, inoculated members of Imperium, allowing them to continue to live without fear of the steam. Giving them a godly appearance with power over death. However, our chemists have been working equally hard and have created a colourless, odourless gas that will affect only the people Bilton inoculated. Therefore, the members of Imperium. A genius approach I'm sure you'll agree. All we had to do was entrap all the members of Imperium in one place where there is an influx of steam. And Imperium provided it for us."

"We know how much you like your little secret societies and meetings," Maddie added. "We also knew that by capturing all of Alium you would gather everyone together. So, whilst you have been telling Archie and the rest of Imperium how amazing you are, Layla has been releasing us from our cages. A few simple guards were nothing for someone of Layla's ability." She turned and smiled at the mechanical character with such identical features. It really was hard to believe that Layla was not human. However, Archie felt her more human, had more of a soul than Roker ever had.

"My followers will just leave," Roker came back at the challenge.

"No, they won't," replied Maddie, "for we have others. Alium has never been strong enough to take on Imperium alone, but you have opened the gates for us. This world knows about us now. They know our ways and our machines. They know your plan and they have united. Since we learnt of your intentions, we have circulated The Daily Verum from town to city across this country. People are ready. They know about Imperium and people will not put up with it. The men in power cannot and will not control the will of the masses."

"The door is protected, you cannot get out of this cavern. There is only one entrance and it is blocked by the people of this world," Layla added. "All I need do is smash this canister and Imperium are immobile." Archie smiled at the beauty of the plan. Using Imperium's own plan against them. He turned and looked at Roker. The man's usual arrogant look was still there but he had the air of a man who had something on his mind. Archie could tell he was worried; that he was thinking on his feet.

"You're bluffing," was his only reply.

"Are we?" Maddie retorted. "Are you really going to take that risk? I doubt that very much. The Ducis is above and more people loyal to Alium are on their way."

"Ahhh, the Ducis. Well, I think you'll find we have a match for that."

"Volantem Mortem!" Archie cried.

"Exactly. Now let us see who has the power." Roker reached to the control panel on his forearm and attempted to turn some dials.

"Don't," Layla ordered. Roker laughed.

"Or you'll drop it? Do it." He walked towards Layla and grabbed the canister. Archie and Maddie both sprinted forward, trying to grab the glass cylinder, helping Layla. This proved to be in vain and, as the four of them tussled, the canister was raised into the air then knocked from the security of Layla's hand. It was clear Roker was not going to be bargained with and had made his mind up. As they scrambled trying to retrieve the glass cylinder before it smashed on the floor, Roker relocated himself away from the chaos, moving to the centre of the circle base. He stood directly upon the fox's head and, after moving several dials on his wristband and pushing a button, the central panel of the floor dropped away and Roker vanished through a trap door. In the confusion with the canister, several other members of Imperium - including Crowle and Bilton - also disappeared.

The attempts to save the canister proved fruitless as the cylinder smashed into hundreds of pieces upon the floor; the clear gas escaping into the cavernous void. Not the end of the world as now, most Imperium would be contained and rendered immobile, but vital members, including Roker, had escaped. Archie moved without thinking and jumped straight down the trapdoor. The shouts from Maddie could be heard fading into the background as he travelled down a spiral slide. The noise behind him led him to believe other members of Alium had the same idea.

After several seconds of spiralling down, Archie reached the base. He found himself in what appeared to be a doorless and windowless room. Maddie, Ida and Krewler followed down the chute into the room.

"It's no use, he's gone. How did he get out?" Archie cried in despair.

"Not so fast lad," Krewler beamed. "Has tha got tha ring on?"

"Of course." Archie recalled the many doors he had opened using the ring and he, along with the others, began searching the wall for some indentation that would allow an exit from the trap they were in. "It's got to be somewhere, come on."

"Got it," Ida exclaimed. Hidden neatly in the mortar between the brickwork, was a small impression - the perfect match for Archie's ring. He pressed it up against the hole and the brickwork moved away in a plume of steam. Methodical, mechanical, almost magical, Archie thought. A long, flame-lit passage was set out in front of them and along it they ran. Unsure of what would be at the end, Krewler took the lead, pointing his weapon forward. The others also produced firearms of some sort as they ran. Krewler reached the end first, and raised his left forearm - fist clenched - to stop the followers. They all froze as he edged to the end of the passage - his weapon poised ready.

"Oh flippin' 'eck," he called as he ran out into the darkness. Archie looked at Maddie as they decided to follow him out. There they could see the giant box being hoisted up into the sky towards the dark clouds above and, what Archie could only assume, was Volantem Mortem hidden away from view.

"They're getting away," Archie exclaimed, "we've got to stop them." Maddie pressed some buttons on her wrist pad and said,

"Help is on its way, we need to get to the top of the Pike." They turned to see both the pigeon tower and Pike behind them in the distance. "Ducis is on its way. They are a bit battered and bruised but ready for action. There is a squadron of Canemvolantes en route. They will start the fight." As they progressed up the hill, they kept a watchful eye upon the giant cube raising heavenwards. In the distance, a slow rumbling sound - a consistent growl and there in the distance over the hill, the squadron of Canemvolantes appeared.

Looking like a volley of torpedoes aiming for their target, the Canemvolantes were not huge, but they were very quick. They would certainly leave an airship behind and in a dogfight in the skies, they would be priceless. About ten metres in length, the entire body looked like a missile, enabling its aerodynamic movement through the air. A tiny module sat at the rear in which a single pilot sat. Air rushed through the gap at the front, rotating the spiral coil at such high speeds it enabled them to stay in the air. At the rear, a propeller spun and could be manoeuvred by the pilot to change the craft's direction. The pale brown bodywork had a dirty white band around it with the Caeli Pirata emblem emblazoned for all to see. Gun turrets poked from the front of the ship, ready for what lay ahead.

Due to the arrival of the squadron, the escape cube of Imperium slowed to a halt. Realising they would be sitting ducks, evasive action was taken and an escape pod jettisoned from the base of the lift. Although only a small craft, like the Canemvolantes, it had a deep green impressive wingspan with a large encased propeller in the centre. Below hung, what looked like a bobsleigh, with its team members sat behind each other in a row. Initially looking like it was plummeting to earth, the craft reared up and shot off into the clouds above, leaving the huge lift swinging in the air.

On the ground, Archie and the others were still heading towards the Pike; the charred shell still smouldering from Crowle's fire earlier. As they wearily ascended the final (and steepest) part of the hill, a small balloon could be seen approaching them. Dropping rapidly through the air, Archie could see Dewey at the edge of the large basket underneath. This came to an abrupt halt as it landed at the top of the Pike and the weary travellers began to climb on board. A simple vehicle with a rather hazardous frame surrounding a large contained fire. Once on board, Dewey shouted some instructions and told everyone to hold on. Archie grabbed the rail at the side of him and with the throw of a large lever, the balloon shot up into the air. The influx of hot air filled the balloon to bursting point. Archie was concerned whether the balloon would hold but his fears were allayed as they poked through the clouds above and found the Ducis. Docking quickly, Archie and the others hastily climbed on board from their escape vessel and proceeded to the bridge where Captain Harrington was waiting.

"Thank goodness you're all safe," he gasped. "We have been monitoring the situation from up here, keeping out of trouble in this thick cloud. Volantem Mortem is in the vicinity but we haven't engaged them yet. It appears to be a stalemate now. A bit of a standoff."

"They'll be waiting to get Roker safely on board. Chances are he'll be there now so I'd prepare for an attack imminently," Maddie replied.

"The Canemvolantes are protecting the area. We should be safe for now."

"Captain," shouted Fizkin from another console on the bridge, "I've had word that Imperium are set to launch their own fighters. ETA one minute."

"Ha, you spoke too soon," Maddie grinned.

"Well there's no time like the present, everyone prepare. Battle stations."

With that, the crew shot into life with people moving erratically from one place to another. A hive of communication and orders were passed from crew member to crew member and Harrington stood in the centre; calm and in control. Stood in front of the huge viewing point on the bridge, Archie could see the

Canemvolantes circling the ship, giving protection. Above them the sky was clear but to the south thick cloud provided the perfect hiding place. As Harrington said, it was a game of chess. Neither side could give their position away for fear of an open attack from with the clouds, so for the last few hours, both the Volantem Mortem and the Ducis remained hidden. Now, however, Alium had decided to show their hand and were ready for battle. Archie gazed into the thick, clouds and saw the enemy fighters, like the one he had seen earlier, emerge from the purple-tinged softness.

It could not have been, but Archie was sure there were hundreds of fighters descending upon the Ducis. The Canemvolantes engaged them and a vicious battle in this game of chess began. The Ducis, like the King, kept at a safe distance. Other smaller ships from the Alium fleet were nearby for protection, some twenty or thirty providing a perimeter, like the bishops, knights and rooks. The pawns continued their battle and both sides took casualties. Archie noticed a brave pilot taking a hit on its propeller and causing it to spin out of control. The back heavy craft plummeted towards the ground and as it did so the pilot must have activated the emergency procedures as the entire front shot off with a mini explosion and a large parachute emerged slowing the vessel down. One of the rooks shot straight to its aid, diving through the air like an arrow. As it closed on the fighter's position it provided covering fire and a large mechanical clasp emerged from the front of the ship. As it reached the troubled vessel, the open clasp surrounded the strings on the parachute and clamped firmly shut, taking the ship and its pilot away to safety. No such luck for the Persona in the Imperium fighters. If they were hit, they were faced with a trip of certain death as no rescuers came to their aid. Another example of Imperium thinking only of the few, not the many.

"Captain, we've had word from one of our fighters. The Volantem Mortem has been sighted to the south in that large cumulonimbus. Much higher up, at an altitude of approximately 49,000 feet," Fizkin reported.

"They'll be watching everything we do, preparing for an attack. We cannot let them get above us," came Harrington's response. He turned to Archie. "Told you it was a game of chess. We know their plan. They will try to get above us via cloud cover and drop all their incendiaries upon us. That would be checkmate for us. But now I know their move I can plan two steps ahead."

"We need to end this, we can't just hide in the clouds," Archie pleaded.

"Leave this to me Archie, I've been doing this for many years," the smug looking captain replied. Archie wasn't happy with this.

"Where's Layla?" he demanded.

"She'll be on board the Salvator, her ship. Out there," Maddie pointed into the distance. Archie could see a ship with large robin crested sails on either side.

"I need to go to her."

"Why Archie you are safe here?"

"I have a plan." Archie left the bridge and moved down the deck. "Dewey, Dewey?" Looking desperately, he finally saw the young man at the edge of the ship dropping Tempus grenades over the side. "Dewey, you know that canister Layla had, the one at the Pike? Is there any more?"

"Er, yeah I think so," Layla had a backup canister, in case anything happened. Why?" he questioned.

"And it works in steam, water vapour? Only against those in Imperium?"

"Yes, and we would have got them all down there if Roker hadn't escaped. What are you planning Archie?"

"What are clouds made from?"

"Er... water vapour! Wow, you may be onto something here. But to drop it you'd need to be higher than the Volantem Mortem. There's no way Harrington can get this ship that high without them knowing. They get on top of us and we wouldn't stand a chance."

"I'm not talking about the ship, I'm talking about a secret spy." Archie turned a dial on his wrist strap and pushed a button. He knew a loyal friend would come to his aid. Abe was on his way. "Now I need to get over to that other ship."

"What do you think you are doing Archie?" He turned and there stood Maddie. For the first time in his life, he felt he was in trouble with his mother.

Chapter 20
A New Day

"I need to do this Maddie, I can put an end to all this," Archie exclaimed, expecting a barrage of threats back from his mother. Maddie stood silently for a few moments.

"Well if you're going to do it, you're going to need some help," she grinned at her son. That was not the answer Archie expected, but the smile was returned to his mother.

"We need to get to Layla as she has another canister. I've contacted Abe, and I will get him to fly it above that giant monster in the sky. Once they are all immobile, we can take the ship safely," Archie explained.

"And I have just the things to get us to her. Dewey, have we got a couple of sets of Avisalas on board?"

"We certainly have Maddie, but are you serious? In the middle of a battle? With Archie?" came the response from Dewey.

"He'll only do something stupid without me, so at least I can keep an eye on him this way." She winked at Archie with a feeling of great pride. Having known her son was a captive for most of his life with his father had killed Maddie daily. She had her son back now, and she was going to make sure the experiences he had from now on was one as a free man. Dewey had disappeared inside the vessel but soon returned with two large, long bags. They were placed on the floor in front of Maddie, and she bent down and unzipped one of them. Archie matched her and did the same with the other. Upon looking at the contents, Archie thought he was assembling a deck chair with a mismatch of wood and fabric.

"What is it?" he questioned.

"Put the leather straps on first, like a backpack. It will all become clear," Maddie explained. Archie did as he was told but felt a little daft applying the strapping. "Dewey, can you add my Avisalas please?" Dewey picked up the assemble wood and material and went behind Maddie's back. Archie could see that he was attaching the package down the length of her back. With a few clicks, he stepped away and moved to Archie.

"Your turn," he grinned at Archie. Archie turned around with his back towards everyone and felt tugs as Dewey attached whatever he had in his hand to the leather straps he was wearing.

"Listen carefully, Archie," Maddie explained, "if you reach down your sides and slightly back you will feel two leather straps. Put your hands through them and grab the two handles there." Archie did as instructed, but felt like he was now being shackled against his will. Was this his mother's unusual way to prevent him from doing anything dangerous? If so, she had succeeded as Archie felt well and truly trapped. "Now turn around and face me. When I say, there is a button on the top of the right handle. Do not press it yet. Only when I say, do you understand?"

"Yes, but what will happen?" Archie quizzed.

"These are like wings Archie and you will be able to glide, but if you press the button too early, you may be blown overboard.

"What?" exclaimed Archie.

"Watch," Maddie replied. "Stand at the edge with the wind behind you, when ready, press the button. Dewey will sort you out; I'm going." She grinned as she moved to the side of the Ducis. She climbed up on to the edge and Archie could see her press the button. In an instant, the thin backpack extended on her back and opened to reveal the material in between. A giant pair of wings. Within the next second, she had disappeared; she flew off the edge of the ship. Archie moved to the side and saw his mother soaring through the sky.

"You need to find the rising air currents Archie, or you'll just go down," offered Dewey as advice.

"And how do I do that?"

"You'll work it out," and with that, he leant forward, patted Archie on the back and pressed the button for him. The next thing Archie knew he was falling through the air. Tumbling rapidly through the air, Archie struggled to control his new appendages but managed eventually to force his arms out wide and the wings filled with air. Now he had stopped freefalling, Archie caught his breath and looked around him. High above he could see the immense presence of the Ducis and a small circling bird that was Maddie. Other ships were in the vicinity, but all Alium. There was no sign of Volantem Mortem, still hiding away in the thick, dense clouds. As he glided through the air, he recalled what Dewey had said before his first flight about rising air currents, so Archie carefully observed the other ships in the sky.

Noticing their flight plans and positioning, he could guess where the rising air currents may be; so, he tried his luck. Swooping into the path of a supposed raising air current, he found himself shooting up into the air. Archie let out a whoop of delight at his newfound skills and continued to rise. The problem however was he did not know where he was rising to. Archie had lost sight of Maddie and was getting gradually further away from the Ducis and closer to the thick cloud. More alarmingly, he was also getting closer to an Alium ship. If the next air current took him up at a rapid pace, he could find himself flying straight into the hull of the vessel. If this caused severe damage to his wings, he would have little hope. He tried to guide the wings away from the Alium vessel, but something was jammed. In his excitement of flying and repeatedly increasing in altitude, something had got caught on the backpack, and he was in trouble. Not only could he potentially fly into the hull of his own friend's ship, but he may even have been blown off course and lost forever. He struggled and tugged at the levers and switches, but nothing happened.

Suddenly he felt something on his back. Turning his head, he saw Abe perched upon his back, pecking furiously at the tangled mess behind Archie. Abe worked rapidly, and Archie could only hang and pray as he was drawing closer to Alium ship. As he approached, he saw it was the Salvator - Layla's ship. Archie was picking up speed now, accelerating further as he got closer to the bow of the vessel. With a final desperate tug, Abe managed to release the tangled mess on Archie's back, and he could move his wings. By changing their position, he was able to fly up above the deck of the Salvator, and by shutting the wings, he performed an unglamourous and reckless landing, leaving him rolling along the bridge and collapsing into a heap in some netting.

Abe fluttered down next to him and cawed loudly. Layla approached him looking slightly concerned.

"Nice landing," she joked.

"Thanks, I try," he smirked back. Suddenly there was a thud on the deck behind them. There landed Maddie, perfectly!

"See, that's how you do it," Layla added.

"I'll try harder next time. Anyway, enough of that." He struggled to his feet, his bones aching from his fall. "Do you have another canister of the gas?"

"Yes, why?" He proceeded to repeat his plan, and Layla smiled an approving grin.

"Well done Archie," she added. She then disappeared from the deck towards the bridge of the Salvator. She returned with a matching gas canister to the one that had been destroyed before. Archie took the cylinder and turned to Abe.

"Now it's your turn, don't let me down," Archie smiled at his Angelus custos. A loud caw came in return, and Abe grabbed the canister in his beak. He hopped to the edge of the deck and took flight into the frantic sky. Archie, Maddie and Layla watched as he gained altitude at it appeared to be just in time as the Volantem Mortem was emerging from the vast clouds to a position above the Ducis.

"Come on Abe; you can do it," Archie willed his raven on. Soon he was out of sight, and all they could do was hope he could manage to complete his quest.

A deafening siren erupted from Volantem Mortem and, from on board the Salvator, they could see munitions being deployed down towards the Ducis. Countermeasures were deployed with the Ducis crew firing flares into the air to intercept the falling artillery. Some were successful, but the Ducis was taking strikes. The squadron of Canemvolantes now intervened, and some pilots bravely took hits to protect their mother ship. From the belly of Volantem Mortem, a large opening appeared, and the crew watched with baited breath as a large circular mechanism was slowly lowered down. It must have been twenty metres in diameter, and Maddie began to panic.

"It must be some weapon; they're going to destroy the Ducis." From their vantage point it was clear that, whatever this contraption did, it was preparing to start now. After it was lowered about thirty metres below the giant beast shadowing the earth, it began to rotate at a considerable velocity. As it did, steam fired out and a strange purple glow emitted from all edges. Above it, the crew could see an immense rocket shaped projectile, pointing vertically down at the rotating disc.

"This is it," continued Maddie. Sparks flew from the edge of the mechanism as it spun faster and faster when it was suddenly dropped. Free falling through the sky it continued to rotate, and the giant rocket shaped vessel was released. As they both travelled through the air, on a collision course for the Ducis, wings emerged from the side of the projectile and it became apparent to the spectators that it was a ship of some kind. Halfway through its fall towards the Ducis, the ship shot into life, with a burst of flames, firing through the rotating circular mechanism. With a magnificent flash and explosion, the vessel disappeared, followed by an immense explosion in the sky, and the rotating device was destroyed. Debris from the blast continued to fall through the air with smaller fragments disintegrating as they dropped earthwards.

"Perhaps it has gone wrong. Whatever Abe is doing, he needs to do it now," Maddie exclaimed.

Archie began to fear the worse for Abe and that his plan had failed as the incendiaries still fell, but suddenly, everything stopped. It was as if time itself had frozen: Imperium fighters fell from the sky, missiles ceased, and the deafening siren on board Volantem Mortem abruptly ended. It was over.

*

Chaos followed - but only for a short period. After Imperium had been immobilised, Alium had to try and restore some order in the world. This was easier said than done. The gates between worlds were now open - continually - and free passage was allowed for all. The fantastic contraptions made their way to Volgaris and, after initially being sceptical, people saw the benefits of the world, many taking trips to see how life was on the other side. Due to the deep-rooted influence of Imperium in all areas of society, new government structures and authority needed to be implemented; not to mention the collapse of the monarchy and abdication of Queen Mathilda. Exiled, she too disappeared to an unknown haven, but her mechanical double remained; a deactivated symbol of what was before and what would come in the future. Alium, under the watchful eye of Maddie, managed to assist in all areas - health, security, education, industry, democracy. It would be a long process, but a hopeful time and for the first moment in many generations, the ordinary person had a life to look forward to.

In the initial aftermath of Imperium's demise, the Volantem Mortem was boarded by Captain Harrington and his crew, and sure enough, the lifeless bodies of Imperium members lay like statues on the ground. Archie's plan had worked. These crew members and those from Romani Grove were able to be rounded up and prosecuted within the lines of the new laws. With such a large number, this was no simple feat, but with all of society pulling together for its own common good, justice prevailed. With no clear leadership, the Persona were eventually defeated by Alium and the average person on the street

In the search of the Volantem Mortem, significant members of Imperium, including Roker, were not found. After Dewey and other crew members had investigated, it appeared the projectile, first thought to be a weapon, was, in fact, an escape pod, and the rotating mechanical device was a portable gate to allow Similis where required (another of Keiler's inventions.) Where they had gone was anyone's guess, but The Colonel spoke to Alium saying the search would continue.

Archie's life had been turned upside down. Not only had his father and house gone, but he had now found his mother. Home was now on the other side of the gate, but he travelled back and forth with his mother regularly to ensure the smooth integration and development of the new positive society. Kat was no longer the scullery maid anymore; a position she had merely taken to observe and assist Archie through his childhood. She continued her role in Alium, assisting Archie and Maddie whenever possible. Layla too relentlessly worked at the integration of new technology into the old society and had become a minor celebrity due to her mechanical abilities. Although not his true aunt, Layla had become, like Kat, a true and loyal friend.

The feelings of despair and hatred for Roker did not pass. Archie felt betrayed and vulnerable. His early life had been eradicated and that what followed was a lie. For this, Archie could never forgive his father.

"I wonder where he is?" Archie asked his mother.

"I don't know Archie, but he has lost his power. We will keep an eye out for Roker as someone like that doesn't just disappear, but, the worlds have collided, and the resulting explosion is nothing but positive. You should be very proud of what you have achieved."

"Achieved?" questioned Archie. His mother smiled.

"Archie, you may not believe it, but you have a big family around you. Me, Kat, Layla, Abe and the rest of Alium. You can feel the change in the air. The integration of worlds, though not perfect, is moving forward. Things can only get better, and for the first time, the future is ours and not controlled by mysterious, unknown forces. You stopped that."

Archie grinned to himself. Looking out into the mechanical city in front of him, he finally realised he had opened his mind to everything, but he could now trust others. His family, his friends. And in the end, that was all that mattered to him.

www.chrisallton.co.uk

278

Printed in Great Britain
by Amazon